Praise for
death drops

A DearReader.com Mystery Book Club pick

"With a terrific premise and an interesting topic, Fiedler's debut shows promise."

—*Library Journal*

"An engaging investigative thriller . . . an enjoyable whodunit."

—*The Mystery Gazette*

"Fiedler has a knack for detailing aspects of acupuncture, massage, yoga, and homeopathy which should provide fertile ground for further adventures of an unconventional, but eminently likeable, doctor."

—*Mystery Scene Magazine*

"*Death Drops* is as engaging as it is educational about natural remedies and full-body health."

—*Herb Companion*

"A fun book to read."

—*BookTrib*

"*Death Drops* is a gem! Entertaining, informative, and with a mystery that had me completely baffled!"

—Gayle Trent, author of *Killer Sweet Tooth*

"An absorbing mystery and entertaining debut."

—Linda Bloodworth-Thomason,
writer/producer of *Designing Women*

Also by Chrystle Fiedler

Death Drops

scent to kill

A Natural Remedies Mystery

Chrystle Fiedler

Gallery Books

New York   London   Toronto   Sydney   New Delhi

GALLERY BOOKS
A Division of Simon & Schuster, Inc.
1230 Avenue of the Americas
New York, NY 10020

First Gallery Books trade paperback edition February 2013

GALLERY BOOKS and colophon are registered trademarks of Simon & Schuster, Inc.

For information about special discounts for bulk purchases, please contact Simon & Schuster Special Sales at 1-866-506-1949 or business@simonandschuster.com.

The Simon & Schuster Speakers Bureau can bring authors to your live event. For more information or to book an event contact the Simon & Schuster Speakers Bureau at 1-866-248-3049 or visit our website at www.simonspeakers.com.

Manufactured in the United States of America

10   9   8   7   6   5   4   3   2

Library of Congress Cataloging-in-Publication Data

Fiedler, Chrystle.
    Scent to kill : a natural remedies mystery / Chrystle Fiedler.
        p. cm.
    Sequel to: Death drops.
    Summary: "In *Scent to Kill*, the second novel in the Natural Remedies cozy series, Dr. Willow McQuade must solve the murder of a producer of a new psychic television show"—Provided by publisher.
    1. Naturopaths—Fiction. 2. Television producers and directors—Crimes against—Fiction. I. Title.
PS3606.I327S34 2013
813'.6—dc23   2012032143

ISBN 978-1-4516-4361-9
ISBN 978-1-4516-4363-3 (ebook)

For my mom, who always believed.

acknowledgments

Many heartfelt thanks go out to: the talented team at Gallery Books/Simon & Schuster, especially Mitchell Ivers, my editor Kathy Sagan, and the production and publicity staff; to Ann Collette, my smart and steadfast agent; to all the reviewers, writers, and columnists who wrote such kind words; to the bookstores that carry my books; to the readers who have enjoyed my work; and to Eve, Anne, and Ellen for their love, support, and guidance. Thank you all!

scent to
kill

Dr. Willow McQuade's Healthy Living Tips

Welcome to my blog! In this series of posts, I'll focus on aromatherapy, which is the use of essential oils to help treat a variety of conditions, and to support health and well-being. I use essential oils when I'm treating clients. Aromatherapy can:

- ease stress, anxiety, or depression
- reduce inflammation
- treat insomnia
- heal eczema
- balance hormonal function (PMS, etc.)
- enhance immune function
- neutralize nausea
- ease aches and pains
- manage migraines and other headaches
- treat upset stomach
- work as an antiseptic and antibacterial

Until next time, I'm Yours Naturally,

Willow McQuade, ND

chapter one

Dr. Willow McQuade's Healthy Living Tips

Lavender (the Latin verb *lavare* means "to wash") is my favorite herb. Not only does it smell terrific, it's calming and soothing and good for cuts and burns, insomnia, diaper rash, tension headache, PMS, and cramps (use with clary sage and Roman chamomile). The phytochemicals (plant-based chemicals linalool and linalyl acetate) in lavender are absorbed in the skin and in the membranes inside your nose, slowing nerve impulses, and reducing stress. An easy way to start using lavender is to put five to ten drops of essential oil in your bath. Add the oil after you have filled the tub so you can enjoy the full benefits of this wonderful aroma.

Yours Naturally,

Dr. McQuade

Nature is the best natural remedy. That's why I was at my favorite beach early on a Sunday morning. It was late August, a week before Labor Day, and the beach felt empty except for the piping plovers skittering across the sand and the seagulls that sat at the water's edge like sentries. Qigong (pronounced *chee gung*), my scruffy black, gray, and white terrier, ran in front of me, sniffing the ground and making fresh paw prints in the sands. The sky above was aqua blue with whipped-cream cumulus clouds.

I'm a naturopathic doctor, and I dispense natural remedies at Nature's Way Market and Café, which is in the village of Greenport, a popular tourist spot two hours east of New York City on Long Island's East End. But I didn't plan to be a shop owner. Last June when I came home for two weeks to visit my beloved aunt Claire, I had no idea that my entire life would change. But after Aunt Claire was murdered and I turned amateur sleuth and figured out who the killer was, it was left to me to carry on her legacy. Owning a health food store is a big responsibility, especially considering I'd never run a business before. So I needed these breaks, this time spent in nature, to keep me sane.

Qigong spotted the seagulls and ran to the shore. As he did, the entire entourage of birds took off in a whirl, flapping wings and cawing. I walked along the edge of the water and watched as the tide lapped its way in. I spotted a beautiful conch shell with a polished orange and yellow sheen but left it where it was, where it belonged.

I picked up a polished stone, skipped it into the water, and kept walking. The sand felt good beneath my sneakers. I sucked in a lungful of sea air and felt the negative ions in the water boost my mood.

Qigong ran up to me, tail wagging. I glanced at my watch. It was time to turn around. We headed back the way we'd come, me pretending to race Qigong down the beach, Qigong happily scampering ahead of me, knowing he would win. At the other end of the beach, we climbed into the Nature's Way van and headed back to Greenport. It was still early, and a Sunday, so there weren't too many people on the streets, but I knew that by noon the town would be packed, as this was the week before Labor Day.

I drove past the colorful and eclectic collection of boutiques, stores, artist's galleries, cafés, and souvenir shops on Main Street, then hung a right onto Front Street, passing more shops and Mitchell Park, which overlooked the harbor. Across from the post office, on the right, was the three-story, yellow, gingerbread Victorian house with red trim that housed Nature's Way on the ground floor. Brightly colored posters in my windows announced everything from ALL SUPPLEMENTS 10% OFF! and WE STOCK WELEDA! to DELICIOUS ORGANIC WATERMELON!

White wicker tables and chairs were arranged on the porch for alfresco dining. On top of the building stood a ship's weather vane, a nod to our village's nautical heritage. I took a right and pulled into the parking lot in back of the store.

An hour later, showered and dressed, I headed downstairs to my office, which was on the ground floor. My bedroom was on the third floor, along with the offices of my friends Allie, who's a masseuse, and Hector, who's an acupuncturist. On the second floor was a yoga studio that featured floor-to-ceiling windows and a lovely view of Greenport Harbor. Across the hall was an empty room that I planned to make one day soon into a place to see patients.

On the ground floor, at the bottom of the stairs, I headed

past the kitchen to the café section in the front of the store, with its yellow tables and chairs, and bookshelves bursting to the seams with volumes on everything from vegan eating to yoga to meditation. An oversize corkboard displayed the daily specials along with funky artwork and photos and postcards from customers around the world.

Merrily Scott, my salesclerk and right-hand woman, was busy serving customers. She dropped plates off at a table by the window that overlooked Front Street, then met me in the kitchen. Merrily wore the Nature's Way uniform, a green apron over a white T-shirt and jeans. Her hair was pulled into tufts all over her head with neon elastic bands. She was energetic and upbeat, which might have had something to do with the large mug of organic coffee she held in her right hand. "How was your walk on the beach with Qigong?" She leaned over and scratched the little dog behind the ears.

"Wonderful. It was good for both of us." I reached into the display case and plucked out an organic blueberry muffin for my breakfast. Although we did outsource our bread to a local organic bakery, Merrily was an excellent baker and made great muffins and creative vegetarian dishes.

"Are you going to be able to handle things here this afternoon by yourself?" I asked. "I have to go to that party at the Bixby estate."

"Better you than me." Merrily went over to the counter, picked up the *Suffolk Times,* our local newspaper, and handed it to me. "It says there are ghosts in that mansion."

"I know. It's kind of freaky." The headline on the front page read BIXBY ESTATE TO BE STAR OF PARANORMAL TV SHOW. The show was called *MJ's Mind* and featured a psychic named MJ who talked to ghosts. I'd been invited by my ex-boyfriend Simon Lewis, a television writer from L.A., to the welcoming party that was being held today from one to five for the cast and crew.

Simon and I had lived together and broken up when I was in L.A. When I moved back to Greenport last June, Simon came here, ostensibly to write the great American novel and try to win me back, but it didn't work. However, he had, like so many people before him, fallen in love with the North Fork and purchased a huge house on the Sound in Greenport. Now he came to Nature's Way almost every morning he was in town for a healthy breakfast. He usually brought his laptop along, sat outside, and worked on the latest episode of his show, *Parallel Lives,* which he had created and produced, a show in the tradition of *Lost* and *Awake*.

Over the past year, we had gradually, surprisingly, become friends. He could be funny and charming, and in small doses I could handle his behavior, which could also be ego driven and somewhat selfish. Now, he had a new girlfriend, Carly Bixby, who was a producer for *MJ's Mind,* which was going to start shooting tomorrow at the Bixby estate. She was also Roger Bixby's soon-to-be-ex-wife.

According to Simon, Carly had filed for divorce in April because Roger had cheated on her, and they were now separated. But since both of them were owners of Galaxy Productions, both of them were here to work on the show for the Sci-Fi channel. No matter how awkward that might be.

I turned to the article about the estate, which said that paranormal activity had been reported by Roger's father and the mansion's then owner, Max Bixby, who had just died at the amazing old age of 111. I could believe it. The photo of the estate made it look menacing, like something out of a horror movie.

Merrily was staring at me, a worried expression on her face. "You might want to rethink going to that party."

"I'm sure it will be okay. I have Jackson to protect me." Jackson Spade was the hunky ex-cop who'd helped me solve Aunt Claire's murder a few months ago in June. We'd been a couple ever since. "Besides, I have to see that lavender farm." Lavender is my favorite natural remedy, and the lavender farm on the ten-acre estate was usually viewed by invitation only.

Two women walked into the store, and I took this as my cue to get some work done. So I grabbed the paper and a bottle of natural raspberry soda and headed into my office, which was directly across from the kitchen and the checkout counter. The space was warm and welcoming with cozy chairs and a couch. Above the doorway was a sign, PEACE, in bold letters. The bookshelves were crammed with natural, New Age, and veggie books. Pictures of healing herbs and various yoga positions lined the walls, along with photographs of Aunt Claire's native Australia, and London, where she once worked as an editor for British *Vogue*.

Aunt Claire had come here one summer to visit her sister, my mother, and fell in love with Nick Holmes, her yoga instructor, and never left Greenport. That was over thirty years ago.

Qigong jumped on the couch and settled in for a nap while I took another look at the front page of the paper. Something about the mansion was unsettling. It's my job as a holistic physician to restore balance and foster well-being. I've been trained to be sensitive to the energy that comes from people, but I'm also sensitive to the kind of energy that comes from places. Even though I was just looking at a photograph of a house, I couldn't help feeling that something wasn't right about that place. Then again, I also have an active imagination. I shook off the feeling and tossed the paper in the recycling bin. I hoped my initial impression was wrong. I was looking forward to an afternoon off.

Since it was Sunday, I spent the rest of the morning and early afternoon ordering online, everything from eco-friendly cleaning products to produce to natural beauty products. Once I was done, I had a feeling of real accomplishment. Perhaps I was finally getting the hang of being a shop owner after all.

I'd just straightened up my desk when Jackson knocked on the partially open door. "Hey, McQuade." He wore a striped blue shirt with a tie, his good black jeans, and boots. He looked dynamite, maybe because his normal attire consisted of a T-shirt with some sort of message and faded blue jeans.

Jackson was handsome in a Gerard Butler kind of way, with a chiseled jaw, to-die-for cheekbones, beautiful blue eyes, and short-cropped hair. He came over and gave me a long, soulful kiss. He felt warm and smelled of sandalwood, his favorite aftershave.

The connection between us was electric and undeniable, and it had been that way from the second we met, in June, right after Claire was killed. He and I solved the murder together and helped send a crazy organic farmer and her deranged nephew to jail. Jackson had loved Aunt Claire almost as much as I did. And now, barely three months after her death, Jackson had become my rock. I knew I could count on him no matter what.

After we kissed, he surveyed my outfit. "Is that what you're wearing to the party?"

I was wearing a pair of jeans, a LIFE IS GOOD tee, and flip-flops. "You're early."

"I couldn't wait to see you." He kissed me again.

"Me, too," I said, gazing into his blue eyes.

"Do we really have to go to this thing? And if we do, is there any way we can avoid your ex-boyfriend Simon? I've had enough of that egomaniac."

Simon would never be Jackson's favorite person, but Jackson

had made his peace with him once he could see that it was over between us, and that Simon was a fixture in Greenport and probably my life.

"Sorry," I said. "Simon's the one who invited us, after all. Besides, he's harmless."

Jackson gave a short laugh. "That, he is not. He takes up too much of your time, and he acts like a child when he doesn't get what he wants."

"All true. But Simon's also been a good friend to me. I didn't tell you this before, but he offered to lend me money—interest free—anytime I need it for the store. He believes in me. He wants me to make the store a big success."

"He offered to lend you money?" Jackson arched an eyebrow. "Why didn't you tell me?"

I shrugged my shoulders. "I didn't think you'd like it."

Jackson was quiet for a moment. Finally he said, "Well, I don't, but maybe he's changed after all. Who knows? Maybe he's actually capable of thinking about someone other than himself."

"Perhaps hanging out at Nature's Way has been a good influence on him. It's a very peaceful place to be."

Jackson rolled his eyes. "Okay, we'll go party with peaceful Simon."

"It's just a couple of hours. And it is kind of exciting. The invitations are highly coveted." I kissed Jackson again. "We'll go to the party, see the lavender farm, and we'll be home before you know it. I just have to get changed. I'll be quick."

Jackson made a face. "No, you won't. It takes you at least an hour to get ready when we go out."

"Not if you help me get undressed."

"I think that can be arranged." Jackson smiled.

• • •

Later that afternoon, the smell of lavender was pungent as we drove toward the Bixby estate in Southold, which was about ten minutes west of Greenport. Being invited to this party seemed serendipitous since I'd recently decided to hold workshops about aromatherapy in the store, and the first one—which would take place tomorrow night—was going to focus on lavender, my favorite aromatic herb. I was hoping that the workshops would both educate my customers and draw new business for the off-season, which would begin next week, right after Labor Day.

I took in a deep breath as we drew close to the estate. "Smell the lavender?"

"Mmmm, you were right. It smells fantastic." Jackson was an amateur gardener with a real passion for roses and lavender.

Since I was driving, I couldn't look at him, but I knew he was smiling. "I'm using lavender as the focus of my first aromatherapy workshop tomorrow night. I'm hoping it will improve business."

"I think it will. But you have managed to put some money away for the off-season, haven't you?"

That question made me uncomfortable. Yes, the store was doing okay, and I'd even managed to save a bit. But I had expenses that came from owning a three-story Victorian that demanded constant upkeep. The roof had been repaired in June right after Aunt Claire had died, the copper piping was replaced in July, and I had to buy a new heater in August. Yes, August.

"Sales have been good, but I still wonder if I'll be able to make a go of it and carry on Aunt Claire's legacy," I said.

"What about the Fresh Face formula? You'll be getting proceeds from the sales, won't you? That should help."

Fresh Face was a unique anti-aging cream that Claire had

created. The car I was driving, a mint-green Prius, was a thank-you gift from the parent company, Green Focus, for finding the formula when it was stolen after Claire was killed in June.

I spotted a small, discreet sign with BIXBY on it and turned onto a dirt road that had surprisingly seen better days. I concentrated on not hitting any of the huge potholes as we traveled toward the water. Now the lavender smell mixed with the salty tang from the bay.

I answered Jackson. "Fresh Face goes on sale next week, but sales will take time to build. We ought to be getting the finished product any day now. I can't wait to see it."

I followed the road past a stand of beautiful white birch trees. A squirrel with a big, bushy tail skittered into the woods. We reached the end of the road and followed the signs to a parking area. I squeezed the Prius into an end spot next to a maple tree.

I got out of the car and checked my reflection in my compact mirror. Not for the first time, I realized how much I looked like my aunt Claire when she was younger, tall and blond, with angular features, good skin, and high cheekbones. I put on a touch of organic lip gloss and decided I was ready for the party, but Jackson had other ideas. He pulled me into his arms and gave me a good long kiss.

"What's that all about?" I asked.

"We're going to be here awhile, so I needed to do that now."

"Good thinking." I kissed him back and took his hand, and we followed the signs to the Bixby mansion. Walking along a narrow path, we came to a small hill. When we reached the top, we could see the house. It was all Gothic spires, pointed arches, steep gables, and towers. It looked mysterious, foreboding, and unwelcoming. Suddenly, I had the same feeling that I'd had this morning when I'd looked at the photo of it in the paper, only this time it was much stronger. I sucked in a breath.

"What's wrong?" Jackson said.

I tried to shake off the feeling, not wanting to ruin our day out. "Nothing. Let's find Simon."

"Do we have to?"

"Yes, we have to." I smiled. We walked down the hill and I spotted three huge, white production trailers parked behind the mansion. Moments later we walked past the front door of the house. Suddenly I spotted movement in one of the downstairs windows. "Jackson," I said in a low voice. "Someone is watching us."

Jackson turned to look, but whoever it was had disappeared. "I think that's your imagination, McQuade."

"You're probably right." I tried to ignore the negative feelings and focus on the day ahead. "Let's go and enjoy ourselves."

chapter two

The aroma of jasmine (*Jasminum officinale v. grandiflorum*) is intoxicatingly sweet, exotic, and floral. It is incredibly therapeutic for a variety of conditions. Jasmine essential oil eases mild depression, anxiety, and tension. It also balances energy and helps you feel more optimistic. It calms coughs and laryngitis, soothes sore muscles, stiffness, and sprains. You can apply it topically, use it on a warm or cool compress, put it in the bath, inhale it from your palm, or put it in your diffuser. It will make any room an oasis.

Yours Naturally,

Dr. McQuade

Jackson and I walked across the freshly mown grass to an impressive yellow-and-white-striped tent about two hundred yards north of the front door of the mansion. A hundred yards beyond the tent was a ten-foot retaining wall that separated the Bixby property from an inlet and, across the water, a public beach with white sand and sparkling blue water.

Simon spotted us, waved, and walked over. He wasn't conventionally handsome, but he had a broody demeanor, deep chocolate-brown eyes, and a slim, athletic build. When we were living together in L.A., he would take a daily run around the reservoir where you could see the HOLLYWOOD sign. Today, dressed in an expensive suit and wearing chic new sunglasses, he looked every inch the successful TV writer.

His show, *Parallel Lives,* had started shooting in August on the Warner Bros. lot, and he'd visited there twice, but he wasn't planning to leave the East Coast again until after Labor Day. I couldn't blame him. It was paradise here—beautiful sandy beaches, crystal-clear blue-green water, and the bustling, picturesque town of Greenport, recently named one of the prettiest villages in America by *Forbes* magazine.

"You made it!" Simon said as he reached us. "I'm so glad you both could come." He kissed me on the cheek and shook Jackson's hand.

"It's a beautiful day for a party," I said, looking up at the clear blue, cloudless sky.

"Sure is," Simon said, and waved at a petite blonde with a pixie haircut, who was coming toward us at a fast, determined clip. She wore designer sunglasses, a little black dress, and five-inch-high, red platform heels.

This had to be Carly Bixby, I thought, the mistress of the mansion, Roger Bixby's soon-to-be-ex and Simon's new girlfriend. Simon had told me that they met at Comic-Con in July in San Diego, and they were both "instantly infatuated." But Simon had also told me that he and Roger did not get along. Mr. Bixby was not at all pleased that his wife had already moved on and was living with her new boyfriend, in his house, for the week of production.

Simon put his arm around her as she came up to us. "This is Carly. She's the line producer on the show. Carly, this is Willow McQuade and Jackson Spade."

"Willow," Carly said in a slightly frosty tone as she sized me up. "Simon has told me a lot about you."

From the way she said it, I gathered that she didn't like that Simon talked about me at all. "It's nice to meet you, too," I said. "Looks like a great party."

"Oh, it is." Carly sounded self-assured. "We wanted something special to kick off our East End shoot."

Simon beamed at her. "Carly is a whiz at organization."

"It was easier than producing a TV show, that's for sure. Would you two like something to eat? The seafood is super-fresh, most of the food is organic, and the cake is gluten free and even decorated with natural food coloring."

That sounded good to me, especially the organic offerings. I had been busy in the store and had missed lunch, a rarity. I was still running on my muffin, a healthy choice but certainly not enough to sustain me until dinner. "Lead the way," I said.

Simon and Carly held hands and walked in front of us. Carly whispered something to Simon, laughed, and glanced back at me. I wondered what she was saying. I got the feeling that she wasn't going to be my new best friend.

"I don't think she likes me," I told Jackson.

"She's probably threatened by you, since you and Simon are close. Not everyone can be as incredibly well-adjusted as I am." Jackson took my hand and smiled at me.

"Obviously not."

"Simon *is* acting surprisingly normal. Not like a jerk at all."

"Perhaps Carly is a good influence on him," I said, not quite believing it. Then again, he and Carly hadn't even known each other a full two months. Like many people, Simon was always on his best behavior in the beginning of a relationship. Then once you got to know him, the trouble started.

But I pushed aside thoughts of Simon and his ability to screw things up when it came to women. If there were any problems, they were now Carly's concern, not mine.

The lavish seafood buffet featured Maine lobster, crab legs, littleneck clams, and oysters on beds of crushed ice that sparkled under the decorative lights in the tent. The many hot entrées ranged from baked, stuffed lobster tails and shrimp scampi to flounder Florentine, broiled scallops, and wild salmon.

Carly, who had organized the event, was clearly health-conscious. There was a huge organic salad and organic corn and lots of side dishes, including organic potato salad, tabouli, and couscous. For dessert, there was an extravagant five-tier red-velvet cake, emblazoned with GALAXY on the bottom, in midnight blue. Planets such as Mars and Saturn were embellished on other tiers of the cake in bright neon colors. On top was a crystal ball and a cartoonish figurine of MJ, the psychic.

We managed to find a table for the four of us and started eating. Every bite was delicious.

"Carly, this food is incredible," I said as I tucked into Maine lobster, littleneck clams with hot sauce, and couscous and a garden salad. "It's all so delicious and healthy."

"And Willow is hard to please," Jackson assured her.

"That's not true," I replied. "I just like organic, humanely raised food that is good for you."

"Me, too," Carly said.

"I have to admit, you two have made me a convert," Simon said, and took a sip of his martini.

A big man with a weathered face and downturned mouth took a seat at the next table. He didn't look to be part of the L.A. crowd that had flown in for the shoot, and neither did the woman who accompanied him. She was thin, with a pinched face and wispy, gray hair. I guessed he was in his late seventies; she looked as if she might be ten years younger. He wore shapeless jeans and a short-sleeved, plaid shirt, and she wore a faded navy cotton shift. To my surprise, a good-looking guy in jeans and a T-shirt who looked like he was in his late twenties, sat down with them.

Simon leaned over to me and whispered, "That's James Russell, the Bixby estate caretaker; his wife, Sheila; and their son, Lucas. They've been here forever, Carly says."

"Nice of you to invite them," I said as I put a dollop of hot sauce on a littleneck clam and ate it. It tasted like the sea.

Carly shook her head. "I didn't. It must have been my ex-husband, Roger. They're not exactly sociable. They live in their own little world, in a cottage on the west side of the property, down by the lavender farm. I'm surprised they're here." She got up and went over to their table. "Thanks for coming, James. I hope you're having a good time. Are you enjoying your meal?"

"Fine," James said, and put his head down and kept eating.

"It's very good," Sheila added. "Thank you for having us, Carly."

Lucas remained silent.

Carly exchanged a few words with them, then came back

over to us and sat down. She took a sip of her martini. "Well, I tried. They aren't the easiest people to talk to."

Simon patted her hand. "Enjoy your meal, honey. Forget about them."

After we finished eating, we left the tent and walked over to the retaining wall. By now, it was midafternoon, the hottest time of the day, and beyond the retaining wall, the beach across the inlet was packed. We lingered for a few moments, surveying the grounds.

Off to the right in the gazebo, I noticed a woman with flaming-red hair piled on top of her head, and dramatic eye makeup in shades of blue and purple. She wore colorful, flowing robes that reminded me of the coat in the musical *Joseph and the Amazing Technicolor Dreamcoat* and red, high-top sneakers that matched her red nails. She was arguing with a man with a graying goatee and tiny glasses, who wore a white linen suit. He reminded me of a younger Colonel Sanders. Both of them looked to be in their early fifties. Simon walked out of the tent and over to us.

"Is that the TV celebrity MJ McClellen?" I asked.

"The one and only," Simon said. "Let me get Carly to introduce you."

Simon disappeared inside the tent and moments later came back with Carly, and we headed over to the gazebo.

"Join us," the man drawled when we reached the gazebo, the argument with MJ clearly over. His accent identified him as coming from somewhere south of the Mason-Dixon Line. "The more the merrier. I've got two bottles of Cristal in the bucket." He tried to hand us two glasses of champagne. Simon and Carly stuck with their martinis and declined.

"No thanks," Jackson said. "I don't drink." Jackson belonged to Alcoholics Anonymous and had been sober for years.

I'd never been much of a drinker either. "None for me, thanks."

"You all are missing out," the man said, taking one of the glasses and draining it. "This is real good stuff. It should be, for the price."

"This is MJ and Rick McClellan," Carly said, making the introductions. "MJ, Rick, this is Willow McQuade and Jackson Spade."

"Nice to meet you both." Rick shook our hands. "Carly told us you two would be coming. I take it you are some kind of natural doctor, is that right?"

"I'm a naturopathic doctor, yes."

"Now what in the heck is that?" Rick gave me a charming smile.

I smiled in return. "Naturopathic doctors take a holistic view, putting body, mind, and spirit in harmony. I work with clients to remove any blockages, so that the body's healing mechanism can work optimally."

"Say what, darlin'?" He cocked his head to the side.

I smiled. It wasn't always easy to explain what I did with patients. "In other words, we try to stop problems before they happen. Conventional medicine is more about treating symptoms, not helping patients become more healthy so they don't get sick in the first place. We focus on body, mind, and spirit. The whole picture."

"Does that mean you need to eat twigs and leaves?" He laughed at his own joke.

"Oh, Rick," MJ said, clearly embarrassed. "Please excuse my husband," she said to me. "I'm afraid he isn't very conversant in alternative approaches. But I find them fascinating."

She, too, had a Southern accent, though hers wasn't as pronounced.

"And you're a cop, right?" Rick said, turning his attention to Jackson.

"I used to be. But I'm off the job now, and on disability." Three years ago, Jackson had been a policeman working in Nassau County. One night he had been chasing a suspect when he slipped on black ice and injured his back. Conventional treatments such as physical therapy and chiropractic treatments hadn't helped, but he found some relief using the natural products that Aunt Claire recommended. Now, with help from me; and Allie, the masseuse; and Hector, the acupuncturist; he was significantly better.

"You look pretty healthy to me." Rick chuckled. He seemed relentlessly upbeat, and I couldn't help wondering if it was real or an act.

"Rick," MJ said, "leave them alone. Just ignore my husband, please. He doesn't have an internal censor, like normal people." She rolled her eyes and sipped her champagne.

"That's okay," Jackson said. "No worries."

I tried to change the subject. "It's so exciting that you're shooting your show here."

MJ nodded. "Yes, Roger and Carly made a good choice. It's unfortunate that his father, Max, isn't still alive. I would have liked to talk with him about his experiences. He used to regularly hold séances in the mansion."

"Really?"

"Yes, he was quite the enthusiast."

"What do you expect to find here?" I asked, curious.

"I'm picking up a lot of negative energy emanating from that mansion," MJ said, and took another sip of champagne. "Perhaps dangerous spirits as well, which can make it quite perilous for those of us who are still alive." She turned to look at the mansion. "I haven't been inside yet, so I don't know exactly what I'll be dealing with, but my research shows that there was a murder here at the end of Prohibition. A caretaker named Daniel Russell was killed."

"Murdered?" I felt unsettled. Getting a negative vibe was one thing, but it was too soon to be dealing with murder again, even if it did happen eighty years ago. "So you think Daniel Russell's spirit is still here?"

MJ gazed at the mansion. "It's very possible. Something terrible happened in that house."

I decided not to mention my own feelings about the place. "If you do find a spirit in there, what will you do?"

"Ideally, I try to understand the spirits and communicate with them so they can move on. But it's not always that easy."

Rick put his arm around her shoulders. "MJ is the best darn psychic on the tube. If there are ghosts in that house, she'll find 'em and show 'em the door."

MJ came up to me while the men and Carly continued to talk. I noticed that she had a slight limp, as if she were favoring her right leg. She leaned in close to me. "I hope you don't mind me saying this, but I'm sensing you had a recent traumatic loss."

For a second that spooked me. How could she possibly have known about Aunt Claire? But then, I reminded myself, I had to keep an open mind. After all, I'd picked up on the negative energy from the house, so it was certainly possible that a psychic such as MJ could sense people's spirits. It was also possible that Simon or Carly had told her about Aunt Claire's untimely death. And if she was doing research on the area, she might have seen a newspaper mention of it. "Yes, my aunt died in June."

MJ looked at me sympathetically. "That was a tremendous loss for you, wasn't it?"

I could only nod. *A tremendous loss* didn't even begin to cover it. Aunt Claire was like a mother to me. She had accepted me the way I was and had championed my career in natural medicine. My mother always wanted me to be MD, like my sister, Natasha, who had graduated from Harvard and considered my chosen career path a waste of time. I'd become weary of trying to convince her that I was a "real" doctor. My training had been rigorous. I'd studied with some of the best in the field, including Ray Richmond-Safer, MD, America's favorite "natural" doctor, bestselling author, and teacher at the highly respected Arizona Center for the Advancement of Natural Medicine.

MJ interrupted my train of thought, saying, "Perhaps I can help."

"What do you mean?"

"We could hold a séance to get in touch with your aunt. It might ease your mind to know how she is doing on the other side."

I shook my head. "I don't think so, but thank you." If there was one thing I didn't need right now, it was a séance. The loss of Claire was still fresh in my mind and heart, and I was still trying to process it.

MJ took my hands and looked deeply into my eyes. "I can sense that you aren't ready, Willow. That is very common. If you change your mind, let me know. I'll be here until next Monday. I also do phone consultations."

I thanked her and went back over to Jackson. As I did, a perky-looking woman, holding a walkie-talkie and a clipboard, with a Bluetooth in her ear, came out of the tent and ran over to us. "MJ, Rick, they want you to make a toast and to cut the Galaxy cake now. Roger sent me to get you."

"Thank you, darlin'," Rick said. "This is Amanda, Roger's assistant. Amanda, this is Willow and Jackson. If they need something, you be sure they get it, okay? These are good people."

"Sure. My pleasure." Amanda smiled and hustled back to the tent.

"How old do you think she is?" Jackson asked me. "She looks like she's about sixteen." She did, wearing a Galaxy T-shirt and jeans, with her long, brunette hair in a ponytail.

"She's probably in her early twenties," I guessed. "But not much older. Seems like being Roger's assistant means she's essentially a gofer."

Back inside the tent, Rick, MJ, and Carly stood beside the table that held the cake. Moments later, they were joined by a tall, slender man dressed in a black linen suit with a cerulean-blue shirt, and no tie. His face was all planes and angular lines, his eyes and hair dark brown, almost black. He picked up a glass of champagne and the microphone from the table. "Welcome, everyone. I'm Roger Bixby. It's good to be home. I decided to kick off the first season of *MJ's Mind* here in South-old because my father, God rest his soul, had his own experiences with the occult. So we're here to check it out and make some great television! Let's toast to that!"

So this was Roger Bixby, Carly's soon-to-be-ex-husband and lord of the manor. Simon had told me that they had separated in April, right before Max Bixby had died, because Roger had cheated on Carly.

According to Carly, cheating had ended his first marriage, too.

Carly took the mike from Roger and gave him a sugary smile. "Actually, Max told *me* about his experiences here and *I* suggested the idea to Roger."

Roger took the mike back and gave her a withering look.

"Actually, we *both* thought this would be a great venue for the premier episode of *MJ's Mind*."

"You can cut the tension between them with a knife," I said to Jackson.

"Another happily married couple." Jackson was divorced himself.

"So set your DVRs for the Sci-Fi channel, Tuesdays at ten! Now drink up and let's get our star, MJ, to cut the cake."

Everyone clapped. MJ waved to the crowd, then pressed a knife into the cake as a photographer snapped photos. The servers brought around slices of cake, and we enjoyed them with coffee.

It was now about four o'clock, still plenty of time to see what I'd come for. "Want to visit the lavender garden?" I asked Jackson as I finished my cake.

"Sure. Why don't we go that way?" He pointed to the tent's back door. "Fewer people to wade through."

"I can't wait to see this," I said as we skirted tables and chairs. "I know I'm going to be inspired."

"Me, too. I've been wanting to add more varieties of lavender in my garden, so I'm curious to see what they have here. All we have to do is figure out where this famous garden is."

"Let's ask Carly."

"Good idea, but where is she?"

Suddenly, we heard shouting coming from behind the tent.

"What's going on?" asked a woman, who was reaching for a second slice of cake.

Jackson answered for both of us. "I don't know, but whatever it is, it isn't good."

chapter three

An effective way to practice aromatherapy is to use an electronic diffuser. It works by sending small aromatic particles into the air. A diffuser can help with respiratory problems, enhance immune response and emotional well-being, and act as an air antiseptic. You can also use a candle diffuser by placing five to ten drops of essential oil in the diffuser and lighting the candle. This method is wonderful for enhancing room ambience and making you feel really good.

Yours Naturally,

Dr. McQuade

Jackson and I stepped out of the tent and spotted Roger Bixby by the retaining wall yelling at Carly, his face turning red. "What were you trying to do in there—upstage me? It was *my* idea to do the show here, and you know it. This is my house!" He plucked a walkie-talkie out of his pocket and shouted into it, "Amanda, I need you. Find me by the retaining wall, behind the tent, immediately!"

"You're deluded, you know that?" Carly retorted.

Rick hurried out of the tent and over to them. "Okay, calm down now, both of you. Let's remember, we've got press here. This doesn't look good, you two fighting."

"Shut it, Rick," Roger said. "Mind your own business."

Amanda walked up to Roger, clipboard in hand. "You needed me?"

Roger didn't look at her, just barked out orders. "Call Larry in accounting and get the new budget breakdown. Leave a message for my tailor and make sure the two suits I ordered are here first thing in the morning. And I need to see tomorrow's call sheet ASAP."

Amanda nodded and scribbled something on her clipboard. "I'm on it." She quickly walked away.

"Amanda, wait just a minute," Carly called.

Amanda stopped and turned around. "Yes, Carly?"

"Did you remember to pick up my prescriptions and those other things from the drugstore?"

Amanda nodded. "I'll do it right after I help Roger."

"Might I remind you, Amanda, that you work for both of us? Roger's needs do not necessarily come first."

Amanda didn't say anything, but she bit her lip. I felt sorry for her. Anyone could see that being caught in the middle between Roger and Carly would be uncomfortable.

"Carly," Roger said, a warning tone in his voice, "stop

throwing your weight around. Amanda is my assistant, and the agreement is that she also helps you when she can." He put his arm around Amanda, and she gave him an adoring look. "She can't burn the candle at both ends. And really, darling, a trip to the drugstore is something you can do yourself. Off you go, Amanda, and thank you."

Amanda scurried away, and Carly's face became a bright pink. "This is outrageous!"

"Is it?" Roger said. "I'm sorry you feel that way."

"Looks like there are going to be some fireworks on the set," I whispered to Jackson.

"Who do you think will storm off first?" Jackson asked.

"That's a tough call."

Roger turned away from Carly, spotted us, and gave me a huge smile. "Now, who is this gorgeous woman?" He came over to me, took my right hand, and kissed it. "I haven't met you before. Believe me, I would have remembered you."

Jackson rolled his eyes. Roger was obviously a player. Fortunately, Jackson was too secure in himself—he was, after all, a former cop, six feet two inches, ruggedly handsome, and an all-around great guy—and our relationship was not threatened. I took his hand and squeezed it.

He squeezed back and smiled at me.

"Let me introduce you to Willow McQuade and Jackson Spade," Rick said. "Willow is one of those natural doctors. She runs that health food store, Nature's Way, over in Greenport. Jackson is a former cop."

Roger ignored Jackson and zeroed in on me. "I hope you're having a nice time, Willow."

"Yes, *we* are, thank you," I said. "We were wondering if we could take a look at the lavender garden while we're here?"

Before he could answer, a younger version of Roger, shorter

with a shaved head, a two-day beard, and Ray-Bans, walked out of the tent and joined us.

"There you are, Tommy. I thought you got lost," Roger said.

"My name is Tom," the younger man just about spat out. "Here's the call sheet for tomorrow's shoot. Amanda said you wanted it ASAP."

Roger took the call sheet and handed it to Carly. "Check this over, will you? Make sure the start time is correct and that everyone we need will be here."

Carly gave Roger a venomous look, but she took the call sheet and started reading.

"Willow, Jackson, this is my brother Tommy," Roger said, ignoring Tom's directive. "Tommy is working on the show, too, thanks to me."

"Yes, thanks to my big bro, I'm the second assistant director." I didn't know much about the pecking order on a film crew, but from the way Tom said it, I got the idea that the second assistant director didn't have too much clout. "But I'm really an artist. I'm a sculptor."

Roger laughed caustically. "You'd be a starving artist if it wasn't for me."

"That's not true," Tom retorted, pushing his sunglasses to the top of his head. "I just sold two pieces."

"That'll keep bread on the table," Roger quipped.

"This is supposed to be a party?" Jackson whispered in my ear. "I am not having fun."

"Me either," I said. The arguing between the brothers reminded me of the contentious relationship I had with my sister, Natasha. She dismissed my profession as quackery and was always undermining me.

"Roger, stop," Carly said, looking up from the call sheet and glancing at me. "I'm sure that Willow and Jackson do not want to hear us air our dirty family laundry."

"We actually just wanted to see the lavender farm," I said.

"Oh, that. Everyone wants to see the farm." Carly sounded annoyed. "Just go up to the main house and ask Mrs. Florrick for the golf-cart key and then follow the signs at the head of the trail by the parking lot to the lavender fields."

We thanked Carly and headed toward the mansion. "She definitely doesn't like me," I said. "She sounded so peeved that we wanted to see the fields."

"It's not you. It's Roger. What a piece of work," Jackson said.

"No wonder Carly divorced him. I wonder who he was having an affair with."

Jackson gave me a knowing smile. "Don't start snooping, Nancy Drew. Let's just have a nice time, okay?"

"There's nothing to snoop, don't worry." But as we got closer to the house, I got that uneasy feeling again, and this time I couldn't shake it off. This time I knew that something was wrong here and had been wrong for a long time. Whatever it was, it was building, gathering energy, like clouds before a storm, and there were going to be some bad results. I glanced at Jackson, debating whether to mention it. Finally I said, "You'll probably think I'm crazy, but I am getting a very bad vibe from this house."

"You're right. That *is* crazy." He rang the bell.

After a few moments, a haggard-looking woman in her seventies with a tight, white bun and wearing a maid's black uniform came to the door. "The bathrooms are behind the house," she said, and started to close the door.

Jackson put his hand on the door. "Thank you. Carly told us we could borrow the golf cart so we could go and see the lavender garden."

The woman looked as if she were being asked to do something below her station. "The golf cart is also around back." She plucked a key off a hook on the wall and handed it to him. "Head toward the gate and take a right, go one hundred yards, and you'll start seeing signs. Follow them to the garden." She closed the door.

"Well, that's a fine welcome," I said.

"I would say something worse, but it's not worth ruining a nice time." Jackson put his arm around me.

We circled the mansion and found the golf cart near the production trailers. Jackson followed the signs for the lavender fields that were posted all along the path and through the woods. Sunlight glinted through the green leaves above us, birds twittered and tweeted, and the smell was woodsy and earthy. I felt much more at ease now that we were away from the Bixby mansion and its unsettling atmosphere. Five minutes later we arrived at the lavender fields and found hundreds of purple, spiky plants waving in the salty breeze from the bay. Beyond the field, we saw a small family cemetery and, to the right, an enclosed garden and a greenhouse and a yellow cottage covered with red roses that were still blooming late in the season.

We took a stroll through the fields, hand in hand, and stopped at each section that featured a different kind of lavender. The gray-green foliage of the lavender plants sported a variety of purple flowers. The sweet scent was intoxicating. I reached down to a Hidcote lavender plant and ran my fingers along the soft leaves.

The fields were definitely worth seeing, especially after the drama at the party. I felt lucky to be here with Jackson, enjoying the beautiful landscape and the peaceful atmosphere. Suddenly, the silence was shattered by the sound of raised voices. This time, it sounded like two men arguing.

Jackson and I hurried across the grounds toward a small hill, above a lily pond, where we found Simon, my ex-boyfriend, and Roger Bixby, Carly's soon-to-be-ex-husband, glaring at each other. Beyond the pond, I saw two golf carts, which explained why they were here at the same time we were. Something must have happened between them after we had left the party.

"I think you like upsetting her. Why don't you leave her alone!" Simon said angrily. He pulled out his phone and texted a message to someone.

"She's my wife!" Roger yelled at Simon. "And this is none of your business."

"She *was* your wife. Only you had a little problem with fidelity." Then Simon's voice softened. "Look, let's not do this. I asked you to meet me down here because I was hoping I could talk some sense into you about the way you treat Carly. But I don't want a fight."

"Well, you've got one!" Roger poked Simon's chest with his index finger.

Simon put his phone in his pocket and took a step back.

"Break it up now," Jackson said as he walked over and got between them. "This is supposed to be a party."

"He's right," Simon said. "Thanks, Jackson."

"Stay out of this, Jackson." Roger tried to push past him to get to Simon, but Jackson grabbed Roger's arm and held him back. "Let go of my arm!"

Jackson seemed amused. "I'll let you go if you behave."

"Do you know who I am?" Roger demanded, red faced and angry.

"Yes," Jackson said calmly. "We just met you about a half an hour ago."

"That's not what I mean. I'm Roger Bixby, damn it!"

"Calm down. Now, I'm going to let go, but you need to stay

put." Jackson took his hand off Roger's arm, but as he did, Roger rabbited and went after Simon, who ran down the hill. Roger tackled him and the two of them rolled down toward a small lily pond. They came to a stop near the edge where the ground leveled out and started punching each other. "Oh, great," Jackson muttered, and started down the hill after them. But before he could intervene again, Carly pulled up in a golf cart with Rick in the passenger seat. The two of them ran over to the pond.

"Stop it, Roger!" Carly shouted. "Leave him alone!"

Roger turned to look at her, and the distraction allowed Simon time to throw a punch. Roger took it on the nose and fell into the pond with a big splash, pulling Simon in after him.

Jackson waded into the water up to his waist. Within moments he had grabbed both of them by their shirts and walked them out of the pond.

"Nice job, Spade," Rick said, giving him the thumbs-up.

"No problem." Jackson let go of Simon and Roger but stayed between them, just in case. "Okay, you two, it's over now. Simon, go with Carly. Roger, clear off."

Simon and Carly headed for her golf cart, while Rick went over to Roger and tried to calm him down. But it didn't work. As Carly and Simon drove off, Roger threw a rock at them and yelled, "That's right, run away! You're a coward, Lewis! I'm not through with you!"

Jackson's jeans and boots were soaking wet, so we decided to leave the party soon after that. Except for the beautiful lavender fields, we were happy to get out of there. Between MJ's predictions of dangerous spirits, the negative vibrations from the Bixby mansion, and all the fighting between Roger and Carly and Roger and Simon, we'd both had enough.

We arrived at Nature's Way around seven that evening. Since it was a Sunday, the store had closed for the day at five. I made us strawberry-banana protein smoothies as a light dinner, and we took them up to my bedroom on the third floor. We spent the rest of the evening relaxing, fooling around, talking and watching TV. When we turned out the lights to go to sleep at eleven, we had Qigong between us and the cats Ginger and Ginkgo (brother and sister cats that Aunt Claire had adopted) at our feet.

But sleep did not come easy. The strange feeling I'd had at the Bixby estate persisted. I woke up at twelve and then at one. When I finally got out of the bed and looked out the window, the bay sparkled like white diamonds under an almost full moon.

"What's the matter?" Jackson mumbled, half-asleep.

"Something about that mansion still gives me a weird vibe. I can't sleep."

"Come back to bed, crazy woman."

I crawled back under the covers and snuggled next to him. He held me close and kissed me. "You're okay. I'm here. The bogeyman won't get you."

"You think I'm nuts."

Qigong jumped on top of us and started to lick both of our faces. Jackson scratched him behind the ears. "Yes, but that's not the point. You need to get some sleep. You've got a busy day ahead of you. Can't you do some of that deep breathing stuff you like?"

"I can try." So while Jackson held me, I concentrated on my breath as it went in and out. Finally, sleep came.

But at 2:05 a.m. my cell phone rang. By the time I got up, went over to the dresser, and picked it up, the call was ended. I took the phone with me back to bed and placed it on the nightstand.

"Who in the hell is calling at this hour?" Jackson said into his pillow.

"I don't know." I crawled back into bed and snuggled up next to him again. I had almost drifted off when the phone pinged, notifying me that I had a text message.

"Now what?" Jackson said.

I reached over and picked up my phone and checked my messages. There was only one, from Simon: HELP! COME RT AWAY! BIXBY ESTATE.

chapter four

Peppermint is good for muscular aches and pain, headaches and migraines, colds, flu, upset stomach, and nausea. The smell of peppermint can also give you a quick pick-me-up. According to a study in the *North American Journal of Psychology,* drivers were more alert and had more energy when exposed to peppermint. Put this into practice by opening a bottle of peppermint essential oil (*Mentha x piperita*) and inhaling a few times. Chewing strong peppermint gum or peppermint mints will also help perk you up.

Yours Naturally,

Dr. McQuade

Jackson and I got dressed, hopped into his black Ford truck, and headed back to the estate.

My stomach churned at the thought of what might have happened. Was Simon injured? Had he gotten into another fight with Roger at this time of night? Did one of the supposed spirits cause havoc?

Jackson didn't say much. He held my hand while he drove, knowing that I was upset. I tried to focus on my breathing, tried to stay calm. I knew that I needed to be clearheaded to handle whatever was next.

Ten minutes later, we arrived at the Bixby estate driveway, but a patrol car blocked the way. I felt sick. "Why are the police here? What is happening?"

Jackson pulled over, parked, and turned to me. "Look, Willow, I know you're worried, but let's just wait and see what has happened first and then we'll decide what to do, okay?"

I nodded, but I could already feel that dark energy coming from the house. Somehow I was sure that whatever had happened here tonight was only the start.

"Stay here," Jackson said, his voice warm and reassuring. "I'll go talk to him and see what I can find out." He got out and went over to talk to the policeman, who was out of his patrol car, pacing back and forth in front of the gate.

Jackson and the cop had a short conversation. The cop used his walkie-talkie to talk to someone, and after he was done, he shook his head no to Jackson. Now what were we going to do?

"What happened? Is Simon hurt?" I asked when Jackson got back into the truck.

Jackson shook his head. "The cop guarding the place wouldn't tell me. But he called your old friend Detective Koren, and Koren told him not to let us through."

Detective Koren had been my nemesis when I was trying

to solve my aunt's murder. Not only were he and his partner, Detective Coyle, ineffective, they also tried to prevent me from helping to find her killer. Of course, they didn't succeed.

"What are we going to do? Simon sounds like he's in a panic. We've got to find out what's going on!"

Jackson turned the truck around and headed back up the road. "I'm working on it." He drove until we were out of sight of the cop car. Then he pulled the truck onto the side of the road, next to the estate's tall fence. "Are you up to jumping the fence? It's the only way we can get in."

"Detective Koren won't like it."

"Too bad," Jackson said, and got out of the truck.

The night was cool and there was no wind as Jackson helped me over the fence, and together we made our way through the woods. Fortunately, Jackson had been a Boy Scout and had come prepared with a flashlight. We followed the small circle of light through the trees, zigzagging where the underbrush was too thick to pass. We could hear animals skittering away, and above us, an owl calling. After twenty or so minutes we made it to the edge of the woods on the estate. Through the branches we could see the mansion, two police cars, an ambulance, and a coroner's van. "The coroner is here. Someone's dead!" I could feel myself starting to tremble. I had sensed something terrible was going to happen here—and now it had. . . . That dark energy connected to this place, it wasn't my imagination. It was real.

Jackson pulled me into his arms. "We don't know that yet. I know this is hard on you, Willow, after what happened to your aunt. Are you up for this? Maybe we should go home and wait and see."

I had discovered my aunt's lifeless body on the floor of Nature's Way in June after she had been poisoned by cyanide mixed in a homeopathic remedy. Three months later, the memory was still fresh, and whatever happened here might add to the trauma. But for Simon, I needed to be strong. "No." I forced my voice to sound steady. "I have to know now."

"Okay then." Jackson pointed to the beach. "See those lights? That is where they are."

I could see klieg lights shining down on the Bixbys' private beach.

Jackson took my hand. "We'll take the long way around the north side of the tent. Okay? You with me?"

I nodded. "Let's go."

We jogged across the grass, which was moist with dew, and headed past the mansion, which looked even more foreboding at this late hour with all the lights off inside. Only the spotlights over the front door were on. I spotted a cop in one of the patrol cars in the driveway, but he was on his radio and didn't see us. We headed for the yellow-and-white-striped tent and snuck around the northern end. When we came out on the other side, we could see activity down on the beach. There looked to be five or six cops and several other people, but I didn't see Simon. "Where is he?"

"Let's go over to the retaining wall to get a better look."

I followed him, and we scurried across the lawn to the retaining wall that separated the estate from the inlet and looked down at the beach. Lights had been set up along the shore. Between them and the almost full moon, it was bright as day. Unfortunately, we were still too far away to see anything. "I don't see Simon!" I whispered.

"We're going to have to go over there to find out what is going on," Jackson said. "If Koren kicks us out, so be it, but at least we tried." He took my hand and we walked toward the stairs that led down to the beach.

As we got closer, I could see the wide stretch of sand, broken by several large boulders and numerous pieces of driftwood. A seaweed trail ran down the middle of the beach, evidence of the last high tide. Waves lapped at the shore. A wooden dock led from the edge of the beach out into the inlet. A powerboat was moored at the end of the dock, and an American flag hung from a post on the stern.

I stepped closer to the stairs. Suddenly, I saw a body underneath the bright lights. I stifled a scream. A man was lying on his stomach with his arms spread out to the side, as if he had been trying to fly. I couldn't see his face, but I recognized the cerulean-blue shirt and the dark, almost black hair. Roger Bixby.

I grabbed Jackson's arm and pointed. "It's Roger! He's dead!"

The cop who was guarding the top of the stairs and the entrance to the beach heard this, put his hand on his gun, and yelled, "Freeze right there!"

"We're not here to cause any trouble," Jackson said, his voice low and calm. "We're here because we're friends of Simon Lewis. He texted Willow a little while ago and asked us to come."

The cop began, "I don't care if the queen of England texted you—"

But he never got to finish. Detective Coyle, Detective Koren's partner, dressed in an ill-fitting blue blazer with a garish green-and-red tie, jogged up the stairs to the landing. He had worked with Koren on my aunt's murder and shared his disdain for my amateur sleuthing. "Fred, what is going on up here?" Then he spotted us and groaned. "Not you again."

• • •

Detective Coyle studied us for a few minutes, fingering his tie, as if we were some mysterious phenomenon he couldn't figure out. Finally he said, "I thought Detective Koren told you two to stay away." He gave Jackson a pointed look. "You don't listen too good, do you, Jackson Spade?"

"Simon Lewis asked Willow to come here."

"Is he okay?" I asked.

"Simon is busy with Detective Koren right now." Coyle's walkie-talkie squawked. He pressed a button on it and said, "Go for Coyle."

Koren's voice blasted out of the handset. "What are you doing? Get back down here!"

Coyle spoke into the walkie-talkie. "We've got company. It's that Willow McQuade and her boyfriend, Jackson Spade. She says she wants to see Simon Lewis."

After a long moment Koren finally said, "Send 'em down."

Coyle turned to us. "You heard the man." He pointed his finger at us. "No funny business."

From the minute I'd suggested that my aunt had been murdered, Coyle and Koren had thought I was meddling. Things only got worse as I pinpointed suspects and discovered clues in my investigation. When I caught the killers, they grudgingly admitted that I had done a good job, but that didn't mean they wanted my help now.

I gripped the banister on the stairs as Jackson and I followed Coyle to the beach. I scanned the area for Simon. Crime techs were working all over the beach, looking for evidence. Cops stood in tight circles, talking, but no Simon.

When we reached the bottom of the stairs, we followed

Coyle to the right, and I finally glimpsed him. Simon was sitting on top of an overturned rowboat, half-hidden in the reeds. He was talking to Detective Koren. Simon's pants were wet below the knee, and his shoes were missing. A few yards away, Carly was sitting on a log that had washed up on the beach, talking on her cell phone, her face blotchy from crying, and a wad of tissues clutched in her hand.

As we walked up, Koren said to Simon, "Now, when did you leave the estate?"

Simon spotted me and immediately came over and hugged me. He smelled like seaweed. "Willow, thank goodness! You're an absolute lifesaver!"

"I haven't done anything," I said, trying to make sense of the scene. It was like something from a bad dream.

"What's going on here?" Jackson said.

"Back off, Spade." Koren drilled Jackson with an angry look. "I'm just asking a few questions. And I only let you two down here to read you the riot act. This is a murder investigation, and you had better not interfere like you did the last time. I'm warning you."

"Murder? What makes you think it's murder?" I sucked in a breath, suddenly feeling light-headed.

I looked over at Roger's body, lying on the beach, his clothing soaked and covered with sand, his face a ghastly, pasty white, eyes staring blankly into space, and I felt bile rise in my throat. It had been less than three months since my aunt had been killed. As I had feared, all the horror that I'd felt when I'd found her body rushed back. For a minute, I couldn't breathe. Jackson gave me a look of concern and took my hand.

"Let's just say that Roger Bixby didn't just go for a moonlight swim."

"What exactly happened?" Jackson said.

Koren smirked. "Spade, you know I can't discuss an active case with civilians. You're not a cop anymore."

"No, I'm not. But I can tell Simon not to answer your questions."

"Simon, listen to Jackson," I said.

"I need to talk to Willow," Simon said to Koren.

"Go ahead, talk to her." Koren slapped his notebook against his thigh. "You've got five minutes, Lewis." He walked over to a crime-scene tech who was now working around Roger's body.

"Thank you for coming, both of you," Simon said. "I'm going to need your help. That detective is asking me all kinds of questions about Roger. I think he sees me as a suspect because I'm with Carly now. And because Roger and I had that fight this afternoon."

"That's not enough to make you a suspect," Jackson said. "And how did he know about the fight?"

"I had to recount my movements from the party on." Simon winced. "There's more. I also just invested in Galaxy Productions. With Roger gone, I'm the primary shareholder."

Talk about bad timing. "Why did you do that?" I asked. "Buy the shares, I mean."

Simon looked perplexed. "Carly asked me to help out. She told me that Galaxy was losing money. Plus I needed the tax break."

Jackson shook his head. "You've created quite a mess for yourself, Simon."

"I know I did. But I didn't kill Roger."

"Okay," I said. "Now tell us what happened tonight, Simon."

Jackson glanced at Koren, who was still talking to the tech. "Make it quick. Koren will be back soon, with more questions."

Simon ran his hand through his hair. "Carly and I left the set and went home around eleven thirty, but she forgot her phone back here. She had to make a bunch of calls to the coast and the numbers were stored in it. She couldn't even contact Amanda, so we had to come back. When we pulled into the drive around midnight and walked toward the production trailer, we heard MJ screaming. We ran over and found her on the beach, standing over Roger's body, which was floating at the water's edge. Carly and I pulled him out."

"What was MJ doing down here?" I asked.

"She said that she was just out taking a walk on the grounds before midnight when she was drawn to the beach because she sensed that something terrible had happened. She gave her statement to the police, and Rick took her back to their cottage on the estate a little while ago. The rest of the crew is staying at the Greenporter in town, so nobody else knows."

"Sounds like Carly is your alibi," Jackson said. "You were with her when the murder supposedly took place, right?"

"The coroner gave a window of from ten to twelve. Koren figures I had time to kill Rick before we left. That's why I need your help, Willow."

"Simon, I don't know what I can do."

"You need a lawyer," Jackson said, squeezing my hand. "Not Willow."

"You really do," I said.

"Carly is taking care of that right now." He pointed to Carly, who was still talking on her cell phone. "I've got a good legal team. Hopefully, they'll be able to straighten this out. But what if they can't? There are plenty of innocent men in prison." Simon took my hands and gazed deeply into my eyes. "Willow, I need you to find out who did this."

"Me? Why me?" I felt flabbergasted. I was no detective.

"You've done it before. You caught your aunt's murderer."

I had solved Aunt Claire's murder because I *had* to. Once I started, I couldn't stop, not until justice was served and her killers punished.

"That was different," I tried to explain. "It was beginner's luck." I felt a whirl of emotions, fresh pain over Aunt Claire's death, worry for Simon, and panic over what he was asking me to do.

"No, it wasn't," Simon argued. "You took that case apart— in a way that the cops never did. Honestly, you impressed the hell out of me, Willow. I know you can do it again."

Carly put her phone in her pocket and walked up to us. She looked totally drained, and her face was red and puffy from crying. "Simon, I just talked to Dick Browning, and he's on his way to LAX." She looked at her watch. "It's three oh two a.m. here, so it's midnight their time. He's going to shoot for a red-eye and be here in the morning. In the meantime, he's contacted an associate in the New York office and asked him to get out here as soon as possible. He said to keep your mouth shut. No talking to the cops."

Simon nodded and put his arm around Carly. "I understand. Jackson said that, too."

"Thank you both for coming out here in the middle of the night, but I think we'd better leave this to Simon's legal team," Carly said.

"Agreed," Jackson said. "Willow, you can't get involved in this."

"Yes, she can." Simon gave me a pleading look. "Please, Willow. Help me."

Nightmares wrecked any chance for peaceful sleep. I kept seeing Roger lying on the beach dead, and Simon's face when he asked me for help. When I woke up at 6:35 on Monday morning, my mind went into overdrive. I couldn't stop mulling over the facts about the crime that I knew so far, which weren't much. I was sure that Simon didn't kill Roger, but the police seemed less certain. I'd received a text from Carly at 3:30 a.m. just after we had arrived home and knew that Koren had taken Simon to the station and was holding him for questioning. I wondered if the lawyer from New York City had gotten him out, or if he would have to wait for his lawyer from L.A. Carly had also texted that she had authorized an autopsy. Hopefully, it would reveal evidence that would help the cops catch Roger's killer.

I tried to turn off my mind and go back to sleep. I snuggled next to Jackson, and he put his arms around me. Qigong was between us, and the cats were at our feet. After the horror of last night, I felt cozy and safe. I concentrated on my breathing and was almost asleep again when I heard the ping of my iPhone, telling me that I had a text message.

"Don't get up," Jackson said sleepily, reaching out for me. "It's still too early."

I leaned over and kissed him. "I'll be back in a minute."

Jackson groaned. I stepped onto the floor and padded over to my purse, which was on the dresser next to the window that overlooked the harbor. Outside, it was a truly glorious Indian summer kind of day, with a bright blue sky and little poofs of white clouds that looked like pillows. The Shelter Island ferry moved silently across the bay, which looked like plate glass. Seagulls wheeled overhead, and a man strolled through Mitchell Park, walking his two pugs. I reached inside my purse, pulled out my phone, and checked my text messages. There was only one, another message from Carly.

"Let me guess, Simon?" Jackson said as he sat up in bed. Qigong jumped on his belly and licked his face.

I nodded. "It's from Carly." I walked back over to the bed and handed him the phone.

Jackson read the message aloud. "EXPECT LAWYER SOON. S STILL AT STATION & WANTS YOUR HELP. C."

I felt my entire body start to shake. This was a nightmare. One I'd lived through before, only three months ago. Granted, Simon was alive, but he was still in a lot of trouble. Jackson put the phone down and gently rubbed my back. "Willow, don't take this on. He has lawyers for this. She says they will be here soon."

"I just feel bad. I know Simon didn't do this." I took the phone from Jackson, walked to the chair, and dropped it into my purse. "I'm going to take a shower." I stripped and headed for the bathroom. Once the water was a nice warm temperature, I stepped underneath the spray and washed my hair with organic shampoo. After that I grabbed the organic lavender-scented soap and started to scrub. Despite the relaxing warmth and heavenly lavender fragrance, my brain was moving a mile a minute. Who would have a motive to kill Roger? Was it business or personal? Did MJ really sense something or was *she* the killer? And I hated to even think about this, but *how* was Roger killed? Surely, that would reveal something about the murderer. I hoped the autopsy results were available soon.

I dried off, put my robe on, and padded back into my bedroom.

"I could hear you thinking from in here," Jackson said, pulling on his button-fly, black jeans, which were now dry. He didn't keep much clothing at my place; he was used to going home to shower. "Is this going to become an obsession like last time?"

I bit my lip and thought about it. "I'm afraid it might be."

"This is not for you." He put his hands on my shoulders and looked me right in the eye. "Let his lawyers handle it."

"How can I when my gut feeling is that Simon didn't do it? He's self-absorbed and needy, but he's not a killer. So who did commit murder? Who do you think did it—and why?"

Jackson dropped his hands and picked up his shirt. "No, you are not dragging me into a murder investigation again." He put his shirt on and tucked it into his pants. "And you are not getting involved, either."

"I can make my own decision, Jackson."

He put his belt through his belt loops. "I'm just trying to keep you safe. Remember what happened last time."

"I know what happened. I solved the case, with your help." Through intuition and hard work and Jackson's assistance, I had managed to find Aunt Claire's killers. I'd had no intention of becoming an amateur sleuth, but I had a knack for it. It might have had something to do with my training. Holistic doctors see the world as having a natural order. When that order is disturbed in a patient, we bring them back into balance with natural cures. So when things on a bigger scale go wrong in the world, such as when my aunt was murdered, I needed to set that right. It had been my only solace. But could I do it again?

Jackson sat down in the comfy chair and pulled me onto his lap. "You did a tremendous job finding your aunt's murderer, but you also almost got killed—and so did I."

"But if Simon needs my help, don't I have to try to help him?"

Jackson blew out a breath. "Do me a favor. Wait until we hear what the lawyers have to say before you do anything, okay? This may just blow over. Can you do that?"

chapter five

Dr. Willow McQuade's Healthy Living Tips

It's easy to transform your bathroom into an aromatic oasis. Not only will you feel like you're at the spa, afterward you'll feel rested and renewed. Just float fresh flowers or orange or lemon peels in the bathwater for a refreshing flower-power bath. You can use lilac, lavender, honeysuckle, or jasmine. You can also trim the aromatic leaves from mint and lemon balm and put them in the water.

Yours Naturally,

Dr. McQuade

I told Jackson that I wouldn't take action until I learned what Simon's lawyers were able to do. If they cleared Simon, I could let it rest. Still, I couldn't stop thinking about it. So I decided to do my Kripalu yoga practice, which is meditation in motion. It helps to move the life force, or *prana*, through one's body, and I knew it would help me center myself.

I put on my yoga gear, a sleeveless, turquoise top and matching cropped pants, put my hair up in a ponytail, and headed down to the second floor to the yoga studio. The cats stayed on the bed, but Qigong trailed after me. The studio had floor-to-ceiling windows, and the space was open and inviting. I pulled a sticky mat from the stack in the corner and put it down so I faced the windows. Qigong curled up in the corner on a pile of blankets.

I warmed up with a few gentle stretches, head-to-knee pose, and spinal twists. Then I moved on to frog, cobra, bridge pose, boat pose, downward dog, child's pose, and corpse pose. After I was through, I sat quietly and did some Pranayama, or yogic breathing. By the time I was done, I felt better; I always did after yoga.

After I got dressed, Qigong and I headed downstairs to my office. It was still early, so Merrily hadn't yet arrived. First I went into the kitchen and made myself a bowl of steel-cut oats and gave Qigong his organic dog food. I also made a cup of chamomile tea to help calm me down. Then I went into the office and had my breakfast. But thoughts of Simon intruded. I decided to call Carly, since Simon was obviously unreachable right now. The call didn't even ring through; it went straight to her voice mail.

I put my phone down and swiveled around in the desk chair as I tried to decide what to do next. Should I go to the jail? Or wait until I heard from Carly again? I decided to stay put for now. I didn't want to get in the way if I wasn't needed.

I swiveled the chair back around and noticed that a new fax was in the tray. It was a résumé from a Mr. Wallace Bryan, applying for work. With the college kids back at school, I was looking for a little extra help for the off-season. He'd added a note that he would stop by this morning. I hoped that he would be flexible about his salary needs, especially since we were going into the off-season and money would be tight. If I had to, I could take up Simon on his offer of a loan. But that would be a last resort.

Putting the résumé in my in-box, I turned my attention to the seminar on lavender tonight. I opened my file that held all the information about the seminar and quickly reviewed the outline I'd prepared. Next, I scheduled several tweets to remind my followers about what was happening at the store tonight, and I posted it on Facebook, too. I also posted a new blog entry I'd written to the *Nature's Remedy* site, about using aromatherapy in the bath.

Still, it was difficult to concentrate when my mind kept going over what had happened last night. As every minute ticked past, I became more and more concerned about Simon. I'd just made up my mind to go to the jail when the front door opened and Merrily yelled hello. Moments later she walked into the office, a huge grin on her face, holding a box from Green Focus. "The Fresh Face cream is here!" She put it down on the front of the desk.

"Finally, some good news," I said.

"What do you mean?"

I didn't answer her immediately. I wanted to enjoy this moment. I had worked hard to find my aunt's formula after she was killed and felt gratified that it was finally ready to go on sale. I grabbed a pair of scissors and opened the carton. Inside were twenty-four boxes of Fresh Face cream. I picked one up and examined it. The box featured appealing shades of green and blue against a cream background and was covered with line drawings of various herbs. The jar in the box was silver with a white top and also engraved with an herbal theme. I opened a jar, dipped my index finger in, and rubbed it on my cheek. It felt like velvet, and the moisturizer was absorbed by my skin quickly. I handed the jar to Merrily. "It's really nice. Try it."

"Okay." She put a dab of cream on her forehead and rubbed it in. "It is nice. But when are you going to tell me what is going on?"

"You'd better sit down." After she took a seat on the couch next to Qigong, I continued, "Simon is in jail."

"Why? What happened?"

I briefly explained what had happened at the party yesterday, including Simon's fight with Roger. "Late last night, MJ, the TV psychic, discovered Roger dead on the beach in front of the Bixby estate. Detective Koren says it's murder, and he's holding Simon for questioning at the Greenport jail."

"Murder? OMG, it's just like three months ago all over again! But why Simon? Just because he's going out with Carly and he had that fight with Roger?"

I shook my head. "There's more. Simon just bought shares in Galaxy Productions. That's the team that's shooting at the mansion. And with Roger dead, Simon now has the controlling interest in the company. That's all they need to know."

Merrily mulled this over. "Are you going to try and find the killer like you did the last time?"

That was the big question. "I don't know." Then my phone rang. Finally, it was Carly. I pressed Accept. "Carly, what's going on? How is Simon?"

"The lawyers arrived at the jail almost an hour ago, right after I texted you. They're in with Simon now."

"What do you think is going to happen?"

"I don't know." Her voice sounded somewhat shaky.

It couldn't be easy for Carly to wait alone when her estranged husband had just been murdered and her new boyfriend was the prime suspect. Plus, I wanted to know what was happening, firsthand. "I'm coming over."

"I don't know what you think you can do, Willow," Carly said not unkindly.

"I'm not sure either."

After a long pause she finally said, "I'll see you when you get here."

I told Merrily about Wallace Bryan, gave her his résumé, and asked her to interview him and check out his references. Then I left a message for Jackson to tell him what I was doing and left the store. As I walked down the path, past my own lavender and echinacea plants, I realized just how much had changed in less than twenty-four hours. It felt absolutely surreal that I was going to the Greenport jail to see Simon.

The jail was an imposing redbrick building with bars on tiny windows. Nervously, I climbed the steps and pulled open the heavy oak door. I found Carly sitting on a bench, sniffling and scrolling through her messages on her BlackBerry. Next to her was a small garbage can filled with used tissues. Obviously she had been crying. Opposite her was a desk manned by an imposing cop with a shaved head and an extra forty pounds. He was reading the newspaper but looked up and said, "Help you, miss?"

"I'm a friend of Simon Lewis."

He looked back down at his paper. "Sorry. No visitors, miss."

"Willow, he's still in with his lawyers," Carly said.

I went over and sat down next to her. "What's going on in there? Will he be charged?"

She shook her head. "I don't know."

"I'm really sorry about Roger, Carly."

"I know, Willow, thanks." She put her phone back in her purse. "Before, I was in shock over what happened. Then I was so busy getting Simon a lawyer that I didn't have time to process the whole thing, but now it's really starting to sink in. I'm going to have to arrange a funeral for Roger." Her voice started to shake. "I really don't know how I'm going to do this." She pulled a tissue out of her pocketbook as tears began to stream down her face.

We sat in silence for forty-five minutes before the door just past the desk opened and two men, dressed in expensive suits and holding briefcases, came out with Simon. Carly jumped up and went over and hugged him. "Are you okay?"

"Get me out of here." Simon looked absolutely awful, unshaven, with a haunted look in his eyes.

One of the lawyers, who looked like a bulldog and wore tiny glasses, opened the door for all of us. We filed out and walked down the stairs.

When we got to the sidewalk, Carly asked, "What happened in there, Dick? Is he cleared?"

The man with a gold Rolex and what had to be a $3,000 suit said, "We need to talk somewhere in private." He motioned to the black stretch limo parked out front.

"No more enclosed spaces. I need fresh air." Simon came over to me and gave me a hug. "Thanks for coming, Willow. Can we talk in your office at Nature's Way? I want to grab breakfast."

"Whatever you want, Simon." I wondered what exactly was going on.

"Carly and I will meet you there," Simon told the two lawyers. "Willow, are you coming?"

Carly whispered something to Simon. He shook his head. Carly probably didn't want me to come. I couldn't blame her; they needed alone time.

Before he could say anything, I did. "I've got my car. I'll see you all there in a few minutes."

When I returned to Nature's Way, I found Merrily sitting at one of the café tables, reviewing a paper on the table in front of her and chatting with a man with a white ponytail and Benjamin Franklin specs. Both of them had cups of tea in front of them. This had to be Wallace Bryan, the retired owner of a health food store in Northport who had faxed over his résumé this morning. With everything else that was going on I was glad that Merrily, as manager, was handling his interview. If she liked him, that was good enough for me.

"Willow!" Merrily said, jumping up from the table and coming over to me. "What happened?"

"I don't know yet. We're meeting in my office once everyone gets here." I smiled at the man with the white ponytail. "You must be Wallace. Thanks for coming in."

He smiled, stood up, and shook my hand. "My pleasure. Your store is wonderful. You have a great selection here, and the place has lots of positive energy. That's very important."

"I think so, too. So how are you two making out?"

"I'm very impressed with Wallace's background," Merrily said. "I think he could be a big help around here."

The front door opened and we all turned around. It was the lawyers. I went over to meet them. "This way, gentlemen." I steered them toward the office. The two men followed, then sat on the couch. I pulled the guest chairs around for Simon and Carly. "Would anyone care for coffee or herbal tea?" Neither of them took me up on the offer.

I excused myself and went to see Merrily. "Can I talk to you for a moment, please?"

"Sure. How can I help?" Merrily was always ready to do whatever needed to be done.

"Hold any calls for me, okay? I don't know how long this is going to take. And if you like Wallace, just do a quick check on his references and then you can hire him. See if he can start right away."

She nodded. "I think he's going to be a good fit for the store, but there's something else, Willow. One of the people from that MJ TV show came in when you were gone. Amanda, I think? She asked for you but I told her you were out. She asked a whole bunch of questions about how natural remedies can help with stress. I told her about herbs and supplements and flower essences, all that stuff. She asked about the massages and acupuncture here, too."

This was an interesting development. "Did she say why?"

"She was gathering info." Merrily shrugged. "I didn't want to pry."

"That's fine." I put it on my mental back burner. I had other things to deal with now. "Thanks, Merrily." I walked to the front door, opened it, and looked east, down Front Street. Simon and Carly were about a block away. I waited for them to get to the store, and we all went inside together.

"Can I have buckwheat pancakes and strawberries?" Simon asked.

I said sure and whipped some up for him while Carly told the lawyers it would be a few minutes. When the pancakes were ready, Simon took the plate and a glass of orange juice and went into my office. Carly and I followed.

The moment we entered, Dick stopped pounding on his BlackBerry and looked up. "I think that Carly and Willow should step outside for this first part, Simon."

"They stay," Simon said, shoveling the pancakes into his mouth.

"Listen to me, Simon," Dick said. "This is important. You and I need to go over a few things." He glanced at us. "We won't be long, ladies."

Simon took a sip of juice, wiped his mouth, and finally shrugged.

Dick said, "Ladies, you mind?"

Carly opened the door and stormed out, so I guessed she did. I wanted to know what was going on, but I could wait if it would help Simon. I stepped out and closed the door behind me.

Carly, ever productive, used the time to make funeral arrangements, while I helped Merrily out by manning the counter so she could just focus on serving customers. Almost an hour later, Dick opened the door and asked us to come in. Carly took the guest chair next to Simon but didn't say anything. I moved my office chair around the desk and sat down.

"Okay, here is what is going on, ladies," Dick said. "The police wanted to question Simon some more. Of course, I can't allow that. But they did say that he is a person of interest. I believe that their investigation into the murder of Roger Bixby will continue to involve him."

"I don't understand this," I said. "Is this just because he's involved with Carly? Or is it because of the shares that Simon purchased? He said he did it for a tax break."

Dick nodded. "That didn't help. Now that Roger is dead, Simon has the controlling interest in Galaxy Productions. But just as important, Simon has fought with Roger on two other occasions, and there were witnesses both times."

"What? You've fought before, Simon?"

Simon shrugged and took Carly's hand.

"So what happens now?" Carly asked. "What do we do?"

"I'm going to put my best PI on this to investigate backgrounds on all the parties involved. But I also need someone who can go on the set and look around without arousing suspicion," Dick said. "Most outsiders I bring in, they couldn't do that. And I don't think we have a lot of time to be coming up with cover stories." He turned to me. "Ms. McQuade, Simon told me what you were able to do in June. I agree that it was impressive work. But I'm not sure that you should be involved. After all, you're an amateur with not much of a track record."

"I agree." Carly nodded. "No offense, Willow."

"None taken." I understood the way Dick and Carly felt. I *was* an amateur investigator, and *I* wasn't even sure I could do this.

"I want this, Dick. She's good," Simon said, a warning tone in his voice. "Make it happen."

Dick looked at Simon for a long moment. "Okay, Ms. McQuade, perhaps you can see what you can find? We need to cover this from all angles. You'll be compensated, of course."

Part of me wanted to disappear, but another part of me wanted to figure out this puzzle and help save Simon. I didn't say anything. Instead I mulled over the decision. Could I do this?

"Carly can get you access to the set," Dick continued. "No one will wonder if you ask a few questions. What do you think, Ms. McQuade?"

Simon leaned over and gave me a pleading look. "Will you do it?"

chapter six

Lemon balm (*Melissa,* which in Greek means "bee") is a lovely lemony-smelling herb. I like to grow it in my garden in front of Nature's Way Market and Café. It works like mint in that it soothes the stomach and the digestive system and helps relieve indigestion, gas, and bloating. It also helps if you are nervous, anxious, or have a little trouble sleeping, thanks to its essential oils, citronella and citrals A and B.

Yours Naturally,

Dr. McQuade

I was just about to answer Simon when the phone rang. I went over to the desk and picked it up. "Nature's Way. Willow, speaking. How may I help you?"

"Hi, Willow. Rick McClellan here." Rick was MJ's husband and a producer on the show.

"Rick, what can I do for you?" Carly and Simon both had quizzical looks on their faces, wondering what he wanted. I was wondering, too. Perhaps this had something to do with Amanda's visit. "I hear that Amanda stopped by this morning."

"Well, here's the situation. MJ and the production crew are all upset about what happened to Roger last night. Everyone's on edge—tense and skittish and just plain scared. MJ thought maybe you could help us, so I sent Amanda down to check you out."

"Help you how?"

"Amanda says you've got lots of remedies for stressed-out people, like those herbs and that massage and acupuncture stuff. Well, that's what we need. MJ, she wants her people to feel good, and even I can see the sense in that. We want to get an excellent show in the can despite this tragedy. Can you come on up and we'll discuss it?"

Rick's request seemed serendipitous, considering that Simon wanted me to investigate Roger's murder on the estate. Working for Rick would give me an even less suspicious way to ask questions. I had learned not to ignore this kind of sign when it came to making decisions. It seemed that I was meant to go back there, although I wasn't keen on doing so because of the weird vibes coming from the mansion. But I believed Simon was innocent, so I told Carly, the lawyers, and him that I would try to find out what had happened to Roger. Then I headed back to Southold. I didn't bring any supplies since I wasn't sure what Rick would need.

I called Jackson on the way but got no reply. I left a message telling him where I was and that I needed to talk to him right away. He wouldn't be happy about my decision, but I hoped he would help me with my investigation.

Ten minutes later, I pulled into the Bixby driveway and parked in the circular drive behind two police cars, a black Mercedes, and a midnight-blue BMW. Qigong had come along with me and thoroughly enjoyed sticking his head out the window. I opened the rear car door, helped him out of the car, grabbed his leash, and we crossed in front of the Bixby mansion. I felt that same negative vibe, only stronger this time, perhaps even intensified by the immediacy of Roger's murder. Was MJ right? Were there evil spirits in that house? I didn't usually give much credence to their existence, but I was starting to wonder. Spending time here would be a challenge.

I walked Qigong over to the steps that led to the Bixby beach. Below us, the police techs were busy at work, still combing the sand for clues.

Beyond the shore, the bay sparkled in the sunlight. I watched as a seagull dive-bombed into the shallow water, plucked up a crab, took off with it, circled, and then dropped it—splat!—on the dock. Life feeds on life. *That seagull is just hungry, killing that crab to survive,* I told myself. But somehow the act seemed horribly violent.

Detective Koren spotted me and headed up the steps with Rick behind him, talking on his phone. Detective Coyle trailed behind.

"Willow!" Rick said, disconnecting the call and putting the phone in his pocket. "Thanks so much for coming." Today he was dressed casually, in jeans and a blue T-shirt with colorful planets on it that said GALAXY PRODUCTIONS: IT'S OUT OF THIS WORLD!

Koren got up so close to me that I could smell his pungent aftershave. He growled, "I thought I told you to stay away, Ms. McQuade."

Qigong didn't like this and started growling back.

"Back off, dog!" Coyle snapped, trying to be macho. He was dressed in what I can only describe as pure Coyle: He wore a shiny, cheap-looking, black suit, an ugly purple tie, and a tie clip that looked like a golf club.

"It's okay, Qigong." I reached down and patted his head.

Koren stepped back and shook his head. "That is one wacko name for a dog. But it figures, coming from you."

I decided to try to educate him. "Qigong is a twenty-five-hundred-year-old type of energy medicine from China. You use breathing techniques, gentle movements, and meditation to cleanse, strengthen, and circulate your life energy, or qi."

"Whatever, *Doctor*," Koren said sarcastically. "You and your doggy need to go."

"Wait a minute, Detective," Rick said. "I asked her to come. I'll be with you in a minute, Willow. As I was saying, I don't think you understand. We've already postponed the schedule for a full day. We need to start shooting tomorrow."

Detective Koren shook his head. "No, *you* don't understand. This is a murder investigation. It takes priority. You'll have to wait."

Rick blew out a breath. "MJ and the crew are here to work. If I don't use them, I still pay. And if we don't get it done this week, I miss my deadline, we have no show for broadcast, and *MJ's Mind*—and possibly Galaxy Productions—are finished."

"That's not my problem."

Rick pulled out his cell phone. "Did I neglect to mention

that MJ and I are very close friends with the governor of your state? Seems he went to college with MJ. I have him on speed dial. I know he won't be happy if shooting on her show is delayed."

Detective Koren shoved his hands into the pockets of his Brooks Brothers suit. It was fun to watch him squirm. I could tell he was trying to figure out how to play this one. Finally he said, "You can shoot starting tomorrow, but this beach is off-limits, okay? And make sure that MJ, the production staff, and the crew are available for questioning when I need them and that no one skips town just yet."

Rick nodded his head. "No problem. I can make that happen. So we're good?"

"You're good as long as you abide by my rules. Break 'em, and I swear, I'll take you all in for obstruction." Koren headed back to the stairs and the beach.

Rick exhaled a breath as he watched Koren go. "Good thing he didn't call me on that one. I'm not sure the governor would remember MJ after all. They were in only one class together. I think it was biology. They shared a frog." Rick chuckled for a moment, but when he glanced at the beach, quickly got serious again. "Now, here's the thing, Roger's murder, God rest his soul, is, of course, really freaking MJ out. I'm afraid it will affect her ability to read the house and her performance on the show. The staff and crew aren't much calmer. Not to mention that there's a murderer on the loose. Things are tense, and I'm hoping you can help, Ms. McQuade."

His cell phone rang. "McClellan here." He listened for a moment. "Hold on. I'll be right with you." He pointed to the caretakers' grown son, Lucas Russell, as he came rolling up in one of the golf carts. "Lucas will take you to the cottage that I thought you could use as a home base while you're here treating the staff. It's next to ours, and Mrs. Florrick, the housemaid, lives behind it. Think about what services you can provide that would help de-stress MJ and the crew. I'll take this call and meet you over there in a few minutes."

I got into the cart and put Qigong on my lap. Lucas put the cart into drive and we took off heading north along the retaining wall. Across the water, over at the public beach, people were enjoying the hot sun and the cool water.

When I was a kid, my mother would bring Natasha and me there. From morning to dinnertime, we'd be swimming and diving in the dredged harbor. When we got too cold, we'd wrap blankets around ourselves and eat Cheese Nips, Oreos, and watermelon and read books. The days seemed endless, and life, full of possibilities.

As we headed away from the mansion, the energy felt lighter and more positive. "You live in a beautiful place," I said.

"It's okay I guess."

"Your lavender fields are lovely," I said, trying to coax Lucas into conversation. "It's my favorite herb. I run a health food store and café in Greenport called Nature's Way, and I'm giving a seminar on lavender tonight."

Lucas grunted.

We rode along in silence past the pond where Simon and Roger had been fighting. I decided to try again to get Lucas talking. It was time to start investigating. "I guess everyone is upset about Roger."

He shrugged and suddenly became talkative. "I wouldn't say that. Not to speak ill of the dead, but Roger was a fool. It's no surprise that he came to a bad end. When Roger was younger, he was always causing trouble, getting into fights over girls, drag racing on the North Road, gambling and getting stoned. But Max used his influence to get him into Brown.

When he got kicked out of there for cheating, he decided to go out West to Hollywood. He convinced his old man to fund his production company. He's been playing producer and living the high life on Max's dime as long as any of us can remember. The man didn't care about anyone but himself. Ask Carly. She knows."

"Sounds like Roger may have made some enemies. The police questioned Carly's boyfriend, Simon Lewis. You probably heard about that fight they had yesterday."

"Roger will pick a fight with anyone. I don't know Simon, but I don't think he did it. This crime has something to do with the past."

"What do you mean?"

"I mean, you can't get rid of bad blood. And that's all I'll say on the subject. Anything else and I'd just be guessing."

I mulled this over, but before I could say anything else, Lucas pointed to two cozy yellow cottages, with red shutters and roofs. "The house on the left is where Rick and MJ are staying. You'll be using the one on the right."

"Where was Roger staying?" I knew Carly was living at Simon's house.

"He always stayed in the main house when he visited, which wasn't often. Mrs. Florrick took care of him, like he was her own son." Lucas pulled up in front of the cottage on the right and stopped.

I thanked him, picked up Qigong, and got out. "You'll be back soon with Rick, right?" I didn't want to be here alone for long, considering a murderer was on the loose.

"Five minutes." Lucas made a U-turn and headed back to the mansion.

The door was open so Qigong ran up the path, inside the cottage, and jumped up on the couch in the small living room.

He obviously didn't sense that anyone else was here, so I relaxed a little. I checked out the kitchenette and an enclosed porch. On the right were two bedrooms that could be used for massage and acupuncture, and a small bathroom. This could work. I'd just have to hope that Allie, Hector, and my yoga instructor, Nick Holmes, were available on such short notice. I sat down on the sofa, took out a notepad, and began to make a list of the services I could provide for MJ and the crew. I also wanted to ask Rick about Roger's murder, but first things first.

I'd just completed my list when Rick came in. "Thanks for waiting, Willow." He sat down in one of the wingback chairs. "So, tell me what you think you can do."

"Well, I can help MJ and your staff with a wide array of natural remedies—everything from herbs to homeopathic medicines, supplements to flower essences and aromatherapy. As Amanda told you, I also work with a masseuse and an acupuncturist at Nature's Way. Both of these practices can be immensely helpful when it comes to dealing with stress and its effect on the body."

"That all sounds great, but what about some stuff for energy? We need that, too. These shoots can get pretty grueling."

"That's easy. I can set up a smoothie bar with herbal mixtures for energy and clarity so that everyone is functioning at their best."

"Good stuff," Rick said. "And how would you handle seeing folks?"

"We could use a sign-up sheet and people could make appointments to see me, have a massage or an acupuncture treatment. I think I can also arrange for my master yoga teacher to hold classes here, which would be wonderful for everyone in terms of stress release."

"Okay, Amanda can handle the sign-up. How would you bill me?"

My cell phone rang but I let it go to voice mail. I needed to focus on Rick and this job.

"I'll just bill you per client, depending on what services they receive and the products I use."

"Just itemize everything and we'll be fine. So when can you get started?"

I needed to make sure that Allie and Hector and Nick were all available. If not, it would be a problem. But I decided to think positively and said, "I can be here around noon tomorrow with my team. How does that sound?"

"Perfect. Afternoons are much more manageable in terms of people coming and going when we are shooting." He got up and shook my hand. "Welcome to the team. Glad to have you here, Willow."

The feeling was mutual. Not only would this provide a nice chunk of new business, it would also give me the perfect opportunity to snoop around undercover and see what I could find out about Roger's murder.

chapter seven

Dr. Willow McQuade's Healthy Living Tips

Bergamot (*Citrus bergamia*) oil has a fresh, sweet-tart, orange-fruit scent. It comes from the outer peels of bitter miniature oranges grown in Italy. Bergamot is a natural antidepressant (for mild depression only). It eases anxiety and is a mood booster. It also keeps skin looking young and clears up acne. Choose an essential oil blend or a skin cleanser that contains bergamot to experience its benefits.

Yours Naturally,

Dr. McQuade

As Rick drove Qigong and me back to the main house, I mulled over exactly what I would need to make this job successful. The minute I got in my car, I would call Allie and Hector. In addition, I needed to call Nick Holmes, Aunt Claire's boyfriend and the yoga instructor at Nature's Way, to see if he could provide yoga classes. Merrily could help me put together the products that I would need.

We were minutes away from the mansion when I received a text from Jackson telling me that he was on his way up here. I wasn't sure what that was about, but I did need to tell him that I'd decided to try to help Simon. I hoped that he would understand.

When Rick dropped me off at my car, standing in the driveway was MJ, the star of *MJ's Mind*. Today, she wore a flowing caftan in shades of red, orange, and bright yellow. Her red hair was pulled into a loose chignon, and she wore large earrings that dangled almost to her shoulders, and her red sneakers. She had her arm around Carly, who was dressed in a short, black skirt and a white, sleeveless tank top, her face and eyes red from crying.

Rick, who was on the phone, jumped out of the golf cart. "I took your advice, darlin', and asked Willow to come up here. She's going to set up a spa thingie for you in that cottage next to ours. Was there anything special you'd like from her?"

MJ plucked the phone out of his hand and gave him a steely look. "Can't you see that Carly is very upset?"

"Of course I do." Rick pulled Carly into a hug. "It's gonna be okay, sweetie. We're all in this thing together."

"I can't do this Rick," Carly said, pulling away from him. "I can't be here now with this . . . circus going on. I need everyone gone."

"Honey, we couldn't leave even if we wanted to. Detective

Koren needs us to stay here in case he has any questions. Not to mention, we are going to be out a bucketload of greenbacks if we pull the plug." Rick ticked numbers off on his fingers. "I've got to pay the crew and the production staff regardless, and take care of their food and lodging, not to mention the rental fees on all the equipment. If we cancel and come back later, it's going to cost us a fortune."

Carly shook her head. "I don't care."

"You're saying that now, but if we don't deliver this premier episode on time, the order for the series from the Sci-Fi channel will be cancelled, and Galaxy Productions goes under. Who's going to hire us after that? You know how this business is. You've got to produce. We have to do this." He put his hands on Carly's shoulders. "And I need you. You're my line producer. I need you to keep us on track and underbudget."

"It's all about money with you, Rick," Carly snapped. "I lost my husband! I'm grieving. Can't you understand that? This morning I made funeral arrangements for Roger, my dead husband. It's Wednesday morning at the Southold Presbyterian Church, by the way. Do you have any idea how that feels?"

"Sweetheart, I don't mean to be insensitive, but weren't you divorcing the man?"

Carly stuck her finger in Rick's face. "You're right. He cheated on me and made a fool of me. I waited up so many nights for him when he didn't come home or even have the decency to call. I hated him for that. He was a real shit." She blinked back tears. "But I loved him anyway."

Carly had me baffled. The night of the murder she hadn't seemed that upset about Roger. Instead, she seemed focused on finding lawyers for Simon. Maybe she had been in shock then; when she arrived at the jail, the reality of Roger's death started to hit her. Still, I wondered: Did she love or hate Roger—or both? For a brief moment I considered if she might have killed him and this was all an act. But she was happy with Simon now, so that didn't make sense.

"Maybe you need to lie down and take a rest for a bit, darlin'," Rick said. "When you wake up, you might feel different."

I plucked a bottle of lavender essential oil from my bag and handed it to her. "You can put a few drops of this on a cloth and place it on your forehead. It will calm you."

Carly shook her head and pulled out a tissue. "A nap is not going to make me feel better. It's going to take a lot longer than that!" She opened the door of the BMW, got in, and slammed it shut, took a hard left, and drove off, dirt kicking up under the wheels of the car.

Rick shook his head. "She'll be back. She's a pro." He turned to MJ. "Now, was there something special you needed from Willow? She'll be setting up shop here tomorrow at noon."

Before she could answer, Amanda pulled up in a golf cart, parked it, and came over to us. Her eyes were red rimmed, as if she, too, had been crying.

"You don't look too good, sweetheart," Rick said, sounding concerned. He glanced at his wife. "Is everyone on this show falling apart at the seams?"

"I tried to tell you," MJ said.

"I'm fine," Amanda said, her voice sounding shaky.

Rick sighed and immediately began dispensing more comfort. "I know this is hard on you. You were Roger's right-hand gal. But we still need you, Amanda. Would you consider staying and becoming our assistant?"

"That's a wonderful idea," MJ said. "We'd love to have you work for us."

Amanda thought it over and finally said, "I think Rick would want me to stay and help you, so I will. But I'm scared."

She shivered. "I mean, who is going to protect us from the murderer? He could be anywhere. Plus weird things have been happening in that house."

"Like what?" MJ asked.

"Like these weird whispering sounds in the library and books flying off the shelf. I almost got hit in the head this morning! It's creepy."

"That's why we are here, darlin', to investigate paranormal phenomena," Rick told her. "As for everyone's safety, don't you worry. I've taken care of that." Rick pointed to the black Ford truck making its way up the driveway. "I've just hired former police officer Jackson Spade."

We all watched as Jackson got out of his truck and walked over to us. He hadn't shaved and wore his favorite jeans, a gray, short-sleeved T-shirt, and boots. He looked *so* ruggedly handsome. He came over to me, gave me a kiss, and shook Rick's hand. "Thanks for thinking of me. Hope I can help."

"Thanks for coming. Appreciate it." Rick turned back to us. "Jackson is my new head of security. Given that we've still got some nut job on the loose, I wanted someone I could trust to keep an eye on things. Jackson is a former cop, so he's the perfect fit." Rick patted Jackson on the back. "It'll be a family affair. Willow will be here, too. I've hired her to provide all that yoga-type stuff for MJ, the crew, and the staff."

"You've got the right person for that," Jackson said. "She helped me with my back. I'm a walking testimonial."

"That's good to hear," Rick said. "I just got the okay from the police, so we can start shooting in the morning. Spade, I'll need you here at eight a.m. That work?"

"Sure."

"I've hired a guard for the gatehouse so we don't have to worry about intruders. That way you can focus on the grounds and the house."

"Sounds good," Jackson said.

We were interrupted by Tom, Roger's brother and the second director, as he rounded the house and came over to us. He was dressed in jeans, a blue Izod shirt, slip-on purple sneakers, and shades and was smoking a big cigar. He had definitely taken to the L.A. lifestyle. I wondered if he had plans to replace Roger as a producer. Had he eliminated his brother so he could take his job? Walking up to Rick, Tom pushed his Ray-Bans on top of his head. "Pierre wants you to come to the production trailer so we can plan tomorrow's shoot."

"Pierre is our director. He's top-notch," Rick said to us. "Just came off of *Ghost Hunters International*. We were lucky to get him." Rick pointed to Tom. "Call Carly. We need her back here so we can go over everything."

"Where did she go?"

"Just call her," Rick said, sounding annoyed.

Tom pulled out his phone.

"Can I talk to you?" Jackson said to me. He took me by the hand and led me away from the group. "I got your message. Is this what you wanted to tell me about? What's going on with Simon?"

"I decided to help him." I told Jackson about my visit to the jail and the meeting in my office.

Jackson shook his head. "Willow, I thought we were going to discuss helping Simon before you made a decision."

"I know, but things happened pretty fast."

"So fast that you couldn't call me?" He pulled out his cell phone and showed it to me. "See, cell phone."

"I did call you."

"But not to tell me this, McQuade." He shoved the phone back into his pocket. "You just told me you wanted to tell me something."

"I have to do this, Jackson. I can't stop thinking about it. If I don't figure it out, and I think I can—with your help, of course—it will drive me crazy. Don't you want to know who really killed Roger?"

"Not really. I want to keep you safe."

"You can keep me safe. I'll be here with you."

Jackson thought about this. "That's a good point, but I still don't like it."

"I know, but will you help me like last time?"

"Well, I'm certainly not going to let you do this alone."

"So?" I kissed him. "What do you say, big guy?"

"Stop trying to butter me up. I'm in."

Jackson said his good-byes, and I walked him over to his truck. "I have to go see my orthopedist for a check-in," he said. "I'll meet you at the store tonight for the seminar."

"Don't forget the lavender." I kissed him good-bye.

"Don't hang around the estate without me." He started the truck.

"I'm going back to the store. Don't worry." I called to Qigong and we walked to my car. Jackson beeped his horn and waved as he headed down the drive. I opened the door. "C'mon, boy. Let's go home."

But Qigong had other ideas. He dashed up the steps dragging his leash and inside the open door of the mansion. I ran after him, following the sound of his toenails clicking on the parquet floor. He led me into the downstairs dining room, which was like something out of the wedding banquet in *Great*

Expectations. The long dining table was set, as if awaiting guests who never showed up—dishes with the Bixby crest, a gold lion on a field of blue; long-stemmed crystal wineglasses; sterling-silver flatware; and fake mums in porcelain vases. And all of it covered in dust.

Inside the house, that negative vibe was so palpable, I almost felt as if I could close my hand around it. I forced myself to stand still for a moment. Was it a ghost? Evil spirits? I wasn't sure, but it felt as if something angry were in the room with me, and that it had been there for a long time and had no intention of leaving. Suddenly, I knew I had to get out of there as quickly as possible. I reached for Qigong's leash, but he took off again, racing out of the room, across the hall and into the library.

This room was filled with floor-to-ceiling bookshelves with a moving ladder that could be used to reach every volume. Above the shelves were large portraits of the Bixby ancestors. None of them looked happy. The only furniture was a beat-up green couch, a La-Z-Boy armchair that had seen better days, and a dinged-up coffee table with a large ashtray on top. The fireplace looked as if it hadn't been used in a long, long time. Not exactly *Lifestyles of the Rich and Famous*. Qigong put his paws on the windowsill behind the couch, looked out, and started barking.

I scurried over, looked out, and saw Tom standing outside the production trailer, talking to Carly, his sister-in-law. Both of them were smoking cigarettes and both of them looked upset. After a moment, they stubbed the cigarettes out, hugged each other, and went back inside. Maybe Tom was just comforting Carly, as any good brother-in-law would, but the detective in me wondered if he had designs on her as well as on Roger's job.

As I picked up Qigong, I noticed crisp, clean editions of

such books as *A Farewell to Arms*, *Atlas Shrugged*, and *The Moving Finger* on a small table near the window. Curious, I put Qigong down, told him, "Stay," and picked up *The Moving Finger* by Agatha Christie. The cover featured a hand with a finger pointing to a portrait of one of the characters in the book. I opened it and found crisp, light brown pages that were frayed at the edges.

I checked the front of the book and realized that it was a first edition. Although in 1942 the book had cost just two dollars, it certainly was worth considerably more now. The other books were first editions, as well. Obviously Max Bixby had been an avid collector. With his death, Roger would have inherited all these books, which had to be worth a nice chunk of change.

Suddenly, I heard strange whispers. I thought about what Amanda had said. The whispers continued, getting louder. I spun around and tried to find the source. What I found was Mrs. Florrick. The whispers stopped. "Did you hear that?"

"I heard nothing." Her tone was brisk, brittle, and no-nonsense.

I wasn't sure I believed in ghosts, but something weird was going on here.

"Now, what are you doing in my house?" Her house? Maybe she had been here so long, she considered the house her own.

"I'm here because Rick asked me to provide natural remedy treatments for MJ and the crew."

"It is my understanding that they will not begin shooting the show until eight a.m. tomorrow morning. What are you doing here *now*?"

"My dog, Qigong, ran inside and I came in to get him." I picked him up again. The one thing I didn't want him to do was "go" on the rug. Granted, it was a worn area rug, but I didn't want to engender any more hostility from the woman. I would be working on the estate for the next week and didn't want any trouble from her.

As I headed to the door, I noticed a crystal ball on a shelf. "Was that Mr. Bixby's?"

Mrs. Florrick nodded. "Yes, Mr. Bixby was very interested in spiritualism. He regularly held séances with his guests when he was alive." This confirmed what MJ had said.

Suddenly, the antique chandelier above us flickered on and off, on and off, then stopped. A large book fell off the shelf above the fireplace and landed on the floor. I sucked in a breath. It seemed that I was experiencing the same phenomena that Amanda had. "Do you know what caused that?" I asked the housekeeper.

I gazed down at the book that had fallen, *A Complete History of Rum Running on Long Island's East End.*

"Too many books squeezed into the shelves is all," she said matter-of-factly. "Max could never pass up a book on rum-running." She bent over and picked up the book.

As she did, I noticed that she had ugly, bulging blue veins on the backs of her knees and calves. Perhaps if I offered a bit of advice, she might help me with my investigation. "Do your varicose veins bother you?"

She straightened up and glared at me. "What business is it of yours?"

"Sorry," I said quickly. "I don't mean to pry. It's just that I'm a naturopathic doctor, and I have some remedies that might help."

She walked over to the bookshelf and, with some effort, shoved the book back in its place. "I've never found anything for it. I'm on my feet all day, and I'm not getting any younger. I wear support hose, but it doesn't seem to help much."

"Have you tried horse-chestnut cream? It helps to relieve

inflammation and itching. I could bring you some from my health food store if you like. I'm Willow McQuade, by the way."

She gave me a long look, then finally nodded. "Thank you, Willow. I think I would like to try that. It's been a very bad time."

"I know. You must be very upset about Roger's death."

"He was a wonderful boy, curious about everything."

"And what was he like as a man?" I asked.

"We didn't see him much, once he went to L.A. Roger turned out to be a lot like his father, had a strong character. He wanted what he wanted, and he didn't let much stand in his way. Tom thinks he's like them, but he's not. He doesn't have that kind of determination." She pursed her lips, and somehow I imagined that she had disapproved of Tom since he was a boy. "You know, I saw you talking to MJ, Rick, and Carly earlier. That Carly was no good for Roger. She's the reason he was going to sell Bixby manor."

This was a surprise. "Roger planned to sell the house?"

"He didn't want to. But she was always pressuring him. She didn't like it here."

"But they were getting divorced. Couldn't he do what he wanted?"

"No. Carly gets half of everything, and that means this house as well. Now, she gets it all. I think it suits her that he's dead now."

I had to ask. "Do you actually think she could have murdered Roger?"

She shook her head and walked down the hall to the door. "I don't know. But Roger had no shortage of enemies. When you are successful, people get jealous and can do awful things." She opened the door and saw us out.

At first I headed toward my car, but then I decided it would be a good idea to take a closer look at the crime scene, if it wasn't roped off. Maybe the police had missed something. It was unlikely but worth a try. I started toward the beach, but Qigong was impatient and pulled away, his leash trailing behind him. He scurried to the steps and ran down to the beach. I went after him, only to be stopped at the bottom of the stairs by a cop. "Can't be down here, miss. This is a crime scene."

"I know, but that's my dog! Qigong," I yelled, "come back here!"

Qigong, who was thrilled to be back on the beach, scampered across the sand, heading straight for a boulder that had been roped off with yellow police tape.

"You've got to get your dog out of here, miss."

"I agree." Before the cop could object, I raced after Qigong.

Qigong took one look at me and decided we were playing a game. He turned from the boulder and ran toward the water, splashing joyously in the surf. "Qigong!" I yelled. "Come here!" I knew it was hopeless. He was having too much fun, and as soon as I got within ten yards of him, he dashed off again.

I felt as if I were starring in an embarrassing video: "Incompetent Dog Owner Chases Dog." I was also sweaty and getting tired. I ran down the beach and around the bend, where I found Qigong sniffing a pile of seaweed on the shore. "Gotcha!" I said as I picked him up. But a wet dog is a slippery dog. He wriggled out of my arms and took off again. He dashed past two policemen on the beach and out onto the dock.

"Boy, he sure listens to you, doesn't he?" said one of the cops.

"Yeah, that obedience training really paid off," said the other, and they both started laughing. I really did not need this.

I followed Qigong out onto the dock, but he U-turned,

zoomed past me back to the beach, and hugged the shoreline back to the bend. Obviously, chasing him wasn't working. I decided to try a different tactic. I stopped running and casually strolled in his direction, thinking this might make him more cooperative. As I rounded the corner, I found him again sniffing around that pile of seaweed. "Good boy," I said as I got closer to him. He looked up at me. He had a red-and-yellow box with ragged edges and a barely legible label in his mouth. I looked at it more closely. It was a disposable camera. I inched closer to him and plucked it out of his mouth just as one of the cops came around the bend. Instinct took over and I plunged it into my pocket, picked up Qigong, looped my hand through his leash, and walked toward the cop. "Got him," I said, trying to sound cheerful.

"Good. Now you need to clear out of here."

I put Qigong down and we quickly walked up the stairs to the lawn and then to the car. Inside, I pulled the camera out of my pocket and examined it. Despite several teeth marks, it looked okay. I should have given it to the cops, but something told me it was important that I keep it. I wondered what was recorded on the camera. There was one way to find out.

chapter eight

The pungent smell of eucalyptus (*Eucalyptus globulus*) is an excellent aromatic treatment if you have respiratory problems such as bronchitis, asthma, coughing, cold, flu, and sinusitis because it breaks up phlegm and bronchial congestion. You can use fresh eucalyptus leaves in teas and gargles to soothe a sore throat and treat bronchitis and sinusitis. Try using an ointment that contains eucalyptus and apply it to your nose and chest to relieve congestion. Putting eucalyptus oil in a diffuser will open your chest and sinuses and make you feel much better.

Yours Naturally,

Dr. McQuade

We have a one-hour photo shop in Greenport, and I decided to drop off the camera before I went back to Nature's Way. On the way home, Simon called asking if I'd made any progress. I told him he'd have to try to be a little more patient. I called Allie and Hector and left messages and talked to Nick, who agreed to teach at the estate. I pulled up in front of Kate's Photo and dropped off the camera. I didn't expect to find a picture of the murderer, but perhaps there would be something useful. Minutes later, I was back in the car and my cell phone rang. It was Allie. "Hey there, I guess you got my message."

"I did and I talked to Merrily and she told me everything. We're available, but I'm kind of freaked-out about working up there since they haven't figured out who killed Roger. How is Simon?"

"Scared. He's definitely a person of interest. His lawyers got him out of jail, but I don't know for how long. Of course he didn't do it."

"Of course not." Allie paused for a moment. "Willow, are you going to play detective again?"

"I told him I would try. I know it sounds crazy. But I can't stop thinking about it and maybe I can do some good. I can't let Simon go to jail for the rest of his life."

"What did Jackson say?"

"He's not happy about it, but he said he'll help me. He's been hired as a security guard for the duration of the shoot so he'll be there to protect us."

"Hector can help, too," Allie said. Hector had been in the marines and was one tough dude.

"With Jackson, Hector, and the cops, I think we'll be okay. Bottom line, it's a chance to make some money, and with the off-season coming, I really need it."

"I know you do. Okay, we'll do it. We'll leave the city in the morning and meet you at noon."

I thanked her and rang off, relieved that my team was in place. I turned the key and drove a few hundred yards west and parked in front of the Curious Kitten, the new antiques store that had just opened next to Nature's Way. (Nan's Needlework, my old next-door neighbor, had closed when Nan retired last month.) I grabbed Qigong's leash, hopped out of the car, and peered through the shop window—at a set of dishes with the Bixby crest.

I couldn't believe it. They were the same dishes I had just seen in the Bixby manor's dining room, though these were clean and shiny. I decided to go inside and poke around. I picked up Qigong and entered to find a man in his sixties sitting behind the counter. He was wearing reading glasses and a sweater with patches on the elbows. He looked up as the bell above the door tinkled. "Welcome! I'm Arthur Beasley."

"I'm Willow McQuade. I've taken over Nature's Way. Claire Hagan was my aunt."

"I'm so sorry about your aunt. Terrible business." He shook his head. "But it's lovely to make your acquaintance, Miss McQuade."

"Willow, please. And thank you. Is it all right if I just browse a bit?"

"That's fine. Just let me know if you need anything." He pulled out a ledger and began to study it.

I scouted out the store. In the back among cookie jars, vintage signs, and colorful dog dishes, I found the rest of the set that was featured in the front window. I examined the crest and determined that it was the same one that I had seen at the estate. I was sure that these had belonged to the Bixbys, but were they the exact same dishes I'd seen in that dusty dining room—or another set? And how did they wind up here? I browsed my way back to the front where I spotted *The Adventures of Tom Sawyer*, *The Catcher in the Rye*, and *The Call of the*

Wild in a glass case. "Are these first editions?" I asked, thinking of the books I had seen in the Bixby study.

Arthur lifted his head. "Oh, yes. We only sell the finest books here."

Before I could ask about the dishes and the books, a short, pear-shaped, gray-haired woman wearing jeans and a T-shirt came out from the back.

"Willow, meet my wife, Agatha. Willow McQuade is our new neighbor, dear." Arthur sneezed. He grabbed a tissue from a box on the counter and blew his nose.

"Nice to meet you," she said to me, then turned to Arthur. "You need to see a doctor. That cold is no better and it's been almost two weeks."

"Maybe it's allergies," I said. "I have quite a few products in my store that can help you, like stinging nettles, which is a natural antihistamine. Zinc can help the immune system, and fish oil helps reduce inflammation. You can also use a neti pot to clean out your sinuses."

"A what?" Agatha asked, looking confused.

"It's a way to irrigate the sinus cavity. You put a quarter teaspoon of noniodized salt or sea salt and a quarter teaspoon of baking soda into a cup of warm water and use it to rinse out the bacteria."

"And that works?" Arthur said.

I nodded. "It's one of the things that might make a big difference. You also might try an aromatic diffuser. The scents of essential oils like pine, cedar, and eucalyptus can open up your sinus passages. Acupuncture can even help. I have a practitioner, Hector, next door who's excellent."

"Perhaps we could do a trade," Agatha said. "Do you see anything in here you might be interested in?"

"The plates in the window are nice."

Agatha nodded. "Yes, they just came in."

I pointed to the case with the first editions. "These are also interesting."

"Indeed they are," Arthur said.

Agatha frowned. "Those are very pricey. Probably more than we would ever spend in your store."

"I understand. Can I ask where the plates and the books came from? Do you buy from estate sales?"

Arthur began to answer, but Agatha cut him off. "Our sources are confidential. You understand."

"Of course." I took out my phone from my purse and told a white lie. "Would you mind if I took a few pictures of the books? My uncle Nick is a collector, and I think these might interest him." I knew that Nick, Aunt Claire's former boy-friend, wouldn't mind being classified as a collector. But his great interests were yoga, herbs and other natural remedies. Agatha nodded and I clicked off a few shots. After I was done, I thanked them and headed for the door. "It was nice meet-ing you. Please come over to see us if you need help with those allergies."

"I will, thank you," Arthur said.

I stepped out onto the sidewalk and looked inside. Arthur and Agatha were arguing heatedly. Since they were distracted, I quickly clicked off a photo of the plates in the window, too. As I walked back to Nature's Way, I wondered how the Beasleys obtained the plates and the books. Had Roger been selling off the goods from the estate so he didn't have to split the prof-its with Carly—or to finance the shoot? Or was it Tom, who clearly needed money? It could even be Mrs. Florrick, supple-menting her income, thinking no one would notice now that Max and Roger were both gone. Who needed the money most? I would have to find out.

• • •

When I walked up the steps to Nature's Way, I found a large box on the front stoop. I checked the return label and saw that it was my order from an aromatherapy company. This was good news since I needed the contents for my seminar tonight. It had been a long day, even for a Monday, but I was determined to do a good job.

Inside, Qigong headed straight for my office. I grabbed the box cutter from underneath the counter and slit the box open and was rewarded with the smell of lavender. Which was not surprising, considering that it contained lavender essential oil along with lavender soap, moisturizer, candles, neck pillows and wreaths, and twenty-four gift bags that held samples of lavender products. I unpacked the box and arranged a display of some of the products on the counter.

Merrily came over to the cash register and rang up a sale. "How did everything go up there? How is Simon?"

"It went well." I told her what Rick and I had agreed on. "The funeral for Roger is Wednesday morning, and Simon was released from jail and he has a good lawyer. But right now I need to focus on tonight's seminar."

"Gotcha. What do we need to do first?"

"Let's push all the tables to the front of the store by the window and set up the chairs here." I motioned to the space to the left of the counter near the door. "Say, six across." I helped Merrily arrange the chairs and placed a gift bag on each one.

Next, I asked her to grab the card table from the storage closet. I placed the lavender essential oils on it, along with two platters, one with the ingredients for stress-relieving smelling salts, and one with empty jars to put the salts in. I also put out two glass vases for the lavender that I knew Jackson was bringing from his garden.

Once that was done, I grabbed a table from the café and put it next to the card table. I placed a bowl of organic punch on it along with recycled cups and napkins and Merrily's scrumptious organic raspberry scones. The guests could enjoy them during the break.

Finally, I felt ready. As I headed into the kitchen to grab some dinner, my phone rang. The caller ID identified an outside caller. I pushed Accept anyway and said hello, but was greeted with silence. "Hello?" I said again.

"You've been asking a lot of questions, haven't you, Ms. McQuade?" said a threatening voice that sounded so mechanical I couldn't identify it. "Didn't anyone ever tell you that curiosity killed the cat? You do have cats, don't you, and a dog, too?"

I felt stunned and sick inside. Did someone know that I had talked to Mrs. Florrick or found the camera or talked to the Beasleys?

"Who is this?" I demanded, but I could hear a quaver in my voice.

"You've been warned." The line went dead.

I immediately called for Qigong, and when he ran out of the office, I breathed a sigh of relief. Next, I ran upstairs to check on Ginger and Ginkgo. I found them lounging on my bed, safe and sound.

I went back downstairs. As I walked up to the counter, Jackson came in with two large bouquets of dried lavender. I went over to him and Qigong followed me. "I just had this really weird phone call." I told him what had happened.

Qigong jumped up on Jackson's legs. "You're okay, aren't you, fella?" He reached down to pat Qigong's head and scratched him behind the ears. Qigong rolled over, and he rubbed his belly, too. "Are the cats okay?"

"They're fine." I took the lavender and put it in the vases. "Thanks for these."

He shook his head. "I knew something like this would happen. Maybe you should reconsider your promise to Simon."

"Jackson, I can't do that. I need to solve this for him and for my own peace of mind. I'll just have to keep a closer eye on my pets. I can take Qigong with me to the estate and put the cats in the office and ask Merrily and Wallace to watch them."

"I think you're crazy," Jackson said, incredulous that I wasn't giving up. "This is only going to get worse."

I looked at the clock over the counter: 6:45. The door opened and five women came in. I said hello to them and then said to Jackson, "Can we please talk about this later?"

He sighed and gave me a kiss. "Yes, we can. I'm going upstairs. C'mon, boy." Qigong trotted after him.

People continued to stream in, excited about the seminar. By seven o'clock, almost every chair was taken. I pushed the phone call out of my mind along with Jackson's disapproval and Roger's murder and focused on what I needed to do.

"Thanks for coming out on a Monday night to learn about aromatherapy," I began. "I think you'll find it worthwhile." The door opened and Carly and Amanda scurried in and took seats in the back. Carly mouthed, "I'm sorry." First, I was surprised to see her, then I wondered if something had happened to Simon.

I refocused. "Aromatherapy is the art and science of using essential oils to relax, balance, and stimulate the body, mind, and spirit. My favorite fragrance is lavender. The lavenders, whose botanic name is *Lavandula,* are a genus of thirty-nine species of flowering plants in the mint family." I picked up a bottle of lavender essential oil. "It's good for stress, tension, and anxiety and can help you sleep better. The use of lavender dates back to the ancient Greeks. Later, the Romans used it to scent their baths. So people have been relaxing, thanks to lavender, for a long, long time."

I explained how to add lavender oil to bathwater or an electronic diffuser, and how it could help with sleeplessness. Then Merrily and I got ready to show people how to make their own lavender stress-relieving smelling salts.

Merrily took the platter with the ingredients, and I took the one with the jars, and we went around the room to pass them out. While we were doing that, Amanda got up and wandered to the back of the store and went into the bathroom. She must have learned where it was when she visited this morning. On her way back, she stopped by the shelf near my office and peered in through the open door. Was she just curious—or snooping?

Once we had handed out the ingredients and the jars, and Amanda had returned to her seat, I said, "First open the jar, then open the baggie with the rock salts and empty them into the jar." I waited until everyone had done so. "Now open the sample bottle of lavender essential oil and put ten drops on the salt." They all did. "Now, the best part, take a good whiff." All put their noses in their jar and took a deep breath. Sighs were heard all over the room. "Can't you just feel the stress melting away?" Everyone nodded. "You can keep it on your desk or on your nightstand." I smiled as everyone clapped. It never failed to amaze me how the simplest things could make such a difference.

I took some questions from the audience and, after that, told the participants that if they liked they were free to browse and shop. Most of them did just that, heading for the essential oils and other products with lavender, which was what I was hoping for. I rang up almost $1,800 in sales.

Most of the participants had made purchases and gone on their way when Simon came in. He went straight to Carly. I finished helping a customer and joined them.

"Anything new?" Simon asked me.

"Nothing new. This is going to take time, Simon. I know it's hard to be patient."

"It is when every time the phone rings or someone comes to the door, I think it's the cops."

"Your lawyers are working on this, and so is the PI they hired this afternoon," Carly said. "Willow can only do so much."

The door opened and Roger's brother, Tom, came into the store. He was wearing ripped jeans, an orange Galaxy T-shirt, and sunglasses. I understood Simon showing up, but Tom? Somehow, I was sure he wasn't there for the lavender oil.

"Carly!" he yelled. "Rick said you'd be here. Want to go get a drink? We can toast to my big bro Roger, and your husband. He would have wanted it that way. No tears, is what I say."

"He sounds like he's already been drinking," Merrily said to me in a low voice. "He must be hurting."

"I think you're right," I said, and winced as Tom spotted Simon.

"What is he doing here?" Tom demanded. He pointed to Simon and said loudly, "You should be in jail."

"I'm going home with Simon," Carly said firmly. "I'll see you on the set tomorrow, Tom."

"He killed your husband," Tom said, raising his voice. "Carly, how can you even go near him?"

The few seminar participants that were left looked at Tom in alarm and scurried out of the store. This was not what I had planned.

I texted Jackson and asked him to come downstairs, just in case there was trouble. It felt like the fight with Roger all over again.

Jackson appeared moments later. "What's going on?"

I pointed to Simon and Tom, who were now in a very loud argument and about to come to blows. Jackson went over to them at once. "That's enough, guys. Let's break it up."

Tom whirled on him. "I don't take orders from you."

"When you're here, you do." Jackson took him by the elbow. "This is private property." He walked him to the door and opened it. "It's time to say good-night."

Tom's face was turning an alarming shade of red. "You can't do this!" he yelled.

"Yes, I can." Jackson pushed him out the door, then closed and locked it.

Tom pounded on the door. "You'll be sorry! I mean it!"

"Just ignore him," Jackson said. "He'll go away."

"Thanks, Jackson," Simon said.

Carly pulled me aside. "Willow, I'm so sorry. I had no idea he was going to come here."

"Is he interested in you?" I wanted to know what exactly was going on between them.

She shrugged. "I think he's always had a little crush on me, being Roger's little brother and all."

"Did Roger know?"

"Yes, but he didn't care. He never saw his brother as much of a threat."

"He didn't seem to think much of him when it came to his profession either."

"No, but Tom actually does have talent. He's a fantastic sculptor. You should see some of his work. But Roger was only interested in how much money Tom owed him. Roger had plenty to spare, but he didn't believe in handouts. In his eyes, Tom was a failure."

"That couldn't have been easy for Tom to live with."

"It wasn't. They'd been estranged for two years until we came back for Max's funeral in May. Roger made amends and asked him to work on the show."

"Why the sudden turnaround?"

Carly shrugged. "He wouldn't say. Just that he owed Tom a favor."

An hour later, everyone had gone home, and Jackson and I were in bed with Qigong, Ginger, and Ginkgo. I felt cozy and safe again. The exact opposite of the way I'd felt after that horrible phone call and the fight between Simon and Tom. The information about Tom from Carly, though, was helpful. Tom had motive. Perhaps he had killed Roger to get his money, his job, and his wife. I'd have to keep a closer eye on him from now on.

"Well, that was interesting," Jackson said.

"Thanks for coming to the rescue." I snuggled next to him.

"No problem. Now, can we talk about how ludicrous it is for you to continue snooping around when you're being warned off?"

"But I've already gathered some good info. And I just took the case this afternoon."

"'Took the case.'" Jackson smiled. "Listen to you, Nancy Drew. Okay, what did you find?"

I told him about my visit to the manor, finding the camera, talking to the Beasleys and Carly, and what Amanda had been doing in the store.

"Interesting that Roger owed Tom for something, even though Tom owed Roger money," Jackson mused. "Maybe Tom had something over his brother."

"You think he got his job on the show by blackmailing Roger?"

"I'm not sure." Jackson picked up the book he'd been reading. "But that was not a healthy sibling relationship."

"Yeah, that's what I think, too. And?"

Jackson gave me a worried look. "And Tom is like a grenade about to blow. Please, Willow, stay clear of him."

"That's not what I meant. What do you think about what I've found so far?"

Jackson thought for a moment. I could almost see him tallying the information in his head. "Okay, objectively, good work. The background info from Florrick about Max and her comments about Carly and Roger's enemies is interesting. So is Lucas's comment about the murder being tied to the past. The part where you took the camera? Not so good. But it will be interesting to see what the photos show. And I agree that it's odd that the Bixbys' dinner set and their first editions appear to be for sale in the Curious Kitten. But if it was Roger who sold them, he owned everything on the estate, so that's not a crime. I don't know about Amanda, but Tom definitely bears watching, from a safe distance. A man with a grudge can be a dangerous thing."

"He could have made that awful phone call before he came to the shop."

"True. Or it could have been someone else."

"Right, but I'm onto something, don't you think?"

"I think you should leave this to the professionals."

I shook my head. "Can't do that." I pulled Ginger onto my lap and started petting her.

Jackson sighed deeply. "Okay, then, like I said at the estate this afternoon, you need protecting. When are you heading up there tomorrow?"

"Noon."

"I'll be there at eight. Be sure you check in with me when you get there." He opened his book and started reading.

I picked up my phone and looked at my notes about the job tomorrow. I realized that MJ had not told me what she needed specifically in terms of treatments. "What do you think about MJ? Is she really a psychic?"

Jackson put his book down. "MJ seems nice, yes, but a psychic, no. It's all a sham."

"So you don't believe in ghosts?"

"There is always a rational explanation for everything."

I thought about the chandelier flickering, the whispering noises, and that book flying off the shelf. I didn't answer him right away.

"What? Don't tell me you believe in ghosts?" Jackson chuckled.

"I think we're foolish if we believe that everything we see is all that exists. I told you about that weird vibe I got from the estate. I'm starting to think MJ's right. It's residual spiritual energy. Why couldn't it take the form of a ghost?"

"I'll believe it when I see it, and *that* is not going to happen. I guess we'll have to agree to disagree, McQuade." He put his book on the night table and reached for me. "Come here."

I picked up Ginger and put her at the foot of the bed, turned off the light, and rolled over to him and gave him a kiss. "Agreed, Spade."

chapter nine

Dr. Willow McQuade's Healthy Living Tips

I always stop and smell the roses by the front walk of Nature's Way Market and Café. I love the rich, sweet floral bouquet and the approximately 275 compounds, which have a myriad of therapeutic uses. For example, if you apply it topically, rose oil can help banish eczema, wrinkles, and acne. If you feel blue, rose essential oil will naturally lift your mood. If you have painful periods, it helps to balance hormones (just put the oil on a warm compress and apply to your lower abdomen). Rose oil also eases nervousness, anxiety, anger, sadness, and grief and can be helpful if you have respiratory problems such as allergies and hay fever. You also use rose oil to help you sleep better and feel happier. For all these conditions, simply put some on your palm and inhale it or put rose essential oil into a diffuser. Your bedroom will smell like an English garden.

Yours Naturally,

Dr. McQuade

I clocked about an hour or so of sleep. Every time I began to drift off, my mind kicked into gear and I reviewed what I'd found out so far. What exactly did any of it mean? I would start by picking up the mysterious photos from the camera that Qigong found.

Tuesday morning I headed downstairs and found Wallace, my new store assistant, in the kitchen, making a stack of organic blueberry pancakes. Two tables were occupied in the café.

"Hi, Wallace. Those look really good." My stomach was grumbling.

He put a pancake on a plate, added a pat of butter and some syrup, and pushed it over to me. "Enjoy."

I grabbed a fork and took a bite. Yummy. "So, how are things going?"

"Pretty good. I'm scrambling a bit since Merrily isn't feeling well."

This was surprising. Merrily hadn't been sick since I'd taken over the store in June. "What's wrong? Did she say?"

He shook his head. "No, but I told her I could handle things."

"I can help you until I have to leave to go to the Bixby estate. I just need to run out for a few minutes right now." I wanted to see those photos ASAP.

"That would be great. But don't rush. I'll be okay."

I thanked him, clipped the leash onto Qigong's collar, and headed out. It was another beautiful day on the East End, sunny with blue skies and no clouds in sight. I took the crosswalk to the south side of the street and walked down Front Street, past the park, a seafood bistro, the bookstore, the florist shop, and the bakery to the photo shop.

I couldn't wait until we got home to look at the photos. When I reached the park, I sat down, and while Qigong sniffed the grass, I opened the packet.

The first few shots were of the beach in front of the estate, the dock, and the boat. The rest were taken from the dock and included shots of the beach, the stairs, the retaining wall, and the mansion. No people were in the photographs, and none of them seemed to have been taken for artistic effect or sentimental memories, and they weren't slick enough for something like a real estate ad. So why would someone take these particular shots? Then I realized—they were all taken in the area where Roger's body was found. What if they were surveillance photos taken by the murderer, part of a planning stage when he or she was considering the best place to kill Roger Bixby?

The rest of the roll was blank. I opened the top of the packet to put them back inside, but as I did I noticed one that I'd missed because it was stuck to the back of a shot of the dock. Prying it loose, I saw that it was a close-up of the first edition of Agatha Christie's *Moving Finger,* the book I'd seen yesterday. Had Roger photographed it—as an example of what he had to sell? Or was someone else planning on cashing in after Roger was dead?

Across the street, I noticed more people heading into Nature's Way. I put my thoughts about Roger's murder on the back burner and went inside to help Wallace. I grabbed my apron, picked up some menus, and seated the two couples who had just arrived. As I put the menus down, I noticed Simon at a corner table by the window. A half-eaten plate of pancakes was next to his laptop. He hadn't shaved and looked gaunt, with dark circles under his eyes.

"Hey, Simon," I said, sitting down across from him. "How are you doing this morning?"

He closed the cover of his laptop. "Not good. My lawyer checked in with Detective Koren, and he said that I am still a person of interest and he'll want to question me again. Though, of course, he doesn't know when."

"Your lawyer said that would probably happen."

"I just want this to be over." He took a sip of his coffee, and I saw a slight tremble in his hand. I wasn't sure if that was too much caffeine or too much stress. "I'm trying to work, but I just can't concentrate, and this script for my episode is due Friday. They want me to come out next week to supervise the shooting and editing, but I can't leave town."

I pulled out the packet of photos. "Simon, I want you to look at something." I set the photos on top of his closed laptop. "I found these, or rather Qigong did, on the beach at the estate. Do they mean anything to you?"

He went through the pictures one by one. "It's just photos of the beach." He pointed to a spot on the shore. "This is where I found Roger."

"Anything else?"

He pointed to a spot on the dock. "That looks like Carly's sweater and sunglasses. See?" He handed the photo to me and pointed to a red sweater and oversize, expensive-looking sunglasses. "So maybe she took the photos. But she has a really good digital camera that I gave her, so probably not."

I wondered if Carly had taken the photos and what, if anything, that meant. As far as I knew, the divorce from Roger hadn't been finalized, which meant she was still technically his widow. Was she selling the first editions? I thought about Mrs. Florrick's saying that Carly was the one who pushed Roger to sell the estate, that she wanted half of everything. Had she killed Roger to inherit it all? I decided to do the tactless thing and ask.

"Simon, please don't take this the wrong way, but is there any chance that Carly killed Roger so she could inherit the house and the estate?"

Simon snorted with laughter. "Are you serious? The place

is a shambles, and Max had mortgaged it up to the hilt. Even if Carly did inherit it, all she'd be inheriting is debt. Besides, Carly was never trying to get money from Roger. She's a trust-fund baby. If you want my opinion, Roger married her for *her* money."

"Good to know." If Simon—and not Mrs. Florrick—was right, it didn't totally eliminate Carly as a suspect, but it might rule out money as a motive.

"Besides," Simon went on, "Carly still has feelings for the guy. She didn't want to be married to him anymore, but she never wanted any harm to come to him. I mean, she's even got a soft spot for Tom, and he's a walking disaster."

"That's what I've seen, too." Carly might have a prickly side, but so far she wasn't the most likely candidate for a killer.

I looked up to see a family of five take a table. "I'd better go help Wallace. Catch you later."

For the next two hours on Tuesday morning, I forgot about the photos, and Wallace and I served a steady stream of customers. I'd just dropped off my last plate of organic buckwheat waffles with honey and fresh peaches when Nick, Aunt Claire's former boyfriend, came in. He wore a black, V-neck, short-sleeved shirt, black yoga pants, and orange Crocs. He looked healthy and at peace.

It was quite a transformation. Devastated by Claire's death, Nick had reverted to old bad habits, such as drinking to excess. I'd confronted him and told him to seek help. He took my advice and returned to his Alcoholics Anonymous meetings. Today, his yoga classes at Nature's Way were more popular than ever. He was a wonderful teacher, thoughtful, intuitive, and kind.

He came over to me and hugged me. "How are you, sweetie?"

"I'm okay. Are you all ready to go to the Bixby estate?"

"I've always been curious about that place, but I never thought I'd be teaching there. It should be interesting."

"I need to tell you something. Sunday night, one of the producers, Roger Bixby, was murdered." I explained what had happened and that I was trying to help Simon.

Nick shook his head. "I always used to think this area was such a haven, so safe, but two murders in less than six months?"

"They're not related."

"Still, you're the one I'm worried about. Do you think you should be involved? You've already been through a lot with your aunt Claire's death, and the murderer could be anywhere on that estate."

"I think we'll be safe. Jackson will be providing security for the production, and Hector has a black belt in karate, and you are a tai chi master."

"At your service," Nick said, bowing to me.

"Plus, the cottage that will be our home base is a good distance from the mansion. You can hold your classes under a beautiful oak tree."

"Okay. I just need to get some mats, blankets, bolsters, and straps to bring up there."

"I need to gather products to place in the rooms and for the guests to use." I also needed to bring horse-chestnut cream for Mrs. Florrick's varicose veins. "I'll meet you out back by the van in twenty minutes."

We arrived at the estate at noon. I stopped at the guard booth and gave the man Nick's, Allie's, and Hector's names so they would be allowed onto the estate. Then I rolled up and parked the Nature's Way van next to Carly's BMW. The estate was abuzz with activity. Crew members hustled into the mansion carrying cameras, light stands, lights, and cables. Production staff scurried from the trailers into the house and back again. But the police were not here today.

I texted Jackson and told him that we were there, and moments later he rounded the mansion and came over to us. He looked fine in his black Galaxy T-shirt, jeans, and boots. He shook hands with Nick and gave me a kiss.

"How are things going? Is Tom causing trouble yet?"

"He's out doing something for Rick, so it's been nice and quiet so far." Jackson pulled four ID badges from his pocket that matched the one he wore around his neck and handed them to me. "Here are the badges for the whole team." I gave one to Nick, who put it around his neck. "Yours is all-access so you can snoop everywhere. I have something else for you." Jackson pulled a small walkie-talkie out of his back pocket. "I've got one and so do Rick and Amanda, so we'll always be in constant communication. Of course you can send me a text or call, too. I'm going to do a sweep of the estate every hour. That way I can keep an eye on you and keep everyone safe."

"Thanks. I really appreciate it." I put my badge around my neck and the others in my pocket. Nick's phone rang and he stepped away to take the call.

"Have you heard from Simon?"

"Yes, he ate breakfast in the café. Jackson, he's in pretty bad shape. His lawyer found out that Detective Koren isn't done with him yet. He definitely wants to see him again."

"No surprise there."

"And I picked these up." I opened the packet and handed him the photos. When he got to the one with the sunglasses and the red sweater, I told him that they were Carly's.

Jackson raised one eyebrow. "Do you think she was scouting the area before she killed Roger?"

"Not really." I told him what Simon had said. I scanned the

lawn. "Is Rick around, so I can check in with him, too? I need to start setting up."

Jackson got him on his walkie-talkie. Minutes later, Rick walked out of the yellow-and-white tent and headed for us, with Amanda trailing him.

"Thanks for coming," Rick said. "I've asked Amanda to help you out."

"Good. I have a sign-up sheet that I'll leave with you." I handed Amanda a clipboard with the sign-up sheet. "This way people can sign up with you, and you can e-mail me the names and the appointment times."

"Okay." Amanda scanned the sheet.

"I made an announcement at breakfast and lunch and told the crew and the production staff to make their appointments for the afternoon, before we shoot at seven p.m.," Rick said. "It looks like it's going to be night shoots all week long."

"Why is that?" Jackson asked.

Rick shrugged. "'Cause MJ says so. She thinks that she'll have better luck connecting with the spirit world at night." He turned to Amanda. "Darlin', can you please go get a cart and drive them to that cottage next to ours?"

"Sure thing." She swiveled on her heel and walked rapidly away.

Rick said to Jackson, "Before MJ sets foot inside, I want to go over the entire house with you and Pierre, our director. We need to know what we're dealing with in terms of rooms, windows, light and shots and any safety issues."

"Sounds like a good idea," Jackson said.

"So MJ hasn't been inside yet?" I asked.

Rick shook his head. "Course not. She always goes in fresh. The show doesn't work unless we get her spontaneous reaction to the mansion—and its inhabitants."

I was curious. "What happens if MJ doesn't find any ghosts or spirits?"

"Hasn't happened yet." Rick winked at me. "We choose our locations carefully."

Jackson turned to me. "I'll check in with you in a bit."

"Can you give this to Mrs. Florrick since you're going that way?" I pulled the horse-chestnut cream out of my bag and handed it to him.

"No problem." He and Rick headed for the mansion.

Amanda pulled up in the golf cart and we loaded the stuff from the van in the back, and Nick and I and Qigong got in the front. We took off, zipping along the bulkhead, salty breeze blowing through our hair.

"Thanks for doing this, Amanda. I hope that you'll come over for a treatment, as a thank-you," I said.

"I'd like that. Maybe even a massage."

Something in her tone bothered me, and I realized that when we'd first met her, she'd been upbeat, efficient. Today she sounded brittle, on edge. "Are you okay?"

"No, not really. I miss Roger. He could be super-obnoxious, but he had a good side, too. He was much better one-on-one than in a crowd." I shot a look at Nick. Did she mean professionally or personally?

She turned the wheel and expertly swerved between two huge maple trees on either side of the dirt path. She increased her speed. Up ahead were two even more enormous oak trees with spreading foliage. She put her foot on the pedal and headed for the space between them. We'd just whizzed past a towering birch tree when, with a tremendous cracking sound, a huge branch fell from the tree. It missed the golf cart by inches.

Amanda put her foot on the brake and we all lurched forward. Fortunately Nick was holding Qigong tightly. Amanda started hyperventilating and tears ran down her cheeks. "It's happening again! I can't work this way!"

"What's happening again?"

"Ever since we got here on Saturday there have been these weird accidents. A chandelier crashed to the floor in the grand ballroom. I-I was in the downstairs bathroom this morning, and when I washed my hands in the sink, the mirror over it cracked right down the middle. And the whispering sounds . . . they're all through the house now, not just in the library."

"I heard those whispers, too," I said. But I hadn't known about the chandelier and the mirror.

"Sounds like it's haunted," Nick said. "That should be good for your show."

"I don't care about that." Amanda's voice rose to a hysterical pitch. "I hate it here. I told Roger this was a bad idea, but he wanted to come. I mean, my God! There's a murderer on the loose!"

An assistant was giving the executive producer location advice? That didn't sound right, unless she was having an affair with Roger. Was she the reason Carly had divorced him? And was Amanda what Tom was using to blackmail Roger? But what I said was "Try to calm down. Take a few deep breaths."

Nick got out of the cart and went over to inspect the branch that had fallen. "This looks like it was sawed off, Willow. You better call Jackson. He'll want to see this." Qigong sniffed around the area on the ground where the branch had fallen. I quickly sent Jackson a text.

Amanda and I got out and went over to Nick. Sure enough, there were jagged saw marks. This was no accident.

chapter ten

Dr. Willow McQuade's Healthy Living Tips

Aromatherapy is effective when it comes to cleaning, toning, and moisturizing your skin. These aromatic recipes from my good friend Jade Shutes, who is the director of education at East-West School for Herbal and Aromatic Studies (www.theida.com) in Raleigh, North Carolina, will make your skin look and feel your best!

Jade's Aromatic Cleanser
2 ounces castile cleansing base (like
    Dr. Bronner's baby soap)
7 drops tea tree oil (*Melaleuca alternifolia*)
5 drops lemon oil (*Citrus limon*)
5 drops lavender oil (*Lavandula angustifolia*)

Wash 2x a day, once in the morning and once in the evening.

Jade's Aromatic Toner
4 ounces witch hazel hydrosol or extract
4 drops tea tree oil
2 drops lemon oil

Jade's Aromatic Moisturizer

Often acne skin types are prone to dehydrated skin due to overuse of alcohol-based toners and/or cleansers. So it's best to apply a soothing hydrating cream after cleansing and toning. To make it yourself, buy an unscented, water-based cream. Put two ounces in a small jar with a lid. Next, mix in the following essential oils: 2 drops German chamomile, 4 drops lavender, and 5 drops frankincense. Your skin will thank you!

Yours Naturally,

Dr. McQuade

While we waited for Jackson, I thought about last night's phone call. Was someone after me? Or was this sawed-off branch aimed at Amanda, who was constantly riding all over the estate on errands for Rick? And if the killer was after Amanda, why? Because she had been close to Roger? Amanda had taken out her cell phone and was now furiously texting someone. She'd wiped her tears away, but her face was as red as a cooked lobster.

Jackson rolled up in his cart and hopped out. I told him what had happened and what Amanda had said. "That does sound strange," Jackson said. "Does Rick know about what has happened? He hasn't mentioned it to me. We were going through the first floor when you texted me. Nothing out of the ordinary was happening."

"Yes, he knows," Amanda said, looking up from her phone. "He thinks it will be good for the show."

"Did he tell the police?" Jackson asked.

Amanda shook her head. "MJ said it wouldn't do any good, that if the police wanted to stop things like that from happening, they'd have to be prepared to deal with ghosts. She says her goal in coming here is to help the spirits move on. So by the time the show is done, these things should stop happening. It can't come soon enough, if you ask me."

Jackson walked over to the branch on the ground and examined the saw marks. "This was done by a human, not a ghost. Let's get it out of the way so everyone can get back to work. Nick, can you help me?"

The two of them worked together and moved it off the path. Once they had, Qigong and I hopped onto Jackson's golf cart and rode to the cottage with him so we could discuss what had happened. Jackson let Amanda get a bit of a head start and then followed behind.

"Are you okay, McQuade?"

"I think so, though that was pretty strange. Were they after Amanda or me or just trying to scare everyone? MJ comes this way and so does Mrs. Florrick. Her cottage is behind the one I'm working in."

"This is what I was worried about. Next time use the walkie-talkie, it's faster. Do you think you can work here?"

"I need the money from this job. Besides, down here, it's not so scary. But I will want to check out the shoot tonight."

"Let me know when you're coming up so I can keep an eye on you."

"You be on the lookout for clues, too. I need your help to do this."

"Will do." He pulled up in front of the cottage behind Amanda and we got out. He opened the door to the cottage, went inside, and checked it out. "All clear. You're good to go."

After Jackson and Amanda returned to the mansion, Nick put his mats and blankets and accessories on the couch and checked out the area around the oak tree where he'd hold his classes.

The air inside the cottage smelled stale, so the first thing I did was open the windows and use the screen door. While Qigong made himself at home on the couch, I started to unpack. I placed the chamomile tea, protein powders, and assorted fruit on the counter in the kitchen and set up the blenders. I noticed the energy mix was missing, though, and called the store. Merrily said she'd be right up and rang off before I could ask how she was feeling. I called the guard and told him to expect her.

Next, I moved into the enclosed porch where I would be seeing patients. The porch was furnished with a comfy couch upholstered in a pretty flower pattern and a matching arm-chair. On the floor was a striped rug that had seen better days.

Through the windows, I could see the twinkling blue bay and a picnic table. A bluebird sat on top of it, pecking at a plate of sunflower seeds someone had put out.

I used an organic spray cleaner on all the surfaces, and soon the space smelled like lavender. On the empty book stand, I put all the herbs, supplements, oils, and homeopathic remedies I'd brought.

An hour later, Nick and I were sitting on the front steps of the cottage finishing up our veggie wraps and fruit soda when Amanda arrived with Allie and Hector. The two of them jumped out and greeted us with hugs and kisses. Allie, a gorgeous, tall, natural redhead with freckles, was dressed in a cute shift dress with a tiny flower pattern and sandals, while Hector wore a bright yellow shirt, khaki shorts, and huaraches that complemented his coffee-colored skin and impressive good looks. Qigong jumped up against Hector's legs, so he picked him up and let Qigong slather his face with doggy kisses.

"How are you doing, girl?" Allie asked me. "Any ghost sightings?"

"Don't say that," Amanda said. "It's creepy enough around here already." She handed me the clipboard with the sign-up sheet. "You're all booked up for today. Allie and Hector have appointments from two to five. Just an FYI, Allie, your five o'clock is with MJ. Willow, you'll be seeing clients from three to five. Dinner is at six. Rick said that you're all welcome to stay and eat with us."

"Sounds good," I said. "Thanks, Amanda."

After she got into the golf cart and took off, Allie said, "What was Amanda talking about when she said it was creepy enough around here?"

I told them what she had said and about the tree branch falling and the more "ghostly" incidents.

Allie frowned. "I don't like the way any of that sounds."

"If we stick together I think we'll be okay," I said. "Besides, we have Jackson, Hector, and Nick to protect us."

"That's right." Hector smiled. "No worries."

Allie took a karate stance. "I can kick some butt, too."

"So we're all set." At least I hoped so.

After Nick left, we cleaned both bedrooms and moved Allie's and Hector's tables in. After that, I put a lavender wreath on each door, lavender candles on the nightstands, lavender soap in the bathroom, and Jackson's bouquets on the windowsills. On the tall bookshelf near Allie's room, I placed the products we could use with clients and/or sell, including massage oils, lavender, rose, bergamot, jasmine, and sandalwood essential oils, which were good for anxiety and stress, and lavender eye masks.

Hector checked his watch. "Just in time. Our clients will be arriving soon. It's one fifty-three."

"Hello? Anyone there?"

I went out into the living room and found Merrily. "Sorry I'm late. I've been exhausted all day. I feel as if it's taking me three times as long to do the simplest things." She handed me the energy powder. "I don't know what's going on with me. The weird thing is, I slept for fourteen hours and I don't feel rested. Plus I feel like I have the flu. Icky, you know?"

"It could be Lyme disease." Long Island has some of the highest rates of Lyme disease in the nation. Symptoms included fatigue, brain fog, headaches, muscle aches, a flulike feeling, indigestion, facial flushing, and more.

Merrily thought for a moment. "I did find a tick on my back after I helped the Audubon Society with beach cleanup last week. But I don't have that bull's-eye mark."

"Only sixty percent of people do." I wrote down the name of my favorite Lyme-literate doctor, an MD who specializes in treating the disease, and gave it to her. "Dr. Cooper will test you and treat you if you have it. Call him today, okay?"

Tuesday afternoon, I saw my first client at three, Sarah Hill, the makeup artist, attractive, in her early thirties, with spiky blond hair and a dazzling white smile. She sat on the couch, and I took the chair, grabbed my pen and notebook, and asked how she was dealing with Roger's murder.

"Not so good," she admitted. "I've been on dozens of shoots in my career, and nothing like this has ever happened. I'm nervous during the day and I can't sleep at night. I mean, Carly warned us that this could be a rough shoot, but I had no idea what I was getting into."

I felt the hair prickle on the back of my neck. "What do you mean she warned you?"

"She told us that both Roger and Tom had bad tempers and also tended to be overly friendly with the women in the crew, but not to take it personally. She said to come to see her if either of them did anything inappropriate. I think she was just trying to avoid a lawsuit. Roger has been sued in the past for sexual harassment."

Carly's warning was news and so was Roger's behavior. I wondered if a woman on the crew or staff had been harassed and may have killed Roger as revenge. "Did Roger bother you, Sarah?"

"He asked me out, but I told him I wasn't interested. I think he was basically harmless."

"What about Tom?"

"Tom is a mess. He's got it bad for Carly, and she just feels sorry for him."

That pretty much lined up with what I'd seen. Right now, though, I needed to help Sarah. "Let's put that aside and focus on you," I said, opening the notebook and finding a fresh page so I could take notes. "How can I help?"

"Ever since we got here, I can't sleep. I keep having these horrible nightmares."

"A cup of chamomile before bedtime is a good start. It's high in nerve-and-muscle-relaxing calcium, magnesium, and potassium. It also contains some of the B vitamins that help you relax. Valerian can also help." I went to the bookshelf and grabbed two bottles and a box of chamomile tea. "Just follow the directions."

When I walked Sarah out, I found Carly sitting on the couch, talking to someone on her phone.

"I'll check in with you later on in the week," I told Sarah as I opened the door.

Sarah threw a glance at Carly and said, "Thank you, Willow," and slipped out the door.

I wondered what the relationship between them was like. Carly ended her call, stood, and looked out the door. "What was she doing here?"

"I like to keep my sessions private, Carly."

"She had a thing for Roger." Carly sighed. "All the females on the set loved Roger. I still can't believe we're burying him tomorrow."

She picked up her bottle of water and sipped it. "Simon said that you two talked at Nature's Way this morning."

"He was upset and understandably so. Have the police called him in again?"

"Not yet. It's like waiting for the results of a pregnancy test." Her eyes sharpened as she looked at me. "Have you discovered anything of value?"

It was a strange metaphor to use, but I didn't pursue it.

Instead I said, "I've just been gathering info here. Not much to report so far." I didn't want to tell her about the photos yet. "We did have an incident when we were headed to the cottage this afternoon. A tree branch that had been sawed off almost crashed onto the golf cart. Amanda says weird things like this have been happening a lot around here."

"I heard about that. They're the kind of things Max was always talking about." Carly shook her head. "And I never believed him." Her phone rang and she plucked it out of her pocket and answered it. "Yes, on my way." She put the phone away. "Rick wants me in the production trailer. Keep me posted, please. The sooner we get Simon out of this mess, the better. And thanks, Willow. Every little bit helps."

I felt that she was subtly undermining me but didn't rise to the bait. "You're welcome. I'll see you later."

I saw my next client and was done in time to take Nick's Yoga-Nidra class under the oak tree. Yoga-Nidra is known as yogic sleep, and doing it is equivalent to getting three to four hours of restful shut-eye. I find it an excellent way to let go of stress, replenish, and renew. It seemed most of the crew showed up for this class. I'd counted twenty-six people when I noticed Amanda pulling up in the golf cart with MJ in the passenger seat. Allie met her at the door with a big smile and ushered her inside.

Knowing that MJ was in good hands, I closed my eyes and tuned in to Nick as he said, "Lie on your backs in savasana pose, legs together, arms by your side with upturned palms. Lower your chin slightly toward your chest. Get comfortable. Let go of your thinking mind. Take a big, deep breath and exhale. Let go of the worries of the day, picture them as clouds floating in the horizon. . . ."

I relaxed and let go of thoughts and worries about Roger's murder. For the moment things were serene and calm. But I knew that this feeling wouldn't last for long.

I was doing a few stretches on the lawn after the yoga class when MJ came out into the yard and walked over to me. "Willow, Allie is just wonderful. Thank you so much for coming here to help us."

"You are very welcome."

"It definitely opened me up. I feel more fortified and focused for tonight's work. Are you going to stay for the shoot?"

"Yes, I'd like to, if that's okay with you."

"That's just fine with me. But I want you to be prepared, Willow. Strange things happen when I enter a house." She took my hands in hers. "We haven't known each other for long, but I feel very close to you, Willow. I want you to be safe."

I pulled my hands away. "What do you mean? Are you saying that being in the house could be dangerous?" Not to mention that a murderer was on the loose.

"I can usually keep the spirits under control. But I haven't been inside yet, so I don't know exactly what I will be dealing with. I expect to find residual energy from Max Bixby, since he just passed, but what I'm really looking for is spiritual evidence of Daniel Russell, the caretaker who was murdered, and his wife, Rebecca. But keep in mind that there may be other presences and they may not be friendly. I wouldn't be surprised if Roger's spirit showed up, and if he does, I can't imagine that he's going to be pleased about having been murdered."

I tried to take that in. "You're saying there might be four ghosts in that house?"

"Could be. So if you sense that a negative spirit is trying to connect with you, just picture a bubble of golden light around your entire body. That will keep you safe. And stay close to that hunky boyfriend of yours, too." She waved to Amanda, who had just pulled up in a golf cart. "I have to go now." She pulled me into a light hug. "But I will see you later. Please, remember what I said."

Amanda returned and gave us all a ride back to the southern end of the estate, dropping us off at the driveway. Allie and Hector had clients to see at Nature's Way, so they had to go. I sent Qigong home with them and asked them to keep an eye on the cats, too. I told them about the weird phone call that I'd received last night threatening my animals.

After they left, I walked Nick over to his car. He was on his way to his AA meeting in Southold. He opened his car door and then hesitated before getting in. He gave me a curious look. "Something on your mind, Willow?"

"Kind of. I've been wondering what Aunt Claire would have thought about this supposedly haunted mansion. Did she believe in ghosts? Would she have taken this job?"

He shut the door and leaned against the front end of the car. "Good questions. Claire always had an open mind, so I think she would have allowed for the possibility of ghosts. And, yes, I think she would have taken this job. She, like you, was a smart businesswoman. She was always open to new revenue streams. Besides, I think our presence here is really helping the crew. They need extra support right now. You're doing a great job, Willow." He put his arm around me. "Does that help answer your questions?"

"It does. I just want to do my best. You know, carry on her legacy at Nature's Way. But I'm also going to go to the shoot tonight, and I guess I'm a little scared." I told him about MJ's advice.

"I suppose it can't hurt to follow her advice," Nick said. "But when it comes to this murderer—whoever he or she is— do me a favor and stick near Jackson. I'm all for golden light, but somehow I'd put my faith in Jackson being the one who will protect you." He opened his car door. "I've got to go now. I'm in charge of refreshments for the meeting, but I'll see you tomorrow." He gave me a kiss on the cheek. "Love you."

He started the car up. "One other thing, Willow. Focus on helping Simon and the people here. That's your real mission. Be careful, yes, considering the circumstances of Roger's demise, but don't let fear rule you."

chapter eleven

Dr. Willow McQuade's Healthy Living Tips

I often see patients who are struggling with depression, but natural remedies can help to cure that blue mood. Essential oils can help, in part because of the proximity of the nerve endings in the nasal cavities and the brain. You can try basil, cedarwood, cinnamon, clary sage, clove, coriander, geranium, neroli, patchouli, peppermint, rosemary, rosewood, sandalwood, thyme, vetiver, wintergreen, and ylang-ylang. You can take eight deep inhalations right from the bottle or put it in a diffuser. Of course, if your depression persists, it's time to see a qualified therapist.

Yours Naturally,

Dr. McQuade

I thanked Nick, blew him a kiss, and headed for the tent, where Jackson and I had agreed to meet. I found a table near the entrance and, while I waited, mulled over what Nick and MJ had said.

About fifteen minutes later, Jackson came in and sat down next to me and put his walkie-talkie on the table. "Sorry I'm late. Rick wanted to go over the shooting plan for this week with everyone. So what happened today after the falling-branch incident?"

I told him what I'd learned from Sarah, and about the warning MJ had given me. "It kind of freaked me out. I wouldn't even go in that house tonight except it might help me with Simon's case."

Jackson shook his head. "MJ's nuts. Don't get sucked into her crazy world. I told you, all that stuff is made up anyway. They can use all kinds of special effects to make it scary. I didn't see any equipment on the tour of the house, but that doesn't mean it isn't there."

I didn't want to get into the "ghost vs. no ghost" argument with Jackson again, so I said, "I talked to Nick and that helped. He told me to focus on helping Simon, MJ, and the crew."

"And staying out of the path of a murderer," Jackson said, putting his head in his hands. "I just wish you would just go back to your store, but I know that you can't do that."

I put my hand on his arm. "If I were *there,* I'd just be worried about you being *here.*" I gave him a kiss. "Now, how did the house tour go?"

"No surprises. No *ghosts.*" He gave me a penetrating look. "Rick and Pierre decided to start in the library tonight."

I thought about what I'd experienced yesterday and wondered if it would happen again. I could believe that the falling book and even the whispers might be special effects, but not the angry "presence" I'd felt in that house. That was real.

Jackson gave me a weary smile. "You're thinking about it again. Let's not talk about this anymore right now. I'm starved. Want to eat?"

Tuesday evening, after a scrumptious, healthy dinner of broiled mahi-mahi, white quinoa, and baked yams, we walked over to the mansion. Jackson turned to me as we entered the front hall. "Are you sure you want to do this?"

"I'm sure. I have to do everything I can to help Simon. Just stay close."

"Rick has a guard for the door to make sure no one comes in when the red light is on." He pointed to a light on a stand at the bottom of the stairs. "So I'll be with you. Don't worry."

We walked through the hallway, which was dark and gloomy and divided the library from the study and led to the stairs. I felt it again. The energy in the house was dense, negative, and uncomfortable. This wasn't my imagination. Something was in here with us. I took some deep breaths, trying to keep calm and focused.

At least the place wasn't deserted. Cables ran the length of the floor, and crew members were running in and out of the library on one side and the study on the other. I spotted Rick, Carly, and Tom talking to a diminutive man with round glasses, dressed in jeans and a denim shirt with GHOST HUNTERS INTERNATIONAL scrolled on the front pocket. "That's Pierre Holden, the director," Jackson told me. Rick waved to us and continued his conversation. We walked up behind them so we could see into the library. The camera was set up across from the couch and, behind that, the bookcases. The pungent smell of incense wafted from the room. The lights in the chandelier were dimmed, and several candles were lit and placed on the fireplace mantel. It was 6:52 p.m.

"Are we ready for MJ?" Rick asked Pierre, who was now behind the camera.

"No, I need a stand-in to check this angle. Where's Amanda? Amanda!"

"She's not here," Rick said. "I don't know where she is." He used his walkie-talkie to call her. "Amanda? Amanda?" After a moment, he reported, "She's not answering."

Pierre looked around the room. "You." He pointed at me. "You're about MJ's height. Can you sit in the middle of the couch so we can get this scene set up?"

"You're a star, baby," Jackson said. "Go for it."

I rolled my eyes, said, "Sure," and walked over to the couch and sat down.

"That's Willow McQuade, Pierre. She's that natural doctor who's helping us out. Oh, and she's Jackson's gal, too."

"Nice to meet you, Willow. Thanks for sitting in." Pierre looked through the lens. "Good. Now please stand up and circle the room."

"Okay." I did as he asked.

Pierre said something to the cameraman next to him, who then took a look through the lens. "That's what I want. Follow her wherever she goes. I'm not sure what is going to happen, but I don't want to miss anything, so look sharp. We'll start in the hallway with Paul on the Steadicam." Pierre went over to a beefy guy with a camera strapped to his body. "I want you to track her, too, so I have coverage to choose from." Pierre turned to me. "Willow, can you walk from the front door to the entrance of the library?"

"Sure." I did as he asked.

The guy with the Steadicam followed me as I walked toward him. Pierre watched the sequence on a monitor near the staircase to the second floor. "That looks good. We're ready for MJ. Rick, make the call."

Rick got on his phone. I hustled across the room back to Jackson. "Now that was interesting."

He grinned at me. "You're a natural, McQuade."

"Okay, people, MJ is coming in," Rick said. "It is crucial that we have complete silence so she can do her job."

"Speed," Tom said.

"Action," Pierre yelled.

When the clock struck seven, MJ opened the door and made her way down the hallway. She wore an impressive purple cloak with white-and-black trim, black ballet slippers, and a tall, black headdress, decorated with faux diamonds. She took measured steps along the hallway, pausing every few steps to stand still and close her eyes. The Steadicam guy tracked her from a few feet away so as not to disturb her.

When she reached the library, she entered the room, walked into the middle of it, and stopped. With her eyes closed, she said, "I'm sensing that Max Bixby is still with us. At least I think it's Max." She looked at the camera. "It would make sense for Max to be here in his favorite room, the library, with the first-edition books he collected and loved so much. If it is Max, I'm not sure why he's still here, but it may have to do with the spirits he connected with when he was still alive. Max Bixby was fascinated by the occult, and this library was also the place where he held a number of séances. Max, if you are here now, can you give us a sign? We don't want to harm you. I just want to connect with you."

She stood still and waited. I glanced at Rick, who seemed to be getting impatient. He was whispering to Pierre and looked agitated. He wanted good TV and he wanted it now. He pulled out his phone and started texting or e-mailing.

"Max, are you here?" MJ circled the room. "Show me."

She moved toward the fireplace, and as she did, a book flew

out from the bookcase and landed right at her feet. MJ didn't seem rattled by this. "We have contact," she said calmly, and bent over to pick up the book. "It is Agatha Christie's *Moving Finger,* a first edition."

I sucked in a breath. It was the same book I had looked at yesterday during my visit.

"You are obviously a fan of mysteries, Max," MJ said as she set the book on the fireplace mantel. "We are trying to solve a mystery during our visit here. The mystery of who killed Daniel Russell, the caretaker."

The lights in the chandelier rapidly flickered on and off, on and off. Suddenly, the room was plunged into darkness except for the candles. I shivered and reached for Jackson's hand. Real or not, this was unsettling.

"Can you help us with this mystery, Max? Is Daniel still here? Or his wife, Rebecca? You asked me to come here by telling your son Roger to invite us. I am here now and want to help."

Nothing happened. Rick continued texting on his phone. Jackson nudged me and whispered, "I'll bet he's contacting Amanda, and she's the one that's making this creepy stuff happen."

"Shhh," I whispered back.

"I'm also here to assist you and any other spirits that may be here in the journey to the other side. It's time to move on, Max. If you help me, I can help you."

The lights came back up and MJ was in the middle of the room. "I'm getting something." She put her hands to her head, stepped back, and slumped on the couch. "It feels like . . . like a swarm of bees are buzzing around my head."

A cold wind swept through the room, and the flames on the candles fluttered. MJ stood up and moved away from the couch. "That's enough, Max. Stop it now." She looked into the camera. "Max's spirit is very angry. He-he just attacked me." She gazed up at the high ceiling. "It's all right, Max, I hear you. I understand that this is your home and you want to stay here. I won't mention going to the other side again." She took a deep breath and stood still. "It's over, Max. Please calm down now."

The wind vanished and MJ looked into the camera again. "I'm going to want to visit him again, but I think that's enough for right now. Thank you, Max."

"Cut!" Pierre said.

MJ went over to the chair by the window and just about collapsed into it. Rick, Tom, and Carly scurried over. Tom handed her a bottle of water. She took a long gulp. "That was difficult. I've never encountered that reaction before. He doesn't want to leave in a major way."

Jackson folded his arms across his chest. "I remain skeptical."

"It seemed pretty authentic to me."

"I don't know if I can go again," MJ said to Rick. "I'm exhausted."

"Just rest and we'll set up in the study. Try it. If you're not getting a connection, we'll go again tomorrow, okay, hon?"

MJ nodded and got up. "I think I'm gonna take myself for a short walk."

As she opened the library door, Amanda rushed in and went over to Rick. Rick seemed to be reprimanding her.

"He doesn't look too happy," Jackson observed. "But if she helped with those special effects, she did a pretty good job."

I thought about this. "If she is responsible, then her freak-out today about the weird events on the estate was all an act."

"It's the best way to divert suspicion." Jackson glanced at the door. "I'd better check in with the guard. Be right back."

I turned my attention to the study. The lighting and cameras were being moved into place. Pierre positioned Amanda first on the wingback chair and then in front of the window.

Twenty minutes later, MJ had returned and they were ready to go again. Jackson, however, hadn't returned. It was too late for him to come in when the assistant cameraman called, "Speed," and Pierre followed with "Action!"

MJ closed her eyes and began to circle the study, but after a few minutes she stopped. "Do you hear that? It's coming from outside."

"No," Pierre said, blowing out a sigh. He obviously was in a hurry to get the take in the can.

MJ opened her eyes and walked over to the window. "Two dogs are in distinct distress. They're not here on the property, but they're not far. They need to be saved. Rick, can you do it?" She gave him a pleading look. "You know how I am. I can't stand it when any animal is being mistreated. I can't do a reading under these circumstances. Rick, fix this."

Rick radioed Jackson and asked him to come in. When Rick explained the problem, Jackson said, "I'll go check it out." He glanced at MJ. "Where exactly did you hear this sound coming from—north, south, east—"

"Out there." She gestured vaguely. "I heard them crying in my mind. They were reaching out to me."

"Right," Jackson said.

Rick went over to MJ. "Okay, Jackson is going to take care of this. He'll find those dogs. Can we get some work done now?"

"How can you even ask such a thing?" MJ chided Rick. "I can't possibly go into the meditative state I need to communicate with the spirits when I'm so worried about those dogs. I have to know they're safe before I can go any further."

Behind MJ's back, Pierre shut his eyes and hit his forehead with the heel of his hand.

Rick tried again. "MJ, darlin', you know our schedule is tight. Can you talk about your reading in a close-up? We can do it in the production trailer."

"I don't think so."

"Please, darlin', while it's fresh in your mind. For me?"

MJ held firm. "No. Ricky, please have someone return me to my cottage. I'm done for today. Have Jackson let me know what he finds." She got up off the couch and walked to the door. Amanda ran after her. Rick went over to talk to Pierre.

A moment later, Pierre said, "That's a wrap. We'll go again at noon tomorrow, after the funeral. We need to get coverage of the rest of the exterior and the rooms we'll be using. Thank you for all your hard work today. Especially MJ. Roger would be proud."

Everyone clapped.

Jackson came over to me. "Do you want to go with me to check this out?"

Like MJ—and Jackson, for that matter—I was an animal lover. "Let's go."

"This is nuts," Jackson said as we cruised down the estate's long drive. "You do realize that we're searching for a sound heard only in MJ's mind?"

"What if she's right? We can't risk *not* helping these dogs if they're in trouble. Besides, she said they're not far."

"Terrific. That's very helpful."

He stopped the truck as we came to the road at the end of the drive. We rolled down our windows and listened.

"All I hear is wind in the trees," Jackson said.

"That's what I'm hearing, too," I admitted. "Wait, no, there is something. It's really faint. I'm not sure it's the sound of a dog crying but—"

"Which way?"

"Turn left." I prayed I was right.

When we got to the disheveled house about half a mile down the road from the estate, the dogs were howling. Jackson and I walked up the broken walkway, and he pounded on the peeling green door.

It seemed to take forever, but finally an elderly man with a walker came to the door. "What do you want?"

"Your dogs sound like they're in distress," I said. "Are they all right?"

"My son takes care of them."

"I'd like to take a look," Jackson said. Then he corrected himself. "*We* would like to take a look."

"Yeah, and who are you?"

"We're with the Greenport Animal Shelter," Jackson lied. He pulled out a card belonging to his friend Georgia, who actually is the head of the local animal shelter, and held it out, his finger deftly obscuring Georgia's name.

It must have looked official enough for the old man because he said, "Fine. Go around," and slammed the door.

We ran along the side of the house and found two bedraggled, long-haired, black-and-tan dachshunds living in a muddy mess of a yard on three-foot chains with collars that were too tight. They had no shelter, water, or food. They were skinny and looked sickly. But still, they stopped howling and wagged their tails when they saw us. It was enough to break your heart.

"Obviously, the son isn't taking care of them," Jackson said. "Let me call Georgia. She'll know what to do." He called her, and she said they were on their way. "We're not going to wait, Willow," Jackson said. "Time to get them out of here."

He strode to the back porch and banged on the door. The man didn't answer. Jackson opened the screen and banged again.

Finally, the man came to the door. "Yeah?"

"I'm confiscating these dogs. You may be charged."

"So what? They're a pain in my ass. Glad to see the back of 'em."

"You should be ashamed of yourself," I said.

"She's right, and don't get any ideas about adopting any other dogs, mister. I've got my eye on you."

Jackson took photos of the dogs in the mess, then the two of us walked through the mud, knelt down, and unchained the dogs. I picked up one, and Jackson took the other. They felt light as feathers and smelled horrible, as if they had been forced to sleep in their own filth. I wanted to cry.

We carried them to Jackson's truck and put them on a blanket in the front seat. I opened my water bottle and used a cup to give them water. They were severely dehydrated. They drank and drank. "I'll wait with them here while you talk to Georgia."

Georgia arrived a few minutes later, along with a cop. Jackson went to talk to the old man with them and came back to his truck fifteen minutes later. "Georgia asked me if I'd take them to the Pet ER in Riverhead since the vet in Southold is closed. She just got another call. Some idiot threw a dog out of a truck. It makes me sick. But I called MJ and she's very relieved that we were able to save the dogs."

"Me, too." I leaned over to give him a kiss on the cheek. "Tell Georgia we'll go, and let's get there fast."

chapter twelve

We all get angry from time to time. In Asian medicine, anger is characterized as Liver Fire Rising. Anger stimulates a contraction of chi, or life energy, and that stresses the liver. Anger can contribute to high blood pressure, elevated cholesterol levels, tight shoulders, back and jaw pain, and ulcers.

Aromatherapy can help you calm down by safely defusing anger. Essential oils that can help you feel better include basil, cardamom, chamomile, coriander, frankincense, geranium, hyssop, jasmine, lavender, lemon balm, lotus, marjoram, neroli, pine, rose, and ylang-ylang. Take up to eight deep breaths from an open bottle of these essential oils, or put it in a diffuser, or in the bath. If anger persists, consider making lifestyle changes to reduce stress and anger or even seek help from a qualified therapist. Letting anger go is one of the healthiest things you can do!

Yours Naturally,

Dr. McQuade

It felt as if Tuesday night went on forever, but it was actually in the early hours of Wednesday morning that the veterinarian on duty at the twenty-four-hour Pet ER examined both dogs and found them to be malnourished, severely dehydrated, and sick with worms. Not only that, one of the dogs had four calcified disks in his back, which must have made life hell in that yard. Both Jackson and I were angry and upset. The dogs were admitted and we were told to call in the morning for an update. We didn't get back to my place until two in the morning.

Our siesta was interrupted Wednesday morning when someone knocked on my bedroom door.

Jackson groaned. "What time is it?"

I squinted at my bedside clock. "Eight oh five."

"That's too early," Jackson mumbled. "Tell them to go away."

I got up, put on my robe, and went to see who it was.

"Sorry to bother you," Wallace said, "but the police are here to see you."

"The police? Why?" The cold finger of fear ran down my spine. Jackson sat up in the bed, now wide-awake.

"I don't know, but they want to see you right now."

"Tell them I'll be down in a few minutes. I have to get dressed. Thank you, Wallace." I closed the door and turned to look at Jackson. "What do you think this is about?"

"Whatever it is, it isn't good. Cops don't stop by this early just for fun."

I took the stairs to the first floor, with Jackson right behind me. I was glad he was there. When I reached the store, I spotted Detective Koren and his sidekick, Detective Coyle, standing by the counter and perusing the café. Wallace gave me a worried look.

Detective Koren spotted me and waved me over. He was dressed in a well-fitting black suit and Ray-Bans. Coyle wore a wrinkled brown linen suit with a garish orange tie. "Ms. McQuade, I need to speak with you," Koren began.

"Why is that?" I tried hard to hide my anxiety.

"The autopsy report is in, and it shows that the victim, Roger Bixby, had what seems to be lavender bathwater in his lungs."

"So, he didn't die in the bay?" Jackson asked.

"No, that's not what it looks like. He also had high levels of barbiturates in his system." Detective Koren flipped open his police-issue black notebook. "We think that Roger Bixby may have been drowned in a bathtub, then moved. Although we don't know how, with a house full of people, that was possible. The interesting thing is that it's the same modus operandi as when that caretaker Daniel Russell was murdered at the estate in the thirties."

"He was drowned in a bathtub and his body was moved?" I asked.

Coyle nodded.

"That's too much of a coincidence," I said.

"Yeah, that's what we thought," Koren agreed.

"How did you know about that?" Jackson said. "You weren't even born then, Koren."

"Hey, we do our research," Coyle answered. "We're *detectives*. We *detect*."

"Okay, then, so why are you here?" Jackson said. "This has nothing to do with Willow."

"I'm here because Dr. McQuade is the only person I know who happens to be an expert in lavender essential oils. In fact, you gave a seminar on lavender on Monday evening, did you not?"

"Please, Koren," Jackson said. "Why would a murderer

need essential oil? It has nothing to do with why Roger died."

"We don't know. It's why we're here," Koren said.

"We've tried to reach Simon and he's not answering," Coyle interjected. "Know anything about that?"

"He's probably asleep," I said snarkily. This was a helluva way to wake up.

Koren flipped to another page in his notebook. "We're still wondering about Simon's motive. We're thinking he did it to get Roger out of the picture so he could have Carly all to himself."

"They were getting a divorce. Roger was already out of the picture," Jackson said. "And we're not talking to you about this."

"Do you think he did it?" Coyle asked me.

"No, I don't," I said.

"Okay," said Koren, flipping a page of his notebook. "But let's say he *did* do it. Did you help him obtain the lavender essential oil that we found at the bottom of the bathtub?"

"No. Absolutely not."

"Then that's all for now," Koren said. "If you see your ex, tell him we want to talk to him again."

At that moment, the door opened and Simon walked in.

Simon didn't notice Koren and Coyle at first because he had his head down and was texting. But after he put his laptop on a table by the window and sat down, he did, and his face fell.

Koren, Coyle, Jackson, and I went over to Simon's table.

"Mr. Lewis. We need to talk to you." Koren looked at Jackson and me. "Alone please."

"I want them to stay," Simon said. "What do you want?"

Koren told him about the autopsy results. "Now, do you know anything about this?"

"No, not at all."

"We were thinking that your ex-girlfriend here"—Coyle pointed at me—"may have given you the lavender oil we found in the tub."

"Simon, call your lawyer," Jackson said. "Do not say a thing."

"You are really getting on my nerves, Spade," Koren said. "This is none of your business."

"It's her business"—Jackson gestured to me—"so it's my business. Willow, would you like them to leave?"

"Very much so."

"Gentlemen?"

"We'll go," Koren said. "But we need to talk to you, Mr. Lewis. Now."

"Willow, call my lawyer." Simon fished out a business card from his wallet and handed it to me. Then he gathered up his laptop, a stricken look on his face. "Tell him I need him now."

After the police left with Simon in tow, I called his lawyer, who said he was on his way. But I didn't have time to dwell on this recent turn of events because the breakfast crowd started to pour in, and Merrily had just called in sick. Because of this, Jackson would have to go to Roger's funeral at the Presbyterian Church in Southold this morning alone and give Carly my regrets. He also promised to call the Pet ER on his way to his house to change and call me with any news.

I pitched in and helped Wallace handle the crowd. Around eleven thirty, Amanda texted me to let me know that both Allie and Hector had appointments at the cottage from two to six. I had appointments at four and five. Jackson called to tell me that he had talked with the vet, who was still evaluating the dogs. I stayed to help with the lunch crowd, too, and finally left the store at one thirty with Qigong, after putting the cats in my bedroom to keep them safe.

Before I went up to the estate, I swung by the police station, left Qigong in the car, and went inside. The desk sergeant told me that Simon was no longer there. I stepped out onto the front steps and called him but got his voice mail. I called Carly and got the same response. Maybe they let Simon go to the funeral with her, I thought. Actually, if Koren and Coyle were anything like TV detectives, they would have gone to the funeral, too.

Jackson showed up at the estate about ten minutes after I did. We set off in one of the golf carts for the cottage where I would be working, and I told him that I hadn't been able to get in touch with Simon again. "Was he at the funeral?"

Jackson shook his head. "I hope he hasn't done something stupid, like gone to L.A."

"I don't think he'd do that. Was Carly at the funeral?"

"Of course. Not a lot of tears, though. But I guess that's to be expected when you're married to someone like Roger Bixby. Or if you had a hand in his murder."

"We don't know that. She's been very upset about Roger's death. Maybe she's all cried out for now. We also don't know what that photo of her sweater and her sunglasses on the dock mean."

Jackson looked troubled. "I know what Simon told you about Carly, and he might be right. But Simon's in love with her, so he may not be the most objective person to ask. And how do we know that Carly's been honest with him? I think I'm going to do a little research and see if I can find out if she really is a trust-fund baby. In the meantime, I'm going to keep an eye on her."

Jackson's phone rang and he pulled over. "Hello? . . . Oh, hi,

Dr. Scott, how are the dogs?" He listened for a few moments. "That sounds good. Thank you so much." He put his phone back into his pocket. "Dr. Scott says they are already doing much better. They've been treated for worms, bathed, and groomed. They're eating a high-nutrition dog food to fatten them up. I'm going to pick them up later, during the dinner break, and take them home."

"Take them home?" I asked, surprised. "You mean, you're going to adopt them?"

"Yup. I've wanted doxies for years, so this seems right."

"That's wonderful!"

"Just following your lead, McQuade. The fact that you rescued Qigong gave me the idea. I'd like to rescue more doxies and other dogs. Maybe even set up a sanctuary on my property. I'm going to look into it."

"That would be fantastic. You're a great guy, you know that?" I leaned over and kissed him.

"I try." Jackson pulled back onto the path. "So, what's the plan for today?"

"First, I want to make sure that Allie and Hector have what they need for their clients. But I don't have appointments until four, so I thought I might do some snooping."

"Just be careful," Jackson said predictably.

"I want to talk to Sarah, the makeup artist. Unless she can do damage with mascara and blush, I'll be fine."

After I checked in with Allie and Hector, I took Qigong for a walk back to the makeup and wardrobe trailer. I wanted to talk to Sarah again and see if I could get more information about Carly and Roger.

The trailer was at the far end of the property, set back from the house. I picked up Qigong, climbed the two steps, and walked in the open door. Sarah was sitting on a couch with a box of Kleenex next to her. A petite brunette, wearing jeans, a tie-dyed top, and flip-flops, pulled clothes from the wardrobe rack on the other side of the trailer. "Hi, can I help you?"

"I'm Willow McQuade, the holistic doctor on-site. I just wanted to check on Sarah."

"I'm Cassidy." She reached down to pet Qigong. "What a cute doggy."

"It's nice to meet you, Cassidy." I turned to Sarah. "How are you doing today?"

She blew her nose. "Not good. The funeral was very difficult."

That wasn't what Jackson had said. If she had been crying, she was in the minority. What exactly was her relationship with Roger?

"In fact, I'm going to go back to the hotel. I'm not needed until later anyway." She picked up her bag and walked out the door. "I'll see you later, Cassidy."

I waited until she was out of earshot, then said, "She seems really upset. I didn't know that she and Roger were that close."

Cassidy seemed uncomfortable with my question. "I don't know about that. I think she felt bad for Tom." Cassidy picked up a few wildly colorful caftans and headed for the door. "If you'll excuse me, I need to go see MJ."

As I stepped out of the trailer, I spotted Tom entering the mansion. Suddenly I knew what I was going to do next.

I put Qigong in the car, checked the call sheet for an address, and headed west. I arrived at Tom's studio in Cutchogue ten minutes later. The address took me to the end of a private road about two blocks from the water. The studio looked more like a shack than a house, with peeling paint and a rotted roof. It was run-down, uncared for, and unloved. It seemed to fit Tom's personality. A rutted dirt road led to the building, but I parked the car on the road, gave Qigong a bone, and walked instead.

Most of the homes in the neighborhood looked empty, which meant they were second homes and only used on weekends or in the summer. Still, I took a quick look around to make sure I was alone before I headed to the front steps of his studio and picked up his mail from under a red brick.

There were two notices from collection agencies, a bill for *Rolling Stone* magazine, and a letter from an E. Thorne without a return address. The back of the envelope was partly open so I helped it along and pulled out a single sheet of paper. It had just two words: *Contact me*. I didn't know what to make of that. I put the sheet back into the envelope and pressed the flap closed.

I put the mail back under the brick and headed around the studio. A large window was on the south side, which probably provided brilliant morning sun. Inside, I saw a potter's wheel, dirty rags, and several half-finished pieces on a workbench. The workroom looked dirty and dusty. I wondered how long it had been since he had done any work here. I went back around to the front door and tried to open it, but it was firmly locked. That wasn't going to stop me. First, though, I went to get Qigong because it was too warm to leave him in the car any longer. When it's warm outside, a car gets hot *very* fast, even with the windows cracked.

I put him on a leash and returned to the back of the studio and found a window that was half-open. I pushed the screen into the room and opened the sash. It took all of two minutes. I leaned in, set Qigong on the floor, and wiggled through myself. Once inside, I padded around the studio and examined Tom's work while Qigong sniffed the floor. One shelf was filled with unfired asymmetrical pots, which I couldn't imagine anyone actually buying. His sculpture, though, was more interesting. The pieces were whimsical busts of mythical beasts. They weren't exactly my taste, but I could see what Carly meant. Each seemed to have a unique and vivid character. Tom Bixby, the walking disaster, really did have talent.

Next, I examined a large oak table. Its surface was covered with dried clay and layers of scattered newspapers. I saw something shiny sticking from beneath the corner of an old *New York Times* sports section. It was a photo of Tom kissing Sarah, the makeup artist, in front of the Universal City Studios sign in Los Angeles. Wow. So perhaps she turned down Roger but went for Tom? No wonder she wasn't happy about his crush on Carly. I turned over the photo to find a date. It had been taken in July, right around the time that Carly had hooked up with Simon. I pulled out my phone and took a photo to show to Jackson later.

After that, I headed into the other rooms. Dirty dishes were in the small kitchen, and a hallway led to the living room, which was sparsely furnished with a sofa and a flat-screen TV. The bathtub was dirty, and the sheets on his bed were a tangled mess. I circled the bedroom and came to a full stop when I found another photo. This one was of Tom and Carly. But it hadn't started out that way. Tom had obviously cut Roger out of the photo and replaced it with himself. Creepy. I took a shot of that, too.

I decided that I'd spent enough time here, but, as usual, Qigong had other ideas. He poked his head into a hole in the wall and started barking, probably at a mouse. I went over to pick him up and asked him to *Shhh!* while I zeroed in on the antique desk next to the hole in the wall. There were more scattered papers, mostly overdue bills. Holding Qigong, I riffled through them and quickly found my third surprise in Tom's house. It was a letter from Roger's production company, Galaxy Productions, dated April 12, 2011:

Mr. Thomas Bixby,

Please accept this check for $31,500 for pre-production services provided during the start-up of MJ's Mind. *A contract for your services on the* MJ's Mind *shoot in Southold, NY, in 2012, exact dates to be determined later, will follow. $1,500 of this amount is payment for the two-week intensive second-assistant-director workshop you have taken at the Creative Film Institute in Santa Monica, Ca. We look forward to working with you.*

It was signed by Roger and CC'd to Carly and Rick.

But there was more, a green Post-it that read, *This is blackmail, Tommy. But I trust you will keep your word and not tell Carly a thing. Destroy this note!—RB.*

I thought about what Carly had said about Roger owing Tom. I was right. That was definitely his euphemism for blackmail.

chapter thirteen

Dr. Willow McQuade's Healthy Living Tips

Menopause is the time when menstrual cycles cease. It's also a rite of passage that can be empowering, enabling you to make changes and start over in midlife. Aromatherapy can be helpful for the hot flashes that are among menopause's most vexing symptoms. Good essential oils to choose include basil, geranium, grapefruit, lavender, lemon, and peppermint. You can inhale these oils directly or put them in the bath. Massages can be especially soothing and calming. To make a massage oil, mix one ounce (28 ml) of one of these oils with twelve drops of birch, rosemary, or juniper.

Yours Naturally,

Dr. McQuade

When I returned to the estate Wednesday afternoon around three, I found Jackson guarding the front of the mansion. The red light was going round and around. Qigong sniffed the grass while I showed Jackson the photos of Sarah and Tom, Tom and Carly, and told him about the letter I'd found.

Jackson shook his head. "I don't know whether to congratulate you or have you arrested for breaking and entry and tampering with the US mail."

"I left everything exactly as it was. And I got some valuable information."

"Yeah, you did. But you took some pretty big risks there. I wish you had waited for me."

"I know. But we need to divide and conquer. Especially since the cops hauled Simon in again. So what do you think it all means?"

"I think it confirms the fact that Tom is interested in Carly, which gives him a pretty good motive for murder. But killing Roger would also stop that blackmail revenue stream. You definitely need to talk to Sarah, the makeup lady, again. She may be able to help you unravel this mess."

"I plan on it." I looked at the red light. "Why are they shooting this afternoon?"

"MJ isn't in there," Jackson explained. "She had kind of a meltdown in the limo on the way to the cemetery, Rick said. She's lying down in their cottage. So, definitely no shoot tonight. They're just taking shots of the rooms that he expects MJ will want to work in, and also the beach during magic hour. You know, right before sunset when you get that golden glow. Rick says it will show the audience that the estate looks welcoming but is actually very scary."

"It is not welcoming," I said. "I'm getting the creeps just standing here."

"Are you staying here for the afternoon?"

"Yes. I have clients to see at four and five."

"I'm going to leave at six and go get the dogs from the ER vet. Want to come?"

"I wouldn't miss it."

By eight Wednesday night, we were back at Nature's Way. The two dachshunds looked as if they'd had a makeover. Both of them seemed 100 percent better. We'd stopped by the Feed Bag, a natural-pet-food store, on the way home and picked up comfy beds, water and food bowls, blankets, pet food, flea and tick control, and, of course, plenty of toys and treats. When we'd reached Nature's Way, Jackson parked his truck in the back and we carried the two boys up to my bedroom. First step, introduce them to Qigong.

Jackson and I sat on the floor between the two dogs and Qigong so we could intervene in case they didn't get along. This worry was completely unnecessary. Qigong took one look at the two dogs, ran over, and tried to play with them. The doxies were a little skittish, but within an hour, the three dogs were lifelong friends. The cats, however, turned up their noses and headed into Allie and Hector's room for some private time. My two friends were in New York City, attending a lecture on a breathing technique called Buteyko.

Jackson went downstairs to get the rest of the pet supplies and fun stuff while I watched the dogs. We'd have to figure out what to call them. Five minutes later, Jackson came back up the stairs with two bags, a frown on his face, and one Simon Jerome Lewis.

Simon looked worse than he had this morning. He hadn't shaved and looked thinner, almost gaunt. He was a shadow of the cocky, attractive guy he'd been just a few days earlier, before Roger had been murdered.

"Look who I found," Jackson said, putting the bags down. The three dogs ran over to greet him and bark at Simon.

"What happened to you today?" I asked.

Simon ran his fingers through his hair. "You saw, they're harassing me now! They brought me in again for questioning because of the autopsy results. I wouldn't answer those questions about the bathroom and the lavender bath oil without my lawyer, and when he arrived, he told me to shut up period, and they let me go. I need to know if you've made any progress."

I hesitated a moment, then told Simon about what I'd found at Tom's house.

Simon listened carefully, then said, "He actually cut Roger's photo out and put his in? And he was blackmailing Roger because he cheated on Carly?"

"As far as I can tell."

"Well, that explains why Tom is so eager to pin this on me," Simon said bitterly. "Because he wanted Carly for himself, and *he's* the one who offed his brother."

"You're jumping to conclusions," Jackson said. "All we know is that Tom was blackmailing Roger. That doesn't mean he killed him."

Simon nodded reluctantly. "I guess I just want this solved, and I know I didn't do it." He gave me a quizzical look. "Who is this Sarah? Have you met her?"

"Yes, she's MJ's makeup person and she was my client yesterday. I saw her today and she was upset. Cassidy, the wardrobe mistress, said it was because Sarah was concerned about Tom at the funeral."

"So Sarah wants Tom, but Tom wants Carly? Have I got that right?" Simon sat on the edge of the bed, then saw Jackson give him a look and got up again.

"We think so, yes."

"I want to go up there."

"When, now?" I said.

"Yes. Carly says they aren't shooting tonight because MJ is a mess. It's the only opportunity we'll have to look around."

"Not true. I can go anywhere in the house and I've seen most of it . . . except the upstairs bathroom," Jackson added, almost as an afterthought. "The police have got it taped off."

"And Pierre may not have shown you everything," I pointed out. "He only showed you the rooms they're using for filming, right?"

"We should go," Simon said. "We need to know what the cops know. It could be our only chance. They'll be shooting at night the rest of the week."

"You two are crazy," Jackson said. "The answer is no."

"Maybe Willow and I can just go," Simon said.

"No!" Jackson and I said simultaneously.

"I'm not going up there without Jackson." I crossed my arms in front of my chest.

"And I'm not going," Jackson said. "That's final."

Jackson eventually gave in. Before we left, we locked the dogs in my bedroom and the cats in Allie and Hector's bedroom to keep them safe. We hopped in Jackson's truck and stopped at Simon's house to pick up a skiff he owned and put it in the back. The plan was to go to Laughing Water beach, which was directly across the water from the Bixby estate, to see if there was a police presence. If not, we'd climb into the boat and row across.

Thirty minutes later, Jackson rolled his truck to a stop at the end of the Laughing Water road. It was a beautiful night, with a clear, dark velvet sky. Pinpricks of starlight and the almost full moon shining overhead were reflected in the inky black water below. We got out and carried the lightweight skiff across the sand to the western end of the beach. When we saw that the lights in the mansion were out and no cops were on the beach, we got into the skiff, and Simon and Jackson paddled across the inlet.

On the other side, we pulled the skiff onto the beach and started to walk up the steps. There, surprisingly, we found Rick, holding a big, fat cigar in one hand and an antique lighter in the other, talking to Amanda.

He pointed his cigar at the piece of paper in her hand. "So just make those changes and then e-mail it to everyone, so they have it tonight, okay, darlin'?"

Amanda put the piece of paper in her clipboard. "Right away." She took off and walked across the grass toward the production trailers.

"What are you all doing? Out for a midnight paddle?"

"It's a beautiful night," I said. "This is one of my favorite beaches."

"Sorry about this whole mess, Simon." Rick clapped him on the shoulder. "You're getting a bum rap, brother."

"Thanks, man," Simon said.

"So what are your thoughts on who killed Roger?" I asked.

Rick shook his head. "Nah, don't know. I'm not a detective, and I'm up to my eyeballs in production matters." He jabbed his cigar in Simon's direction. "But from what Carly told me, and after meeting you, I don't think you have it in you to kill. Maybe some weirdo just came on up here and knocked him off."

"Unlikely," Jackson said, then changed the subject. "So, what are you doing out here, Rick?"

"Just enjoying this excellent cigar. It's my reward for getting through this hellacious day. MJ is still very upset. Not to mention, now we're behind. We've got a lot of ground to cover tomorrow. We just finalized the new call sheet. Amanda will distribute it tonight." Rick lit the cigar with the lighter and blew several smoke rings.

"Nice lighter," Simon said. "Vintage?"

"It was Roger's. He got it from Max. Old Mr. Bixby used to use it when he frequented speakeasies in New York, back in the twenties." Rick took a short puff and pointed the cigar at the sky. "Now, Roger, that boy was different, God rest his soul. He treated his body like a sacred temple, for all the good it did him. He'd sooner fight a rattlesnake than smoke, so he gave it to me."

Rick went silent for a moment, then said, "Roger was my best friend. Known him for ten years. You know we met at Jerry's Deli in Studio City in California? He was sitting next to me, reading the *Hollywood Reporter*. I commented on the cover story about Steven Spielberg, we starting talking, and ended up taking a three-hour lunch. Instant friendship. He could be a prick, but I sure do miss him."

He glanced at his watch and said, "Well, I'm all in. Time for bed." He walked over to a golf cart that was a few yards away. He pointed the cigar at us. "Have a good evening. It'll be a busy day tomorrow. We start at eight, Spade. See you then."

"Okay, now what?" Simon asked as Rick walked away.

"We go inside and start at the top and work our way down," Jackson said. "Good thing I've got a key."

"Yes, it is," I said. "Aren't you glad you came?"

Using small flashlights, we crept silently through the first floor, found the staircase, and headed up to the third-floor bathroom, where we slipped under the yellow police tape. Black powder was everywhere, including the old-fashioned claw-foot tub. The room had the faint smell of lavender.

"Okay, we're here. Let's take a look around, although it's unlikely we'll find anything that Koren and his team haven't," Jackson said. "Don't forget your gloves."

We all put on the latex gloves that Jackson had insisted we bring so that we wouldn't leave prints.

I stared at the bathtub and shuddered. Roger had been killed here, and Daniel Russell before him. I wasn't sure how much longer I could stay in this room. "Let's do this quickly," I said.

Simon put his hand on the wall and leaned over to look inside the tub. "Ow!" He pulled his hand from the wall and looked at it. "I got a splinter!"

"Will you shut up, Simon?" Jackson said. "Do you want the entire estate to hear you?"

I quickly examined Simon's hand. Sure enough, a good-size wood splinter had gone right through the latex glove. I went over to the medicine cabinet, where the beam of my flashlight picked out tweezers and Band-Aids. "You got lucky."

"Hurry," Simon pleaded. "It really hurts."

Jackson rolled his eyes. "Simon, you wouldn't last a day in prison."

"That's why we're here, Spade. So I can stay *out* of prison!"

"Cool it," I said.

Simon stripped off the glove and I pulled a one-inch splinter out of his hand. I took a small bottle of tea tree oil from my pocketbook, and used a few drops to disinfect the wound, then topped it off with a Band-Aid. I put the tweezers and box back inside the cabinet and tried to close it. But the door to the cabinet wouldn't shut. I picked up my flashlight and directed it to the back of the cabinet. I could see a small gap and something else. It wasn't the wall—it was metal, almost like a second, smaller cabinet behind the one I'd opened. I tried to pull off the medicine cabinet's false back, but it wouldn't budge.

"I think I found something."

"Now that's interesting," Jackson said, as he peered into the cabinet. He pulled the false back off easily and set it on the floor. Behind it was a three-foot-by-three-foot square box inserted into the wall. Jackson flipped open its metal lid and directed his flashlight inside.

He gave a low whistle. "Look at this."

Inside was an old-fashioned rotary dial phone, along with a series of switches with small, worn placards below them. I read the placards aloud: "'KITCHEN, DINING ROOM, DOWNSTAIRS BATH-ROOM, BEDROOM 1, BEDROOM 2, BEDROOM 3, AND BEDROOM 4.'"

"It looks like some sort of control panel," Jackson said.

"It is," Simon said. "I saw something like it on TV once, I think on *Columbo*. It's like an early version of special effects. You can use it to make a house seem haunted."

Jackson gave me an I-told-you-so look.

Simon pointed to the switches. "These control all the lights." He picked up the telephone receiver. "And this is con-nected to a system of pipes that carries sounds throughout the house." He put the receiver down again. "Now, if they wanted to make a ghost appear, they would just need a sheet of glass and lighting to illuminate the person playing the spirit."

"Maybe Max used it during his séances to impress his guests," I said. "Mrs. Florrick said he was into that."

"And now Rick could be using this to make MJ seem like a star," Jackson said. "It's a way to get sound effects into the show when MJ does a reading, like those whispers you heard, Willow. Remember, Amanda did disappear during the shoot." He ran a finger along the inside of the cabinet. "It's not dusty so it's been used recently."

I didn't want to admit to the possibility that MJ was a fake, but the evidence pointed to trickery—or at least enhancement.

Simon gazed around the room. "This house looks like it was built in the twenties." Besides being a TV writer, Simon was an architecture buff. He used to swoon every time *Architectural Digest* came to our L.A. apartment.

"So?" Jackson said.

"So that was right around Prohibition," Simon said. "This system we're looking at could have started out as a means of communication when a shipment of illegal liquor was due." He pointed to the window next to the cabinet. "Someone could stand sentry here and, when a boat flashed its lights, give the signal to someone else to go out, meet the boat, and get the booze. I'm guessing that later Max adapted it to entertain his friends."

"Maybe. Let's keep looking." I walked over to the closet at the foot of the tub and opened the door.

"Looking for another false back?" Jackson asked.

"You read my mind." I knocked on the wall behind the shelves of towels. "It sounds hollow." I used my flashlight to examine the wall.

"What are you doing?" Simon said as he came over. "Did you find something?"

I began taking the towels off the shelves, stacking them on a vanity. Then Jackson pulled the empty shelves off the wall. He took a step closer and used his flashlight to examine the wall again. Finally, he pushed on the right side. He pushed again, and this time, with a noticeable click, a door opened.

"Yes," I said, finally answering Simon's question. "We found something."

"It's a secret passage." Jackson stared at me in disbelief. "I'm beginning to think you really are Nancy Drew." He shone his light inside. "And there's a staircase." He pushed away the fraying cobweb at the top of the stairs and stepped down.

I felt a thrill of excitement as I followed him down. The house still spooked me but not quite as much, now that I knew that some of what I had experienced were special effects. I was in a Gothic mansion, following a secret passage. This was *almost* fun.

Simon trailed behind us as we continued down a gray-brick staircase that twisted and turned. The walls were also made of brick and looked medieval. The steps were worn and slippery, so I gripped the metal rail at every turn. The air was musty and dusty and I started coughing. As I descended, I could hear what sounded like mice or rats skittering ahead of me. Okay, I thought, not so much fun.

Jackson stopped and directed his flashlight to the step in front of him. "I think someone was here before us. It's a footprint. See?"

I pointed my flashlight at the step. There, in the dust, was the faint outline of a shoe. "That's a good clue."

"Could be. I'm thinking we should go back up so we don't ruin the rest of the evidence if there is any."

"Wait a minute." I pointed my flashlight at the metal rail and a feeling of dread swept through me once again. This was definitely *not* fun. There on the railing was a tufted piece of cerulean-blue thread. I sucked in a breath. "This *is* how they got Roger's body to the beach. That's the same color as the shirt that he was wearing."

At midnight, Jackson pulled his truck into a spot behind Nature's Way and we got out. As I climbed the steps, I noticed that the large spotlight was on behind the Curious Kitten, the shop I had just visited on Monday. When I got to the deck, I looked over the fence. Arthur and Agatha Beasley were unloading boxes from a white truck. Several boxes were already by the back door.

"Kind of late to be doing business," I whispered to Jackson.

"Let's see if we can hear anything." Jackson pulled me down so they couldn't see us. Luckily, we could peer through the slats on the deck.

Arthur reached into the truck and said, "We shouldn't be doing this." He glanced around nervously and carried a box to the back door. He set the box down, opened the door, and put a trash can in front of it so it would stay ajar.

"Oh, grow a pair, Arthur. It's too late to turn back!" Agatha was carrying a smaller box. "This stuff is going to be worth a fortune, so stop your whining!"

"Okay, okay." Arthur pulled out another box, put it on the ground, and pulled down the rear door of the truck. The two of them went inside their store.

"That was weird," I said, opening the back door of Nature's Way.

"They're obviously up to no good," Jackson said, following me in. "But I'm not a cop anymore, and they're not our problem. Let's forget it for tonight. I want to see the dogs and go to bed. It's been a long day."

"Good idea." But, first I put the Beasleys on my suspect list.

chapter fourteen

Tea tree oil is a must-have for your natural remedy aromatherapy tool kit. It contains terpenes and other phytochemicals that are effective antiseptics and anti-fungals and are absorbed into the skin. You can use it diluted (pure tea tree oil can be irritating to the skin). Just mix it with an equal amount of water and use it to clean wounds, stings, and burns. In addition, it's effective at treating fungal infections in the toes and fingernails. It's also an important component in oint-ments, creams, and salves for treating athlete's foot, acne, ringworm, jock itch, and shingles. For sinus and respiratory problems, such as sinus infections, cold, and flu, just inhale tea tree oil as steam. If you have dandruff, look for a shampoo with tea tree oil or put a few drops in your favorite shampoo.

Yours Naturally,

Dr. McQuade

Thursday morning, while Jackson, Qigong, the doxies, Ginger, and Ginkgo stayed in bed, I threw on my yoga clothes and padded down to the yoga studio on the second floor.

I went through a short yoga practice; then I got comfortable, closed my eyes, and allowed my breath to fall into a natural rhythm. Gradually, my mind began to quiet, and I settled my attention on my breath and meditated for twenty minutes or so. Sometimes when I meditate, things that are confusing become clear. I'd been hoping that this session would clarify something about the case, perhaps give me some perspective that I was missing. When I opened my eyes again, I wasn't any clearer about the case; there were still too many suspects with no clear line to the murderer. But I did feel calmer and ready to reenter my day.

I joined Jackson and the animal menagerie in the bedroom. We had fun playing with the dogs and watching them wrestle with each other. Even the cats seemed a little more accepting. They didn't flee the room, but watched all the canine activity from the top of a bookshelf. Afterward, Jackson headed home to get the dogs settled with the dog sitter and then head up to the estate. He took Qigong with him, since I was planning to make a stop and didn't want to leave Qigong in the car. I quickly showered, got dressed in my Nature's Way tee and a pair of black shorts, and went downstairs.

I was relieved to find Merrily back at work. I found her taking free-range eggs and organic cheeses from the fridge. "Wallace just brought me orders for eight omelets," she told me. "I am the Omelet Queen."

"It's good to have you back. How did things go with Dr. Cooper?"

Merrily put a pat of butter in a frying pan. "You were right. He said that my symptoms sounded like Lyme." She cracked three eggs into the pan and mixed them with a fork. "He sent my blood work to that place you mentioned in California. He said we should have the results in ten days."

"Good, that's the first step. Do you feel good enough to work? You can rest in my office anytime you need to."

Merrily picked up a grater and began to grate cheese. "Thanks, that should help. I'll need to do some ordering and stuff anyway, so I can rest then. What are you up to?"

"I'm headed to the library."

After our visit to the mansion last night and Simon's comments about the age of the house and the possible uses of the equipment in the cabinet, and that secret tunnel, I wanted more information about Prohibition. Plus, when Koren had come to Nature's Way, he had said that Roger's murder was almost a copycat of Daniel Russell's murder. Since Jackson was busy getting his doxies settled, I called Simon, told him what I wanted to research, and asked him to join me. It would be better for him than just sitting around the house worrying all day long.

I got into my Prius and drove down First Street, past the Salamander Café and year-round residences, to the Floyd Memorial Library. The imposing building was covered with ivy and fronted by two stone lions.

I parked and walked around to the front of the building, where I found Simon sitting on the stairs, wearing torn jeans, a PARALLEL LIVES T-shirt, and shades. He pushed his sunglasses up on his head, got up, and kissed me on the cheek. "Thanks for doing this, Willow. Carly said she thought it was a good idea, but I think she's just humoring me."

"How is she holding up?"

"Not so good this morning. The police are questioning her."

"Why are the police questioning Carly?"

"Well, according to her lawyer, they always question the spouse. Especially if a divorce is pending and there's money involved." Simon rubbed his unshaven chin. "Carly should be okay, though. She was on conference calls with Galaxy execs almost all that night, working out the budget for this season's shows. One of the guys in L.A. recorded the calls, so she's covered. Besides"—he gave me a wry smile—"I'm still Koren's favorite suspect. I think he's just got to convince himself that she wasn't my accomplice."

"Well, let's see if we can get any help here." I headed into the library.

I went straight to one of the computers and punched in the word *Prohibition*. Nearly three dozen titles came up on the page.

We wrote down a few of the call numbers, then found four shelves devoted to Prohibition. Simon grabbed as many books as he could carry, while I tried to be more selective and focused on Prohibition on Long Island and the East End. I snapped up *Rum Row: A Long Island Retrospective*; *East End Rum Running*; and *Fishermen to Rum Runners*.

We settled in at a table in the corner under a window and started skimming. Simon started to flip through a book called *Prohibition: A Lesson in Abstinence*.

"That looks like a page-turner."

"It isn't," Simon said as he quickly scanned the pages. "But it does say that Prohibition was declared on January sixteenth, 1920. It also says that rum came from the West Indies and the Caribbean, and whiskey from Canada and Europe."

I held up *East End Rum Running*. "It says here that large sailing ships carried the rum and whiskey to an area in the Atlantic Ocean three miles from the north shore of Long Island. Any closer and it was illegal to transport liquor. The ships anchored there, and then fishermen and whalers would go out and get the liquor and bring it back to shore on their boats. Sometimes they had to outrun the coast guard."

"Interesting," Simon said. "But that's not going to keep me out of jail. What else?"

"Let's see if we can find any references to the Bixbys or Daniel Russell or the estate." I located the index and went to the *B*'s. I turned the book to show Simon. "There are plenty of references to the Bixbys." I turned to the first one. "Okay, this is the introduction to the Bixby family." I skimmed the pages and summarized the copy. "Max Bixby, a textile manufacturer, was said to be one of the most successful rum runners on the North Fork. Bixby never confirmed his side business, but it was widely known in the area."

"So it's like I said. Max, or one of his guys, probably used the switches and the pipes in the cabinet to help them unload more safely and quickly. But what does this have to do with Roger's murder?"

"Be patient. Let's see if we can find a reference to Daniel Russell." I went back to the index and ran my finger down the page until I found a reference to *Russell, Daniel*.

"'Tragedy at the Bixby Estate,'" I read. "It says that Daniel Russell, the caretaker of the Bixby estate in Southold on the East End of Long Island, was murdered on April nineteenth, 1933, in the last days of Prohibition. 'Russell, who was a fisherman and rumored to be the right hand to Bixby in his rum-running enterprise, was just thirty years old. Russell was discovered on the beach in the front of the estate and believed to have drowned.'"

Simon pulled the book closer to his side of the table and continued reading. "'However, the autopsy revealed that he had freshwater in his lungs. After an investigation, police determined that he had been drowned in the upstairs bathroom in lavender bathwater and carried to the beach. Max Bixby and Daniel were seen arguing hours before he turned up dead. Bixby was considered a suspect but was never charged. The case remains open to this day.'"

Simon's jaw dropped. "The two deaths are almost identical. Which means that whoever killed Roger knew exactly how Daniel Russell died." He looked at me. "Do you think Roger's death could have been revenge for Daniel's, all those years ago?"

"Possibly. Or maybe it was set up to look that way—to frame someone who knew Daniel."

Roger began to tick off names on his fingers. "That would be the caretaker, James Russell; his wife, Sheila; and maybe that scary-looking housekeeper, Mrs. what's her name."

"Florrick. But she seemed very loyal to the Bixbys. She knew Roger and Tom when they were kids. She was very upset about Roger's death. Plus his death may mean she's out of a job."

"I guess you could say the same thing for the Russells," Simon said reluctantly.

I glanced at the stack of books and then at my watch. "I've got to get up to the estate, so I'll have to do the rest of my reading at home. I'm going to check out some of these."

"I'll get the rest."

We checked out the books and left the library. When we reached the sidewalk, I said, "Aren't you supposed to be writing a script?"

Simon groaned. "I'm better at procrastination, but you're right. I do need to get that first draft done." He kissed me on the cheek and walked over to his red-and-black Mini Cooper. "Keep me posted."

"Will do." I got back into the Prius. I was about to pull out when I spotted Amanda, taking several books out of the back of her rented Jeep and heading up the steps to the library. It looked as if she was doing her research, too.

I waited until Amanda left, then went back inside and asked if any books about Prohibition had been returned. The librarian seemed surprised but went to the shelf behind the desk and picked up three books. She pushed them across the counter to me. Not surprisingly, all of the books focused on the history of Prohibition on Long Island. I checked out the additional books and left.

When I arrived at the estate, Qigong ran up to greet me. He and Jackson had just emerged from the production trailer closest to the mansion.

"How are the doxies?" I asked Jackson.

"Good. I've got Katie, the pet sitter, coming by at ten, two, and six to take them out into the yard and play with them. And I've decided to name them Rockford and Columbo, you know, detectives."

"Like you." I reached into the Prius and grabbed a few of the books from the library.

Jackson glanced at the books. "Doing your homework, McQuade?"

"I told you I was going to the library to research Daniel Russell's murder."

"That's right, you did. Let's have lunch and you can tell me about it."

I put Qigong on a leash and we headed inside the tent. Today we had our choice of a dozen gourmet pizzas and a salad bar offering everything from organic sprouts, sliced mushrooms, shredded carrots, peppers, and Parmesan cheese to a dozen types of organic dressing.

I put the books down on a table and got in the food line. I chose a slice of pizza with organic, fresh mozzarella, basil, and plum-tomato sauce and a spinach salad. Jackson went for a plain slice, plain green salad, and grabbed two passion-fruit iced teas. On the opposite side of the tent I spotted Pierre eating with Tom. As usual, Tom seemed aggravated about something. Pierre listened but didn't seem to be enjoying the conversation. Finally, he took his phone out, said something to Tom, got up, and left. Tom slammed his bottle of water on the table and looked sullen.

Jackson was watching them, too. "Tom is just a little ray of sunshine," he said as we sat down and started on our food. "I imagine the police will question him at some point."

I told him what Simon had said about the police questioning Carly.

"The lawyer is right," Jackson said. "They always question the spouse. And with this murder, they've probably already taken statements from most of the crew. So what did you and Simon find at the library?"

"That Max was a suspect in Daniel Russell's death."

Jackson stopped midchew. "That's news. Did it say why?"

"They had argued, just like Simon and Roger." I speared a forkful of salad. "I also confirmed what Koren said, that Roger and Daniel were both killed the same way. Maybe the murderer copied the method to distract the police."

"Smoke and mirrors."

"And I saw Amanda there. She returned books about Prohibition on the East End." I pointed to the stack on the table.

"The fact that Amanda was there doing research kind of backs up my theory about them faking it, don't you think, McQuade?"

"Well, MJ said they always research a site whenever they go on location. So it makes sense that they would research Max Bixby and Daniel Russell. But that doesn't mean MJ's a fake. I wouldn't discount her that easily."

Jackson gave me a skeptical look.

"She heard the doxies crying when no one else did," I reminded him.

"Maybe she just has off-the-charts excellent hearing."

I rolled my eyes at him. "You're reaching, Spade."

He bit back a smile. "Okay, we'll table the issue of MJ's peculiar powers for now. What's next?"

"I want to talk to Lucas about Daniel Russell's murder. It was his grandfather, after all. I figure his father, James, must have told him all about it. Maybe James will talk to me, too."

"I guess that's a plan. Just watch your back, McQuade."

Jackson told me that Amanda had leased an extra golf cart for us, so Thursday afternoon I took that to the cottage where both Allie and Hector were in session. I found the schedule on the kitchen counter and it showed that I had appointments from three to six, and both Allie and Hector were booked from two to six. I put a note on the counter to tell them where I was going, took my cell phone and Qigong, and left. My mission was to get fresh lavender from the lavender field next to the cottage where Lucas, James, and Sheila lived. Hopefully I could get a few bouquets—and also some info from the family that would help me solve this mystery.

I decided to walk to the lavender farm, which meant that I had to cross in front of the cottage where Rick and MJ were staying. MJ sat on the porch reading. She was wearing a light blue caftan with gold trim and flip-flops, a modest outfit by her standards.

"Willow, hang on a minute," she called out. "I was hoping I'd see you today. Tell me, what did you think of our show the other night?"

I hesitated, then decided I had to know. "How much of it was real?"

"All of it, of course. Why would you even ask such a thing?"

Did MJ *not* know about Amanda and the special effects in the upstairs bathroom? If that was true, I didn't want to be the one to break it to her.

"Willow," she said more carefully. "Do you think I'm a fake?"

"No." I realized it was true. "It's just that . . . I'm not sure how these shows work, whether or not some of the things—like the book flying off the shelf and the lights dimming—are . . . enhanced."

MJ straightened her spine, and even with the crazy caftan, she looked dignified and formidable. "Pierre tapes my readings as they happen. I can tell you that, personally, I have never used a special effect. I'm surprised at you, Willow. I thought you were open to the spirit realm." A phone rang from inside the house, and she sighed. "I have to get that. But it's important to me that you understand that what I'm doing is genuine. Please, come tonight and see for yourself." She opened the door and went inside.

Feeling confused, I left MJ. Either she was an excellent liar or she was the real thing. If she was authentic, maybe they weren't adding effects, unless they were doing it without her knowledge. That no dust was on the secret compartment behind the medicine cabinet implied that *someone* was using special effects. Could it have been Max?

I followed the path that led from MJ's cottage in a westerly direction through the woods, hoping it would put me in the general area of the lavender fields and Lucas's house. I was using a leash with a long lead, so Qigong was able to run ahead of me. The path circled underneath overhanging trees, past saplings, and between tall bushes and field grasses.

I reached the end of the path and saw the pond that I remembered from the day Simon and Roger had been fighting. Despite that, it seemed idyllic and peaceful. I spotted another path and headed north to try to find the caretaker's cottage.

In the distance I heard the sound of a revving engine and the whine of a blade cutting wood. Great, I thought, so much for enjoying the quiet. But the noise soon stopped, and it was quiet again. The two of us kept walking. Around the next turn, a large, open field was filled with chamomile flowers. Bees, butterflies, and birds hovered over the fragrant blossoms. I waded into the chamomile field and picked a bunch to use for tea later. I was so involved in my task that I didn't notice that Qigong was missing.

I looked around, sure that he was somewhere nearby. "Qigong?" I called. "Qigong, where are you? Come here, boy!"

But there was no response. No answering bark or eager little dog racing toward me. I called again and felt fear tightening around my chest. "Qigong!" I called again. Frantic, I dropped the flowers and ran down the path, shouting his name.

The path dead-ended at a garden that was next to the Russells' house. I did a quick scan of the neat rows of flowers and herbs. No Qigong. Then, at the edge of the garden, I noticed an old shed, its door ajar. I ran to it and peered into the dark interior. I felt a surge of relief as I heard Qigong's familiar bark. It sounded as if it was coming from the direction of the house. But before I could even turn in that direction, someone shoved me hard. I stumbled into the dark shed, then heard the door slam behind me. I pushed back against it and then heard a sound that chilled me. A bolt sliding closed.

"Let me out!" I shouted, pulling against the door. "Let me out of here now!" Through the door I could hear Qigong barking. "Someone help me, please!"

The inside of the shed was dim and stifling hot. Thanks to a small, high window on the back wall, I could just make out some of the contents: a lawn mower, a gas can, a shovel, clippers, and gardening gloves. I wasn't sure how, but one of these items was going to help me break out. I picked up the shovel and banged it against the door, but it didn't budge.

Okay, stop panicking! I told myself. Then I felt like a complete fool. Why on earth was I trying to pull off a jail break when I had a cell phone and could just call Jackson? Shaking my head in disgust, I pulled out my iPhone and hit the On button.

I felt my heart sink as the screen showed a bright red battery. I hadn't recharged my phone last night. And probably not the day before, either. It was dead.

Somewhere outside, Qigong began to yelp, and I felt panic racing through me again. I jammed my uncooperative phone back in my pocket and picked up the shovel. If I had to take this shed apart, I would, but I was going to rescue my dog. I remembered the phone call I'd received at Nature's Way on Monday night. The one in which the mechanized voice threatened my pets. Was that someone making good on that threat? I thrust the shovel against the door again and again until the muscles in my arms were trembling.

I'd stopped for a moment to get my breath when I heard Lucas's voice. "Who's in there? You okay?"

"Yes, but my dog isn't. Open this door! Please!"

"Sure thing." I heard Lucas slide the bolt on the other side of the door, and then it was open.

I stepped outside, blinking against the bright light. "I need to find my dog. Qigong?" His barking had become panicked. My heart was in my throat.

"Sounds like he's that way." Lucas pointed at the house.

We ran toward it, following the sound of Qigong's barking. When we rounded the porch, I called for him again, and he began to whine. I raced up the steps and onto the porch, where he was tied to the barbecue grill. Whoever had done it had used his leash to secure him. I untied him and gathered him in my arms. "It's okay, boy," I told him, burying my face in his soft fur. "You're safe now.

"Thank you," I said to Lucas. Then, for the first time since he'd freed me, I really looked at him. He was carrying goggles and a chain saw. Instinctively I backed away.

"What's wrong? Why are you looking so spooked all of a sudden?" He followed my gaze to the chain saw in his hand. "Oh, this old thing." He carefully set the saw down on the porch. "I guess a man holding a chain saw is not a reassuring sight."

"I appreciate you understanding." I still kept a wary distance.

Lucas raised his hands high. "I'm unarmed, I swear. And I'm not going to hurt you. So, will you please stop looking at me like I'm a serial killer?"

Something in his tone broke through my fear, and I felt myself relax a little. Then I felt myself relax a whole lot more as I heard the sound of a golf cart and Jackson rolled into sight.

"Willow, are you okay?" he called.

"I'm fine. Lucas and I were . . . just talking."

Jackson parked the cart and came up onto the porch. His eyes went to the chain saw on the floor. "Is that yours?" he asked Lucas.

"It belongs to the estate. We use it to trim trees."

"Well, then, were you the one who sawed the branch over the path that almost fell on Willow and Amanda on Tuesday?"

"Hell, no. I've been working on clearing an area near the house the past couple of days. My mom wants to put in a vegetable garden on the other side of the shed, in the field."

"So who locked me in the shed?" Before Jackson could get upset, I said, "It's okay, no harm done. I'll explain later."

"Beats me," Lucas replied. "Anyone could have locked you in there. And I don't know who took your dog, either. What were you doing over here in the first place?"

"I was hoping to get a few bouquets of lavender to put in the guesthouse where we're working."

"My dad doesn't like strangers in the fields. But I guess it'll be okay. It's over here. . . ." He walked ahead of us, showing the way.

Jackson, Qigong, and I followed Lucas back to the garden, which I now realized was beautiful, filled with roses, zinnias, morning glories, cosmos, and sunflowers. "I'll get you some shears," Lucas said as he opened the door to the shed. He pulled out a pair of shears and handed them to me, handle first.

Jackson looked inside the shed. "So you don't lock this?"

"No need," Lucas said.

"There is if someone is using your equipment to harm someone."

Lucas didn't reply, just closed the door, and pointed to the lavender fields beyond the house. "The lavender is that way. Take all you want."

We watched as Lucas climbed the steps and walked onto the porch. Sheila, his mother, came out of the house, and the two spoke for a moment before Lucas went inside. She wore a faded flowered sundress, an apron, and sneakers. Her hair was twisted into a bun on top of her head and her face looked stressed. She was carrying a bowl of water.

Jackson walked over to her. "Do you know anything about what happened to Willow and her dog? Someone shoved her into the shed and took him." He pointed to Qigong.

"And tied him to this," I said, pointing to the barbecue.

Sheila shook her head. "I don't know about the shed. I found the dog and didn't know who he belonged to." She put the bowl of water down for Qigong, and he lapped it up. "I got this for him because I thought he was thirsty."

"I'm just glad to have Qigong back. Thank you." But I couldn't help wondering if Sheila had something to do with what had happened. The house, like the Bixby mansion, had an odd, uncomfortable vibe. It didn't seem as dark and menacing as the mansion, but something about this place didn't feel right. As we walked past, I noticed several blue bottles labeled LAVENDER OIL in a carrier on the steps. I nudged Jackson and pointed at it. "That's lavender oil. Do you think someone in this family killed Roger?"

"Could be. Or someone took it from here." Jackson shook his head. "I think we're accumulating way too many suspects. We're going to have to start winnowing down the list."

We went over to the lavender fields, and Jackson started clipping sprigs of lavender.

Before he had enough for a bouquet, James Russell, Lucas's father, walked up to us with a shotgun. "This is private property."

Jackson stood up and wiped his hands on his jeans. "You can put that gun away," he said calmly. "I just wanted to get a few bouquets of lavender for the cottage where my girlfriend is working. Your son said it would be okay. I'm Jackson Spade. I'm providing security for *MJ's Mind.*" He held up his security ID. "And this is Willow McQuade."

James Russell leaned the shotgun against a fence post and arched a bushy eyebrow at me. "So, you're staying on the estate?"

"No, I'm just working here." I stood up and wiped my hands on my shorts. "I'm a naturopathic doctor. I dispense natural cures, and we're also giving massages and doing acupuncture to help MJ and the crew."

"Don't you know that there was a murder here on Sunday?" He gave me a hard stare.

"We know," I said. "But we're trying to help Rick and MJ."

James laughed. "You'd be better off worrying about yourselves. That murder was just like the murder of my old man, Daniel Russell, during Prohibition. Something very strange is going on here. Something you don't want anything to do with."

"I did some research about the estate," I said, "and it mentioned your father and Max Bixby."

"Did your research mention that my father worked for Max in his rum running business? Or that they had a fight and Max killed him?"

"It did, actually," I said. "So why wasn't Max arrested?"

"The family was too powerful—and too rich. Max bought off my mother by giving my whole family lifetime jobs. He guaranteed us generous salaries and tenancy here. He told her, 'Your family will never want for anything.' But it was the devil's deal she made. The one thing I want, we'll never get—and that's justice."

"Max is dead now," Jackson said. "There's your justice."

"That's not justice. He lived a long life. He deserved worse."

James Russell pulled a flask from his pocket and took a long drink. "Roger came back a few months ago to see Max before he died. Minute the old man's dead, he decides to sell the estate. I told him that he can't do that. He owes us. But he wouldn't listen to me. Now he's dead, too, and good riddance."

chapter fifteen

As human beings, we have all had our hearts broken or suffered a loss. When we cry, it helps provide an emotional release that lowers blood pressure and muscular tension. Chemicals in tears include endorphin, which is a natural anesthetic and helps relieve the pain of loss. Essential oils can also stimulate chemical changes in the brain that can soothe you when you're hurting. Add eight to ten drops of essential oils such as cedarwood, clary sage, cypress, geranium, hyssop, marjoram, orange, rose, rosemary, or sage to your bath after it's filled. When you let the water drain out, visualize your sadness going down the drain. Keep in mind that time is a great healer. You *will* feel good again.

Yours Naturally,

Dr. McQuade

I returned to the cottage with the two bouquets of lavender and a lot of questions. Did James kill Roger to keep him from selling the estate? Was Lucas involved? And who had trapped me in that shed, and why? Only Jackson and MJ had known I was going there.

My musing was interrupted by my first client. Kelly, the accountant, had irritable bowel syndrome. I suggested more fiber, water, and activity; fewer fatty foods; cutting down on caffeine and carbonated sodas; and taking enteric-coated peppermint oil and clown's mustard. Next, I saw Samantha, Kelly's assistant. She had adult acne, so I recommended taking probiotics with bifidus and using tea tree oil on pimples. My final appointment of the day was with Martin, an assistant cameraman, who had strained his wrist. I suggested resting it as much as possible, wearing a brace, and applying topical arnica oil and taking homeopathic arnica.

I had dinner with Jackson since I was staying for this evening's shoot. After we ate, I put Qigong in my car with the windows wide-open and asked Matt, the guard at the door, to watch him, and we went inside the mansion.

Tonight, Thursday evening, they were shooting in the study. Rick, Carly, Tom, and Pierre were talking when we came in. MJ was seated in an old, beat-up wingback chair, eyes closed, preparing to contact the dead.

Jackson looked around the room and said in a low voice, "Please note that Miss Amanda is not here. She's probably waiting upstairs to do special effects."

"You may be right, but I still think that MJ is the real deal."

Carly spotted us and said something to Tom, who glared daggers at Jackson and me. Clearly, he was still furious about being thrown out of Nature's Way three nights ago.

Carly came over to us. "Thanks for taking Simon to the

library this morning, Willow. It was good for him to get out."
She made it sound as if I were babysitting him.

"It's always good to have help with research," I said. "I'm
glad that he was there."

She pulled the sunglasses off the top of her head and hooked
them on the front of her T-shirt. It reminded me of the photo
I'd found that showed these same sunglasses and her sweater on
the dock. "His lawyer is still working on getting him out of this,
but every little bit helps."

I knew I was not a professional investigator. Still, I'd been
working pretty hard to solve the mystery of Roger's murder and
get Simon off the hook. Certainly more than a *little bit*. "Glad
to do it," I said without showing my irritation.

"She's doing a great job," Jackson said, and put his arm
around me.

"Simon told me what you found," she said. "But I'm not
sure that it means anything. Have you discovered anything new
this afternoon?"

Now she was really getting on my nerves. Jackson must have
sensed it because he told her what had happened at Lucas's
house.

"Oh, James," Carly said, sounding bored. "James is always
talking about Max and how he killed his father. But there is
absolutely no evidence that he did, none at all, and Roger never
told me that he was going to sell the estate. I think that James
was making that up, too."

James had sounded truthful to me, but I let her comments
pass.

MJ got up then and started to pace the floor.

"She's ready," Carly said. "I've got to go. I'll see you later."

"Everybody settle!" Tom yelled. MJ sat down again in the
wingback chair.

Martin, the assistant cameraman yelled, "Speed!" and Pierre yelled, "Action!"

MJ got up and began to circle the room, just as she had the night before. She stopped near a window with a view of the bay. "I'm sensing the spirit of a young woman who is very sad. Her name starts with an *R*. Is the *R* for 'Rebecca'?" She waited a moment. "Yes, this is the spirit of Rebecca Russell. She was married to the caretaker Daniel Russell at the time of his death."

MJ put her hand to her chest, and as if on cue, tears began to stream down her cheeks. She pulled out a tissue, dabbed her face, and looked into the camera. "Her love was taken from her too soon, and she is still very grief-stricken. That's why she is still here." MJ took a deep breath. "What do you have to tell me, Rebecca?"

At that moment, the windows started rattling violently. A window shade snapped up and spun around and around.

MJ seemed unperturbed. "That's not necessary. I hear you. I'm listening."

The lights in the chandelier flicked on and off again. Suddenly the room seemed colder.

MJ looked straight into the camera. "She wants me to tell you that the rumor is true. She wants justice for her husband."

MJ's reading was unsettling. As I drove home Thursday night, I wondered if she would connect with Daniel Russell as well. If she did, would he give us the real story on his death? That would make for some exciting TV. And then another thought occurred to me: She knew Roger when he was alive. Would she try to contact him now that he was dead?

I was putting clean sheets on my bed when Jackson walked

in the door with the two doxies. He'd gone home to pick them up after the shoot wrapped. Qigong jumped off the chair and ran over to meet them. Jackson greeted me with a kiss.

"That's nice," I said, gazing into his eyes.

"Very." Jackson kissed me again.

I looked at the pile of clean linens that were still stacked on my dresser. "If we finish making up the bed, we can lie down."

"Good idea."

The dogs settled in the comfy dog bed under the window and watched us. The cats lounged in the chair.

"What did you think of MJ's reading tonight?" I asked.

"Interesting. I wonder how they got that window to shake and the shade to go up."

"Maybe it *was* Rebecca's spirit." I grabbed a pillowcase and threw it to him, then slid another on the pillow closest to me.

"Nah." He grabbed a pillow and put the fresh pillowcase on it. "That can't be it."

"Ye of little faith," I teased. "What about Carly? Would it kill her to acknowledge the work I've been doing?" I picked up the comforter and spread it on the bed.

"She doesn't believe in you like Simon. You really can't blame her for that."

"I guess not."

Jackson lay down on the bed and patted the space next to him. "Forget about MJ and Carly. I've got a better idea of how you can spend your time."

I climbed in next to him. "Oh, really?"

He pulled me close. "Really." He kissed me.

I woke up Friday morning to find a note from Jackson on the pillow next to me:

Happy 3-Month Anniversary! Dinner tonight? Love, J.

I'd forgotten in the midst of all the craziness, but he had obviously remembered that it had been three months since we had first met in June. It was the only good thing that had come out of Aunt Claire's death. We'd met when he came into the store for remedies for his bad back, and he had become my partner in investigating and solving her murder. Since then we had only become closer, and I already found it difficult to picture my life without him. I pulled my cell phone out of its charger on the nightstand and called him.

I left a message that I loved him and dinner sounded great. He was probably busy settling the dogs with his sitter and preparing to go up to the estate.

I got up out of bed and groaned. I felt stiff, probably from attacking the shed with the shovel yesterday. So I did a few yoga poses and a Loving Kindness meditation and took a quick shower. Before I went downstairs, I settled the cats in my room and locked the door. I didn't want to take any chances that they would be harmed by whoever had called me on Monday night.

I headed downstairs. Today, Friday, was the official beginning of Labor Day weekend, and Merrily and Wallace were serving a hungry breakfast crowd. I just hoped Merrily could handle it with the way she was feeling. I waved to her as I walked into the office.

Qigong settled on the couch and I settled in at my desk. My mind was on Jackson and on the case, but I did need to do a few things before I left for the estate. First, I checked my e-mail and found a note from my editor at *Nature's Remedy* magazine about a new assignment. She wanted me to write a story titled "Don't Be Rash," about natural ways to get rid of a variety of rashes. I had a lot of information on this subject, so I immediately e-mailed her back and said yes. Thankfully the deadline was September 15, which meant I could get through the Bixby shoot and Labor Day weekend before I had to start writing. Next, I reviewed the order sheets and saw that all the stock we were running low on should be in by tomorrow.

I picked up the *Suffolk Times* on my desk and thumbed through it. On page two was a story about the burglary of a weekend home in New Suffolk. I thought about the merchandise Arthur and his wife had unloaded the night before last. I wondered if I should tell Koren about it but decided against it. I had enough to handle right now.

I went back out into the store and over to Merrily, who was at the counter, ringing up a sale. "How are you feeling today?" I asked.

"Still tired, but resting in your office helps. Thanks."

"No problem. So, are we ready for the weekend? The order sheets look good."

She nodded. "Wallace and I went over everything and got what we needed. The order should come in this afternoon." She went over to the counter and picked up an envelope and handed it to me. "This came for you yesterday."

I looked at the envelope. It had my name printed on it but no return address. I opened it and found a single sheet of white paper with block letters cut out from a magazine that read:

Back off or you'll be sorry.

"How did this get here?" I asked, trying to keep my voice steady. Just six little words, and I could feel fear sweeping through me. "Did someone hand-deliver it?"

"Search me," Merrily said. "Right after we finished with the lunch crowd, I noticed the envelope sitting on the counter here. It had your name on it, so I held it for you."

"You didn't see anyone put it there?"

"No, and neither did Wallace. I asked him." Her eyes

searched my face. "What's wrong? Why are you asking all these questions?"

I showed her the note.

Merrily shuddered. "This is getting scary, Willow. Someone doesn't want you investigating for Simon."

"No kidding." I hadn't even told her about the falling branch or getting locked in the shed. "But they're not going to scare me off. For one thing, Simon is depending on me. And for another," I said, suddenly understanding. "If they sent me this letter, I must be getting close to finding Roger's killer."

When I pulled into the driveway in front of the Addams family mansion Friday afternoon, crew members and production staff were hustling in and out of the Bixby house. Jackson was in a heated discussion with Tom, who wore ripped jeans, a white, sleeveless T-shirt, a thick silver chain around his wrist, and shades. He was trying too hard to look cool. I got out of the car with Qigong and started toward them, but as I did, Tom gave Jackson the finger and stormed off.

"What was that about?" I asked Jackson.

"I think he's drinking on the job," Jackson said as he watched Tom head to the tent. "Rick asked me to talk to him. I told him I'm in AA. But he doesn't want to listen to me."

"So what are you going to do?"

"Wait. He's probably close to bottoming out now that Roger's been murdered."

"Especially if he's the one who did it. The stuff I found in his studio points in that direction."

"True," Jackson said. "But Roger had lots of enemies besides Tom. Keep in mind, Roger was the one who was pay-ing Tom off and giving him a job. Tom may be unhinged, but that doesn't mean he's deranged enough to destroy his major lifeline. I think one of the reasons he's such a mess now is that Roger's gone, and he's terrified of what will happen without his brother to support him. He might have had motive to kill him, but he had an equally strong motive not to."

I nodded. "Okay, Tom's iffy but possible. Same for Carly. So that leaves James Russell, trying to avenge Daniel's death. And maybe Arthur and Agatha Beasley, who are somehow selling off all the Bixby first editions. And who else?"

"Well, I keep thinking about that phone message and wondering who on this set could possibly know that you have cats," Jackson said.

I mulled it over. "The only one I can think of is Amanda. She was poking around at the store that day. I remember she looked into my office."

"And there's a good chance she knows about the third-floor bathroom, which means she might know about the secret passage."

"Plus, she's done all that research for MJ," I said. "She knows about Daniel's murder; she would have the information to re-create it."

"So we add her to the list." Jackson looked around. For the moment, we were alone. "Now, on to more enjoyable matters." He pulled me close and I could feel the heat between us. "Happy anniversary, Willow." He kissed me. Qigong jumped on Jackson's legs, wanting attention. Jackson reached down to pet him. "And to you, too, buddy."

I smiled. "It's really been a wonderful three months."

"There's more where that came from." Jackson kissed me on the tip of my nose. "Are you free for dinner? I thought we could go off campus."

"That sounds wonderful. But I need to show you something first." I pulled the anonymous letter from my bag and gave it to him. "I think it's from my mystery caller."

He read it and handed it back to me. "It might be. It could also be from whoever locked you in the shed yesterday. Obviously, they want you to stop snooping. So, maybe you are closer to finding out the truth. Let's eat and we can discuss."

When we entered the tent, Rick, who had his cell phone plastered to his ear, waved us over to his table. Pierre, the director, was also at the table, on his phone and scribbling in a notebook. Tom, Carly, Sarah, and Cassidy, the wardrobe mistress, were standing on line to get lunch.

Rick ended his call. "Hey, Willow, how you doin', darlin'?" He looked at Jackson. "How did it go with you know who?"

"Not so good. He isn't ready to admit he has a problem."

"Aw, hell." Rick petted Qigong. "Tom would have to be a pain in my ass about that, too."

Jackson shrugged. "It takes time for some people to come around."

"Well, don't let me hold you up. You two gonna eat? I think you'll like what they're serving, Willow. It's all vegetarian and all organic. It was MJ's idea. Meatless Fridays."

"Good thinking," I said. "Where is she?"

"She's lying down. We're going to try to shoot this afternoon to make up for the time we lost because of Roger's funeral. But I still think we'll be here until Monday. We'll wrap things up on Labor Day. Can you two stick around till then?"

"I can," Jackson said.

"I think so," I said. "But I just have to check with Nick, Allie, and Hector."

"Good enough," Rick said. "Now, let's get some grub. Pierre, you eatin'?"

"Hold on," he said into the phone, and pressed it against his chest. "I have to get this done first. The lab that Roger decided to use screwed up the dailies. I only got half of them back."

"What's missing?"

"MJ's meeting with Max."

"We need that!" Rick said, sounding stressed. "That's the best footage we've got so far."

"I know that," Pierre said. "Not to speak ill of the dead, but Roger's mind was not in the game. I've never seen as many screwups as we've got on this shoot. It's amazing that we have cameras."

"Fix this, Pierre," Rick said.

"I'm working on it." Pierre put his phone back to his ear.

"I don't need this," Rick said as the three of us, along with Qigong, got in line. "Pierre shouldn't even be working on this. Roger was the unit production manager, as well as executive producer, and now that he's gone, we're all doing double duty."

While Rick took another phone call, I pulled out my phone and texted Allie, Hector, and Nick and asked about their availability this weekend. I heard back from Nick immediately, who said he was available and would be teaching Slow Yoga tonight. I thanked him and slipped the phone back into my pocket.

Tom still hadn't been served. Carly, Cassidy, and Sarah were still behind him along with half a dozen other people. We could hear him complaining, "Why is this taking so long? Do these caterers think we have all day?"

"They've had a lot of people to serve. We're almost there," Cassidy said, trying to calm him down.

Tom raised his voice. "Don't you people know that time is money?"

"Tom, you've got to control yourself," Carly said, her voice soothing.

Ignoring them, Tom turned to Rick. "Tell them, Rick. We got to get a move on!"

Rick sighed and ended his call. "Calm down, Tommy. You'll get fed soon."

Tom spun around, stepped toward Rick, and jabbed his finger into his chest. "Don't call me Tommy!"

I was standing right behind Rick and I could smell the liquor on Tom's breath. I looked at Jackson, who nodded and mouthed, "He's drunk." He turned to Tom and said, "Get back in line, Tom. You need to eat something."

Qigong growled.

"Shut up, Jack, and you, too, mutt," Tom said as he walked back to his original place in line.

"Tom, cool it," Carly said in a stern voice.

"Please don't make a scene," Sarah added. "You don't need to do this."

"No, he doesn't," Cassidy said. "But he is. I swear, of all my cousins, the Bixbys are the craziest."

Tom wasn't listening. He grumbled until he reached the serving station. There, things just got worse. "Give me a cheeseburger," he said to the server.

"It's vegetarian, Tom," Carly said, sounding exasperated. "Pick something else."

"Fine," Tom said. "Give me a meatball sub."

Cassidy rolled her eyes. "*Vegetarian* means 'no meat.'"

"All right then, give me a turkey sandwich."

Rick sucked in a breath and walked up to Tom. "Get a veggie burger and fries. People are waiting, *Tommy*."

"I am not eating some damn vegetable burger!" Tom leaned forward and pushed the tray of freshly made Gardenburgers on the ground. Fortunately, the server got out of the way. But Rick wasn't so lucky. Tom whirled around and punched him in the nose. "And I told you not to call me that!"

Sarah screamed. Qigong started barking uncontrollably.

Rick held his face and groaned. He gave Tom a death-ray look. "You punk! You're fired!"

"You can't fire me," Tom yelled. "I have a contract signed by Roger. He was my boss, not you!"

Jackson grabbed Tom's arm and pulled him away from Rick. This seemed to appease Qigong, who stopped barking. Jackson plunked Tom into a chair at Rick's table, across from Pierre, and put his hand on his shoulder. "Stay put."

"God, Tom, can't you behave?" Pierre said, looking up from his notes. "It's like working with a five-year-old."

"Shut up," Tom said.

"Grow up, *Tom*. You and your brother are the same. I thought when he was gone, we might have some peace around here, but no such luck."

For a brief moment, I wondered if Pierre should be a suspect in Roger's murder. But he'd need more of a motive than aggravation.

Tom tried to get up. Jackson pushed him down again. Tom glared up at him. "Do that again and I'll have you fired!"

Pierre grabbed his notebook and his phone and walked up to Rick. "You and I need to talk when you get back." Pierre gave Tom a withering look and left the tent.

"Do you want me to call the police?" Jackson asked Rick.

Rick shook his head. "No, don't do that. We've had enough trouble with them already." He groaned again. "This really hurts. Can you take a look, Willow?"

I walked up to Rick and pulled his hand away from his face. His nose was swelling, and the area under his right eye was already black-and-blue. "I need a napkin filled with ice, please," I said to the server. She grabbed a cloth napkin, reached into the cooler, filled it with ice, and handed it to Rick. He put it on the side of his nose.

"It's really throbbing."

"He needs to go to the ER to get an X-ray," I said.

"I'll take him," Carly offered.

Rick shook his head. "I need you here if I'm going to be gone. Get Amanda." Clearly Amanda had quickly become his go-to person, just as she had been for Roger. "I also need you to go and see MJ and tell her what happened, okay? Tell her not to worry. I need her mind clear for the show."

Carly pulled out her walkie-talkie and called Amanda. Amanda ran into the tent a few minutes later. Her face blanched when she saw that Rick was holding ice on his nose, but she quickly agreed to take him to the ER.

Rick took the ice pack off his nose and pointed at Tom. "You're drunk. Go home."

"I can work."

"I don't want you here. Go. Come back when you've sobered up."

Jackson released Tom, who left the tent mumbling expletives. He stalked toward his car, Sarah and Cassidy following him. Jackson and I with Qigong on his leash weren't far behind.

"He shouldn't be driving," Jackson shouted, and sprinted toward the car, trying to reach it before Tom did.

Sarah got there first. "I'll drive," she said, deftly slipping between Tom and the car door and taking the keys from his hand. "I'm going to take you to your studio. And you're going to sit there quietly and not give me any trouble. If you even say a word, I swear, I'll call the police."

"Call me and let me know when you get him there safely," Jackson said, handing her a card with his number. "If I don't hear from you in twenty minutes, *I'll* call the police."

Meanwhile, Carly was walking Rick to his car. Amanda got to Rick's Mercedes first and opened the passenger door for Rick, but as she leaned in to help him into the car, her cell phone dropped out of her back pants pocket and tumbled onto the driveway. Qigong grabbed it and ran, pulling his leash out of my hand. "Qigong!" I knew that he would chew through the cell phone "skin" in seconds.

I ran after him, calling his name, and finally caught up to him at the guard booth. I grabbed his collar. "Qigong, sweetie, let me have it." He thought about it for a moment, then dropped it at my feet. He'd left four tooth marks, two on the top and two on the bottom. "It's okay, I've got it," I yelled to Amanda.

But as I wiped it off on my shirt, I noticed a text-message conversation that she had probably been having when she got Carly's SOS. I glanced at Amanda but she was busy helping Rick into the car. I took a closer look at the screen. The first line was from someone named Annie.

HOW R U DOING?

MISS L.A. NOTHING SAME SINCE ROGER DIED. I THINK C KNOWS.

THAT SUCKS.

ALSO THINK C MAY HAVE KILLED R OR HIRED SOMEONE TO DO IT!

Now, this was interesting. I looked up from the screen. Rick had settled into the passenger seat, but Amanda was staring right at me.

I kept my expression calm, walked up, and handed her the phone. "Sorry. I'll be glad to replace the skin for you."

She glanced at the text and then at me and shoved the phone into her front pocket. She rounded the car and opened the driver's door.

"Remember to call and update us, Amanda," Carly said. "MJ will want to know what is going on."

"I will, don't worry." Amanda got into the car and took off down the road, leaving a dusty cloud in her wake.

chapter sixteen

Osteoarthritis is the most common form of arthritis. It manifests when the cartilage that cushions our joints degenerates over time. But you don't have to be old to get it. Knee OA is a common ailment for thirty- and forty-year-olds. One of the first symptoms is stiffness in the morning, usually in the hips and knees, but you can feel OA almost anywhere. Here's a topical pain relief blend from my friend Jade Schutes, director of education at the East-West School for Herbal and Aromatic Studies:

> 1 ounce vegetable oil (apricot kernel or sunflower)
> 7 drops of black-pepper essential oil
> 4 drops lemongrass essential oil
> 4 drops helichrysum (everlasting) essential oil

> Massage on painful joints as needed.

Yours Naturally,

Dr. McQuade

Jackson and I went back into the tent and finally got our veggie burgers, sweet-potato fries, and passion-fruit iced teas. We made camp at Rick's table, which was still vacant.

"Well, that was exciting," I said.

"And then some. Quite a Friday afternoon, huh? It's bad enough Roger was knocked off, but Tom is out of control. He really got Rick good."

"You were great."

"Aw shucks, ma'am, just doing my job." He'd just picked up a french fry and popped it into his mouth when his cell phone rang. He finished chewing and answered, "Spade here." He listened for a moment. "Okay, no worries. I'll be right there."

"What's going on?"

He stood, picked up his plate, and grabbed his iced tea. "My dog sitter is sick and she needs to go home. I have to go pick up the dogs. I'll eat this on the way."

"How are you going to take care of them and do your job?"

"I'll take 'em for a walk to tire them out, and I'm sure they'll sleep in the car for a while. I'll bring their dinner, some treats, and toys and a couple of bones. They'll be fine."

"Well, if you need help, let me know."

"I will." He leaned down to kiss me good-bye. "Be back soon."

As he left, Cassidy walked past the table with her tray. "Hey," I said. "Want to join me?"

"Sure." She sat down at the table.

"That was a scene, wasn't it?"

"It was classic Bixby," she told me. "I mean, I should be used to Tom's shenanigans by now, but somehow he always takes me by surprise. I just can't believe that a grown human being would throw temper tantrums like that. But then, Roger was the same way. Max was subtler, but he had his own techniques for manipulating things to get what he wanted."

I remembered something then. "You said you're a cousin to the Bixbys?"

"That's right. My mom, Monica, and their mom, Aunt Evelyn, God rest her soul, were sisters. We all grew up together in Great Neck. We used to spend summers out here."

"That must have been fun."

She took a bite of her burger. "It was, lots of fun."

"Is that how you got the job on the shoot—through Roger?"

She nodded. "Yes, but I've worked on a ton of shows. I even worked on Simon's show, *Parallel Lives*. I'm good. That's why he hired me. It wasn't nepotism."

"So, you know Simon?"

She nodded. "I was hired by his line producer, but the costume designer and I conferred with Simon about what sort of costumes he wanted. He's very charming and well liked."

"Really?" This was a surprise. Simon could be charming, but he could also be immature and self-centered.

"Yes, he's good to his people. Even the non-union staff get health insurance for free, which is way unusual. He's great about overtime, and we always have amazing caterers. And the Christmas presents are insane. Last year, everyone got iPads. He's very cool. I know that the cops think he killed Roger, but I don't buy it."

"Whom do you think the police should be looking at then?"

"Not Tom," Cassidy said at once. She gave me a frank look. "I know he must seem like a complete jerk to you. I'd think the same thing if I didn't know him better. It's the alcohol that's got him. He needs treatment. But he's not a bad person underneath."

She picked up her phone, which I hadn't heard ring or signal an incoming text. She took a moment to read something, then said, "I need to get back to wardrobe. Carly wants us to start at two." She picked up her tray, which contained mostly uneaten food. "I'll see you later."

Rick was back on-site within the hour. I knew this because he radioed me at the cottage and asked me to bring him a smoothie, since he was finding it difficult to eat. When I arrived back at the big house, Jackson had just arrived with the doxies, and they were running around the front lawn with Qigong, happy to be outside. Jackson was talking to Amanda and Rick, who now sported a bandage on his nose.

I handed Rick the smoothie. "How are you feeling? That looks pretty bad."

"They took X-rays—it's definitely broken—and gave me painkillers, which help. I owe Tom one." He took a sip of the smoothie. "Hey, there's MJ. She'll want to see your dogs, Jackson." Rick pointed to the golf cart in the distance. It looked as if Lucas was driving. "Then we've got work to do."

A few minutes later, MJ climbed out of the cart and went over to Rick. "You look awful, honey. Are you okay?"

"The ER doc says he'll look worse tomorrow," Amanda said.

"I'm okay," Rick said. "But I don't know what we're going to do about Tom."

"He seems determined to self-destruct," Jackson said. "That's not easy to stop."

"Jackson's right, honey," MJ said. "But I don't feel good about just cutting him loose. Then he might really do something desperate. I'll talk to him about getting into treatment, though I don't know if he'll listen." She looked at the dogs. "And who do we have here?"

"These are the dogs we rescued. This is Rockford." Jackson pointed to the bigger of the two doxies. "And this is Columbo."

"You named them after detectives, just like you. How clever." MJ bent down and petted the dogs. "Aren't you the cutest little things? How could anyone be mean to you?"

"I'm glad you told us about them," Jackson said to MJ.

MJ gave him a gracious smile. "I knew they were in distress. It would have been a crime not to try to help them."

Lucas got out of the golf cart, holding a plate of brownies covered in clear wrap and a small bound book. "Mom heard what happened and she made these for you, Rick."

"Please thank her for me." Rick peeled off the wrap, took a brownie, and scarfed it down. "Good stuff. Anyone else?"

"And here's the book you were asking about," Lucas said to Amanda. "Mom says to keep it as long as you want."

Amanda looked a little uncomfortable and quickly tucked the book under her arm. Jackson caught the motion, looked at me, and mouthed, "More research?"

"Okay," Rick said. "Time to get back to work. We're burnin' daylight." He turned to MJ. "Do you want to go back into the library today, so you can try to talk to Max again? I know you wanted to shoot at night, but we have time now and we need to catch up."

"We can do it now, but I want to try and talk to Daniel in the study first. He won't be in the library, because that's where Max hangs out. I've made contact with Max and Rebecca, but I need to contact Daniel to get a complete picture of activity here."

"Your wish is my command," Rick said.

• • •

I didn't need to see patients until later in the day, so I decided to stick around for the Friday-afternoon shoot. Jackson, though, needed to guard the door, so I was on my own. I entered the mansion and found Mrs. Florrick in the hallway, using an old-fashioned feather duster to clean the light fixtures in the hallway. I stopped to check on her. "How are you feeling, Mrs. Florrick? Did the horse-chestnut cream help your varicose veins?"

She actually smiled at me. "Yes, I'm much improved. Thank you."

Pierre and Rick passed us, heading for the study. "I'm telling you he needs to go," Pierre was saying. "I can't work with him, Rick. He disrupts everything."

Rick pointed to his nose. "You think I'm happy about him being here? But he does have a contract signed by Roger."

Mrs. Florrick watched them walk away, shaking her head. "I'm not happy about having this TV crew in my house. I can't wait for them to leave."

"What do you think of what MJ is doing?"

She shrugged. "I'm surprised that Max is hanging around. Rebecca and Daniel I've seen more than once. They can't seem to move on." Not for the first time, I was impressed that Mrs. Florrick saw the ghosts, too, and didn't seem to be bothered by them, whereas I felt something sinister in the house, and even MJ had been rattled by Max's ghost.

"Where have you seen Daniel?" I asked.

"He appears in different parts of the house, but he always returns to the scene of his death, the upstairs bathroom. If MJ wants to talk to him, that's where she should do her reading."

I left Mrs. Florrick and walked to the doorway to the study. I wanted to tell MJ what Mrs. Florrick had said about Daniel, but MJ was talking with Rick, Carly, and Pierre while Sarah touched up her makeup.

I noticed Amanda in the corner, reading the book that Lucas had given her. Rick called for her and she left the book on a table by the window. I started toward the table, wanting to at least see the title, but the group finished talking, and Amanda walked back over to get her book and headed out of the room. Was she going up to the third-floor bathroom? Pierre, Rick, and Carly went over to the television monitor and sat on stools that faced it. Sarah came and stood next to me.

"Are you okay?" I asked her. "That thing with Tom was rough."

"I'm fine." Sarah said, her voice was cool. "Excuse me." She walked out of the room and into the hall.

"I need quiet on the set," Pierre yelled. "Action!"

MJ began to circle around the study as she had done before. "I'm back again, my spirit friends. This time I'd like to talk to Daniel Russell, who used to be the caretaker for the Bixby estate. Daniel, are you here?"

MJ continued to pace around the room. "Daniel, dear. I need to talk to you." She waited a few moments and turned to look into the camera. "Sometimes this happens. Psychic readings aren't like just turning on a TV. The spirits have to want to make contact." She smiled but she looked uncomfortable. "Let's try again. Daniel Russell, please answer me. Daniel? Please show yourself."

She waited another moment, closed her eyes. "Max? Rebecca? Are you here?" She waited some more, then finally opened her eyes and yelled, "Cut!"

Rick hustled over to her. "MJ, what's wrong?"

"I can't connect. It's extremely frustrating."

"Let's take a break, everyone," Rick said.

"But we just got started." Pierre sounded annoyed.

"Take five," Rick said, ignoring him.

MJ sat down in one of the leather chairs, and I went up to

her. "MJ, I was talking to Mrs. Florrick, and she said that you might have better luck communicating with Daniel if you go upstairs to the third-floor bathroom where he drowned. She said she's seen him there before, that he keeps returning to that place."

MJ took my hand. "Sweetheart, I have to go where the vibe takes me."

Fortunately, Rick agreed with me. "Hon, a reading in the bathroom is just too good to pass up in terms of the wow factor. I don't know why I didn't think of that." He called Pierre over. "We're going to move up to the third-floor bathroom."

But at that moment Detective Koren and Detective Coyle entered the study with Jackson and two men wearing jump-suits, gloves, and carrying large suitcases. Definitely crime techs. "That's not going to happen," Koren said as he motioned to the stairs. "We're not done up there yet."

Since Koren and Coyle had interrupted the shoot, Pierre decided to shift gears and do close-ups of MJ discussing her feelings about the Bixby mansion and her conversations with Max and Rebecca. The plan was to shoot in the upstairs bath-room that night if Koren okayed it.

"What are Koren and his techs doing back here?" I asked Jackson when we were back outside.

"He's obviously going to have the crime techs go over the room again before he releases it. I don't know what he thinks he's going to find this time. I hope that Simon didn't touch any-thing when we visited."

"I don't think so," I said. "We were all wearing gloves." I looked at my watch. "I need to head back to the cottage. I have clients to see."

"Don't forget dinner," Jackson said. "I've made reservations for seven at the Lobster Claw."

The Lobster Claw was a new restaurant in Greenport. They had opened in July, but neither of us had been there yet, and I was looking forward to trying it. "Can't wait," I said, and kissed him. "Keep me posted on Koren, okay?"

"Yes, dear." Jackson smiled.

I went around to the back of the mansion to get the golf cart. As I did, I noticed Amanda coming out the back door. She still had the borrowed book under her arm. She saw me, waved, and went into the production trailer. On impulse, I decided to follow her.

I climbed the steps to the trailer and found the door open. Inside were two long tables, one on either side of the trailer. Several laptops were on the tables, along with a few desktop machines, cell phones, an adding machine, two overflowing ashtrays, stacks of copy paper, and a flurry of candy wrappers. A cooler on the floor held dozens of cans of lemon-lime soda.

Amanda was the only one in the trailer and sat at the end of the table that faced the mansion. She was animatedly talking to someone on her cell phone while sipping a Red Bull. "No, I really think she knows." She listened. "No, I don't feel safe here. Not after what happened." She saw me, said, "Call you back," and put down the phone. "Hi, Willow. Do you need something?"

The book she'd borrowed from Sheila Russell was on the table next to her laptop, and now I was close enough to read the title: *Notes from the Lavender Farm.* Was this a journal or a history of the lavender farm?

"I was just wondering if you knew if you were going to be able to shoot tonight," I said. "I don't want to miss it."

"Don't know yet. The police are still up there." Her cell

phone rang, and she picked it up again. "Go for Amanda." She got up and walked to the front of the trailer. As she did, I moved a little closer to the desk and the book. While Amanda kept talking, I picked up a ruler and used it to draw the book toward me, inch by inch. I had almost moved it to the edge when Amanda ended the call and turned to face me. I quickly hid the ruler behind my back.

"Do you need anything else?"

"No, I'm good," I said.

She turned around and made another call. That was all I needed. I pulled the book toward me, grabbed it, and stuffed it in the top of my pants, pulling my T-shirt over it. Thank goodness it was a small book. I walked up to her, mouthed, "Thank you," and left the trailer. She would realize soon enough that the book was gone and that I had probably taken it, so I scurried behind the mansion, found a golf cart, took off, and didn't stop until I reached the cottage.

chapter seventeen

Dr. Willow McQuade's Healthy Living Tips

Anxiety can make you feel as if you've had ten cups of coffee! Recently I showed the students in my aromatherapy seminar how to make stress-relieving smelling salts with lavender. This is another variation that is effective. Make it and carry it with you to de-stress on the go.

4 drops of ylang-ylang oil
7 drops of mandarin oil
2 drops of vetiver oil

Yours Naturally,

Dr. McQuade

The book was a journal written by James Russell, Lucas's father and Daniel Russell's son. Unfortunately, the handwriting was pretty illegible. Interestingly, it also contained drawings of the lavender farm, the garden, and objects from the shore, like shells and starfish. James had also noted what the weather was like for each day with crude markings, such as a sun or half sun or a cloud with raindrops. James had started the journal a year ago, which meant he probably had something to say about Max's death. But on the date of his passing, April 22, the page was blank except for a little sun symbol.

I flipped through the book again, looking for any mention of Daniel, Rebecca, or Max but didn't find anything. I checked my watch again. My first client would be here any minute. I closed the book and shoved it into my bag so I could show it to Jackson later.

I spent the next few hours Friday afternoon focusing on my clients. I gave the stressed-out production secretary, Sally, a bottle of lavender essential oil and told her to take ten deep inhalations. I suggested that the electrician, Billy, who suffered from osteoarthritis, try cayenne-pepper cream to decrease the amount of a neurotransmitter, called substance P, which relays pain messages to the brain.

When I was done seeing patients, I checked my messages. A text from Jackson said he was taking his dogs home and would meet me at the Lobster Claw.

Not an hour later, I was showered and wearing a new little, black linen dress, spiky black heels, and a silver necklace with a peace sign that had been Aunt Claire's. I chose an oversize, black, antique clutch I'd found at a yard sale, mostly because I knew I could fit James Russell's journal in it. I fed the animals and settled them into the upstairs bedrooms, locked the doors, and headed downstairs. When I reached the first floor, I found a note from Merrily on the counter: *We sold out of Fresh Face cream today! Need to order more ASAP! Congrats!*

I had always believed that Aunt Claire's special herbal anti-aging formula would be a big seller. I hoped this was an indicator of how it was faring nationwide.

I headed for the door, feeling good about the sales of the cream and my intimate dinner with Jackson. But I hadn't had time to get him a present. He loved to read, so I decided to go next door to the Curious Kitten and see if they were still open.

The books I had seen in the window a few days ago were gone, but the door was propped open. I stepped inside. "Anyone here?"

Arthur hustled out of the back and came to the counter. "Ms. McQuade! How is my new neighbor?"

"I'm looking for a nice copy of a detective mystery, maybe Raymond Chandler? I don't have enough money for a first edition. But it looks like you sold most of those."

"We're always getting more in."

"How do you acquire them?" I still wondered if they had come from the estate and what that might mean.

"Various ways," he said, leading me briskly toward a bookcase that was marked MYSTERIES.

I thought about the story I'd read in the *Suffolk Times* about the string of burglaries on the North Fork. Were they stocking their store by stealing?

"I've got plenty of choices for you." He studied the shelves, then pulled out a copy of *The Long Good-Bye* with a blue-and-green cover but no dust jacket. "This is a first US edition but a second printing from 1954. I can let you have it for, say, ninety-five dollars? That's a good price."

"That sounds fine." Knowing that Fresh Face was selling in the store allowed me to breathe a bit more easily about money.

That, and the money I was making at the estate this week. "Can you wrap it?"

He walked back over to the counter. "I can put it in one of our silver bags." He showed me an elegant-looking bag with THE CURIOUS KITTEN embossed on it. "Will this work?"

"Great." I paid for the book, said good-bye, and walked a few blocks down Front Street to the Lobster Claw. Jackson was waiting inside.

"Hello, McQuade." He kissed me. "You look great and you smell like lavender."

"You look great, too." He wore a cool blue blazer with a pale blue shirt underneath, a blue tie, and his best jeans. His after-shave smelled incredibly good.

The host of the restaurant picked up two menus and said, "Your table is ready, Mr. Spade." He led us to a table next to the plate-glass window at the front of the restaurant. We could see Front Street and Greenport Harbor beyond. The interior of the restaurant was clean and contemporary, with white walls and tablecloths, black-and-white prints of Greenport from the last century, and a chrome-trimmed bar. Light jazz was playing in the background. The place was packed, which wasn't surprising, considering it was Friday evening and the beginning of Labor Day weekend.

When our waiter came to the table, we both ordered iced tea. I was tempted to order a glass of wine but didn't want to make Jackson uncomfortable.

He read my mind. "Order some organic wine. It's okay, I don't mind."

I smiled and said, "No, I'm fine," and put the silver bag and the diary on the table.

The waiter thanked us and walked away. Jackson pointed to the bag. "Now, what is that?"

I pushed it across the table toward him. "It's an anniversary gift for you."

He took a small, gift-wrapped box out of his inside jacket pocket and pushed it toward me. "And this is for you."

"Should we open them at the same time?"

"Sure. Let's do it." He reached into the bag while I unwrapped the box. He held the book up. "This is great, Willow. You know I'm a big Raymond Chandler fan. Thank you."

"You're welcome." I pushed the wrapping paper aside and opened the box. Inside was an exquisite pair of silver earrings in the shape of peace signs. "I love them. They're the perfect match to Aunt Claire's necklace."

"I know. That's why I got them. I pay attention."

"Yeah, you do." I put the earrings on, leaned across the table, and kissed him.

We spent a few minutes scanning the menu and decided on warm lobster rolls with hand-cut french fries and fresh New England chowder. After we ordered, Jackson pointed to the journal. "What is that?"

I showed him the book and told him how I had "borrowed" it from Amanda. He picked it up and flipped through it. "I don't like the way you got this, but I understand why you did it. Did you find anything interesting? To me it looks like a *Farmer's Almanac*."

"The date of Max's death was blank. No comment whatsoever. I think that's intriguing, considering how much James hated him, don't you?"

Jackson put the book down. "People are weird. You can't always figure them out so easily."

"I can't figure out this case at all." I picked up the book and slid it into my purse. "I think our main suspects are Tom, because he hated his brother and is in love with Carly and is completely out of control; and, I hate to say it, Carly, because Roger repeatedly cheated on her and she might inherit the estate. Also, Amanda suspects her. I guess Amanda could be a suspect, too, if Roger jilted her, but there's no evidence of that." A new possibility occurred to me. "Do you think Sarah could have killed Roger because of his treatment of Tom?"

"From what I've seen of Sarah, that's a reach. I think she cares about Tom and would love for things to work out between them. But I don't get the feeling that they've ever been close enough for her to commit murder on his behalf."

I fingered my peace-sign necklace. "Okay, next, James Russell because of his father's death and the fact that Roger wanted to sell the estate. But he would have had to have help. He's too old to have done it by himself."

Jackson opened two raw sugar packets and put them in his iced tea. "Right, I don't see him dragging Roger down that secret passage without having a coronary. Though maybe Lucas helped him."

"Maybe. Next, what about Rick and MJ? Or even Pierre? He was really annoyed that Roger did such a lousy job."

"I don't see either Rick or MJ doing it. Rick is all about getting the show produced, and both of them needed Roger alive as an investor. Pierre being annoyed isn't enough of a motive."

"What about Cassidy, the wardrobe mistress? I forgot to tell you that she's Tom and Roger's first cousin."

"Really?"

"Yes. Maybe she had a grudge against Roger because of something we don't know about. I talked to her after you left at lunch. She doesn't think Simon or Tom did it, but she didn't say anything more than that."

Jackson looked thoughtful. "You've got plenty of suspects, but you don't have enough on anyone, yet. You need to keep investigating. Something will break, usually when you least expect it. I'll help as much as I can." The waiter set two steaming bowls of clam chowder on the table. "Let's enjoy our dinner. We'll be back in the middle of this soon enough."

"Right." But I couldn't help asking a few more questions. "Are they going to shoot tonight? Did Koren grant permission? Did he find anything new?"

"Yes, they're shooting tonight at eight. The cops released the scene. I didn't see the techs come up with any new evidence, but they could have put it in their bags. I guess you want to be there when they shoot, right?"

I nodded and grabbed two raw sugar packets and added them to my iced tea. "I need to gather more info, like you said." I picked up my soup spoon and tasted the chowder. "This is outstanding."

"Mmmm," Jackson agreed. "I mean, the food at the estate is tasty, but it's nice to get away and try something new, with you." He reached across the table and took my left hand.

"Exactly." It felt so good to be out with Jackson, just the two of us enjoying a romantic evening together. That's when someone tapped on the window next to us. It was Simon.

Simon looked even more haggard than the last time I had seen him. His hair was unkempt and stuck up from his head at all sorts of wild angles. He hadn't shaved, and he had a stain in the middle of his Greenport sweatshirt. He waved to us, then came inside and plopped down in a chair at our table. So much for our romantic evening. Jackson rolled his eyes. I mouthed, "I'm sorry."

"Didn't you get my messages?" Simon asked before either of us could say anything.

I realized that I hadn't checked my messages since this afternoon. Did this have to do with Koren's revisiting the upstairs bathroom to find more evidence? "Has something happened?"

"No, not yet, but I'm going crazy." He ran his hand through his hair. "I need to know what's going on. You need to call me back when I call you!"

The diners at the tables near us all turned to stare. "Calm down, Simon," Jackson said. "Willow is doing the best that she can."

"I know that. It's just nerve-racking wondering if—and—when I'm going to be arrested."

I decided not to tell him about Koren's return visit to the estate this afternoon. Instead I said, "We've got plenty of suspects. We were just going over everything." I told him what we had been discussing, though I omitted any mention of Carly.

The waiter arrived and put two tantalizing plates in front of Jackson and me. Full pieces of lobster fell out of the crusty rolls, and the fries looked crisp and delicious. My mouth started to water.

"It sounds like you've been busy," Simon said begrudgingly. "Sorry I went off. Can I have a fry?" I pushed my plate toward him and he took two. He suddenly noticed the opened gifts on the table. "Wait a minute. Am I interrupting some special event?"

"You could say that." Jackson picked up a fry.

"It's our three-month anniversary, Simon," I said. We both looked at him, hoping he would get the hint.

"Well, then, let's celebrate." He grabbed another fry off my plate. "Drinks are on me."

An hour later, Jackson and I were back at the Bixby estate, watching the camera crew set up for Friday night's shoot in the bathroom. Simon, of course, had wanted to come, but neither Jackson nor I thought that was a good idea. We'd already spent our anniversary dinner with him, and Jackson was still fuming.

Pierre decided to set up the camera equipment opposite the tub and shoot from there. Since it was a large bathroom, MJ would still have plenty of room to move around. Right now, she was in the bedroom across the hall, getting her makeup done by Sarah.

We watched as Pierre worked with the lighting techs. Tom should have been there, too, but he was AWOL even though Rick had asked him to come in. Right now, Rick was talking to Carly about production matters. Amanda stood by the bathroom door, on hand if Rick needed her. I glanced at the bathroom cabinet, wondering if she had indeed been the one creating special effects to enhance MJ's readings.

Once they were done setting up, Pierre asked Rick to go get MJ. For tonight's shoot she was dressed in a gold robe with gold jewelry and gold ballet slippers. Her hair was up in a tight bun, and she wore giant gold hoop earrings. A cameraman tracked her movements as she stepped onto the landing that ran along the top of the stairs.

Slowly, almost hesitantly, she entered the room. She seemed to give a little shudder as she saw the tub. She turned to address the camera. "I have to be honest. I never wanted to come up here. Two people have been murdered in this room, in this very bathtub." She closed her eyes. A moment later, they flew open. She stepped back from the tub and pointed at it. "This is the center of the spiritual unrest in this house. There's a powerful residual energy left over from the two murders in this room. Anger and betrayal and an endless thirst for revenge." She paused a moment. "And I can sense that both of these deaths were fueled by lust."

I exchanged a glance with Jackson. That was new information.

MJ took a couple of deep breaths and stood in the center of the room. "Now, I am going to try to contact Daniel Russell, the caretaker of the Bixby estate, who was drowned in this tub during the last days of Prohibition. Daniel, are you here?"

Suddenly the lights went out. "Daniel, is that you? Turn the lights back on, please." The lights came back on. "Thank you very much, Daniel. Now, what is it you want me to know?" The lights flickered again. "I know you are upset, Daniel. What do you want to tell me? What happened to you on that night so long ago?"

She circled the room, stopped quite suddenly, and looked directly into the camera. "He says he was lured up here by a friend, someone he had trusted. When he entered the room, he was hit on the back of the head. He woke up lying in the bathtub long enough to see the face of his murderer."

The lights flickered rapidly, and the sound of moans and pounding noises filled the room. The lights went off and the room was again plunged into darkness. "Daniel? Daniel? Who was it that killed you? Daniel? Daniel!" The lights came back up. MJ looked directly into the camera. "He's gone."

The pounding sounds stopped. I noticed that Amanda was inside the doorway now. Rick stood next to the medicine cabinet. Had he or she turned the lights on and off and created the sound effects?

"Cut!" Pierre said. "What the hell was all that noise?"

"I don't know," Rick said. "MJ, do you want to continue?"

She went over to the window opposite the tub, pushed it open and looked up. "It's almost a full moon. I want to come back when the moon is full and try to contact Daniel again. But now I'm going to try to contact Roger, since he also died in this room. He may have passed over to the other side already, but I still want to try to talk to him."

Pierre got the camera rolling again as she took a few deep breaths. "Roger? It's MJ. I need to talk to you. Are you here?" She circled the room again.

The pounding started up again, even louder than before. Jackson and I looked at each other. "It sounds like it's coming from the secret passage," I whispered to him.

"Let's see if anyone else knows about that passage," Jackson said. "It could be our murderer."

I scanned the room. Pierre and Rick didn't seem to know what was going on. Just outside the doorway, Cassidy began whispering to Sarah. Only Amanda seemed to be trying to avoid looking at the closet. In fact, she inched toward the doorway.

"Amanda knows," I whispered to Jackson.

"I see that."

MJ turned from the window and pointed to the closet. "You need to let him out."

"Let who out?" Rick said.

When MJ didn't reply, he turned to Amanda. "Take a look."

Amanda looked uncomfortable and, for the first time, didn't jump to do Rick's bidding. "I can't." She backed away from the door. "I'm scared."

Rick blew out a breath. "Jackson, can you do the honors?"

Jackson entered the bathroom and opened the closet door. The pounding continued. He stepped inside and began handing towels out to one of the lighting techs. Then I could hear him pulling out the shelves. Rick went over to the door and looked in. "What in hell are you doing?"

"It sounds like someone is trapped behind this wall."

"Trapped behind the wall? What are you talking about?"

Amanda seemed to be about to say something but stopped herself. But Carly looked at Cassidy and said, "It's a secret passage. They used to use it during Prohibition."

Jackson played dumb. "Do you know how to get it open?"

Carly hesitated a moment, then nodded and stepped into the closet. I could hear the click of the door to the secret passage being opened. Then she gasped. "What are you doing in there?"

We all watched, shocked, as Tom stumbled into the room and collapsed into a heap on the white tile floor. Blood trailed down his face and onto his T-shirt from a nasty-looking gash in his forehead. Carly knelt down beside him. "Tom, what happened?"

Tom opened his eyes. "Someone tried to kill me."

chapter eighteen

Dr. Willow McQuade's Healthy Living Tips

If you have the flu, using aromatherapy will comfort you. You'll need a diffuser, but once you have one, you won't want to be without it! One of the best aromatherapy blends is Antiviral Plus from Leyden House (www.leydenhouse.com). When the diffuser saturates the air with this combo of eucalyptus, lavender, tea tree oil, clove bud, and geranium, it will help to relieve your stuffy head, cough, fever, and congestion in the lungs. Running a diffuser in your house may also help keep other members of the family from coming down with the flu by helping to eliminate airborne viruses.

Yours Naturally,

Dr. McQuade

I quickly grabbed a hand towel from the towel rack. The gash over Tom's right eye was bleeding profusely. I put the folded towel against the gash and pressed hard. "Can you apply pressure?" I asked him. "It should slow the bleeding."

Tom nodded and held the towel as Carly and I helped him to a seated position, propping him up against the wall. Then, I went to the sink and got him a glass of water.

"Tom, what happened?" Carly said.

"I was out on the back lawn and someone came up behind me and whacked me on the head."

"Did you see who it was?" Jackson asked.

"No, they hit me really hard." He leaned back against the wall, and I saw a trickle of blood slide beneath the towel and down his cheek.

Rick looked worried. "How long have you been in the—what's it called?—the secret passage?"

"I don't know. I came back here around five to talk to Rick and Pierre. I wanted to apologize."

"Well, that's a new one." Rick touched his nose gingerly.

"Rick, stop it," Carly said. "We need to take care of him."

"Someone needs to take him to the ER," I said.

"I'll do it," Carly said. "And don't tell me I can't, Rick. I'm going."

Tom Bixby had been one of my prime suspects in Roger's murder. But now that he had been attacked himself, I was thinking, not so much. I guessed that he might have injured himself—or got someone else to do it—to divert suspicion, but it was unlikely. After all, the police were still focused on Simon.

When we got back to Nature's Way Friday night, Jackson and I talked for a long time about what I should do next. We concluded that it was a good idea to do more in-depth research on the Russell family. That Daniel's and Roger's murders were so similar could not be a coincidence. The past must be connected in some way with the present. I also realized that I hadn't talked to James's wife, Sheila, yet, and that might yield answers, too.

After that, we celebrated our anniversary in style with champagne and slept late. When I woke up Saturday morning, the sun was shining and a cool morning breeze wafted through the bedroom. I felt Jackson's arms around me, holding me close. Columbo was tucked under his chin, Rockford was at my feet, and Qigong was between us. The cats slept in the dog bed. It was a wonderful cocoon, one I didn't want to leave. After the letter I'd received and Tom's being hit on the head, I felt more on edge about being at the estate. Plus, time was running out. As Rick said, the production would leave on Monday.

When Jackson headed home with his dogs, I showered, dressed, picked up James Russell's diary, and went downstairs. Qigong trailed after me. I planned to use the morning to research the Russell family.

I found Wallace in the kitchen making blueberry pancakes. "Hi, Willow," he said cheerfully. "How are you this fine Saturday morning?"

"I'm well, Wallace." I watched the pancakes cook in the pan. "How are things going?"

"Can't complain. Merrily and I have everything under control. You don't need to worry."

"That's good to hear." Especially since my mind was on Roger's murder more than the store. But that's why I had a manager, to pick up where I left off. I hoped that Merrily felt up to the task today. "So where is Merrily?"

"She'll be here in a few minutes. She had to stop at the pharmacy to pick up a prescription."

That must mean she got her test results back, I realized.

"Your friend Simon is here, though." Wallace pointed the spatula at the corner table where my ex was sitting.

I went over to him and sat down. He was in the middle of eating a short stack of buckwheat pancakes with humanely raised bacon and fresh-squeezed orange juice. He looked the same as last night—tired, haggard, and unshaven.

He stuck a fork into a pancake and said in a monotone, "Carly told me what happened last night. I guess that means that Tom is no longer a suspect." He put his fork back down without eating.

"It doesn't look that way, no." As Wallace went by, I asked him for a plate of blueberry waffles and watermelon slices. "I'm going to spend the morning going over those books from the library and this diary I found." I pushed it across the table to him. "Maybe you can help me."

Simon lifted his head up. "I'd like that. It keeps me from thinking about possibly spending the rest of my life in a cell. My lawyers tell me the police are not finished with me yet."

"What did they say exactly?"

"That I shouldn't leave town and to make myself available for questioning."

"They've been saying that all along."

"Exactly." Simon pounded his fist on the table. "I'm sick of it! I can't concentrate. I can't write. I need to go to L.A. next week to supervise the filming of my episode. I need this to be over."

I put my hand on his fist. "Calm down. I think we're getting closer. Really, I do. We just need more information. You can help me with that. It will make you feel better."

He picked up his fork and put it down again. "I'm not even hungry."

I picked up his fork and handed it to him. "Eat first for brainpower, then we work."

• • •

After we finished breakfast, the two of us went into my office. I assigned him the books from the library while I concentrated on the journal. I sat behind my desk, while he took the couch next to Qigong, who was already taking a nap.

"What are we looking for exactly?"

"Any new information about the Bixbys and the Russells."

"Okay." Simon picked up a book from the stack on the coffee table in front of him.

I opened the diary again and scanned each page. About forty-five minutes later, I came to a notation for last Sunday, the day MJ, Rick, and the rest of the production staff and crew arrived at the Bixby estate. *MJ and R came over. Discussed TV shoot. Nothing new from R. Same B.S. This will be a problem. Talk to LB.* I read the notation to Simon. "R must mean 'Rick.'"

"What do you think 'This will be a problem' means? And who is LB?"

"No idea. I definitely need to learn more about Mr. James Russell. Have you found anything?"

"The Bixbys are mentioned in connection with rum running, but that's all. The only mention I can find about Daniel is what you found in the library." He closed the book he'd been reading. "Are there any museums around here? Maybe they could tell us something."

"Simon, you're a genius. I know just the place."

The Maritime Museum was located in Greenport at the foot of Third Street, in a former railroad station, adjacent to the Shelter Island ferry dock and the Long Island Rail Road stop. I hoped that we might find something that would move me one step closer to solving the case. We decided to walk over, since it was just a few blocks from Nature's Way.

The museum was a bright, airy space with white walls, hardwood floors, and a second story accessible by a staircase. For a small museum it had an impressive collection that included exhibits on the maritime heritage of Greenport; and displays on menhaden, or bunker, fishing, along with information about the thriving oyster industry before the hurricane that wiped it all out in the thirties. There were also nautical flags, lighthouse lenses, model ships, and lots of photos depicting maritime history.

The volunteer who manned the information desk was busy chatting on the phone and typing something on the computer. Two people were also waiting to talk to her. Rather than get in line, I told Simon we should each take a floor and get started looking for information on the Bixbys and the Russells. I needed to be at the estate by one, and it was already eleven twenty. We split up and started looking. I took the bottom floor and scanned the walls as I slowly walked toward the east end of the building.

Fifteen minutes later, Simon leaned over the railing upstairs and called down, "Find anything yet?"

"No, keep looking." I added under my breath, "And have a little patience." Sometimes Simon reminded me of a little kid on car trip, always asking, "Are we there yet?" But about thirty seconds later, I came to a black-and-white photo from 1930 on the wall of three men on a fishing boat in Greenport Harbor with a giant swordfish at their feet. One of the men in the photo looked a lot like Roger. I looked at the plate under the photo: MAX BIXBY, DANIEL RUSSELL, AND RON TURNER CATCH ONE OF LARGEST SWORDFISH EVER ON EAST COAST. It was amazing how much Roger Bixby resembled his father, Max. Both had angular faces and serious, dark brooding looks. Daniel Russell seemed more lighthearted, with a thatch of blond hair and a friendly smile. Ron Turner was big and burly, with a full beard and bushy eyebrows. The name Ron Turner was familiar, but I couldn't remember why.

"I've found something," I called to Roger. He scurried down the stairs and stood next to me. I explained who the men were. "I think the three of them, besides being fishermen, were rum runners."

"That's what it said in the book. But who's this Turner guy?" Simon pointed to the stocky man with a ruddy complexion wearing waders.

"The name is familiar, but I can't place it. There's no one on the set named Turner, is there?"

"Not that I know of, but I can check with Carly."

He was texting Carly when it clicked. "I think I know," I said. "I got a card from the Turners when Aunt Claire died. I never met any of them, but maybe they're related to this guy in the photo." I pulled out my phone and called information for his number.

It turned out that Ron Turner was the son of the Ron Turner in the photo. I found his wife, Cynthia, at home. After we talked about Aunt Claire and how they had worked together to close the pet shop in Greenport that was to be filled with puppy mill dogs, I asked her if her husband was at home. She told me he was fishing and where to find him.

Half an hour later, we arrived at Laughing Water beach, located directly across from the estate. Simon and I traipsed across the powder-white sand to the edge of the shore. I took

Qigong off his leash and he ran down the beach to where Ron Turner was standing with his fishing pole cast out into the bay. He wore a denim shirt, jeans, waders, and aviator sunglasses. He looked to be in his late seventies, the same age as James Russell. Like his father, he too sported a beard and had bushy eyebrows that looked like fat caterpillars.

He reached down to pet Qigong and gave me a smile. "Cute dog."

I rubbed Qigong's back. "Thanks, he's a rescue."

"I've got two greyhound rescues of my own at home. They're such sweet dogs." He took his sunglasses off and clipped them to his shirt. "You must be Willow McQuade. My wife called and told me you'd be coming." He stuck out his hand. "I'm Ron Turner. We were both real sorry about your aunt. She was the best. She really helped me out with the arthritis in my hands. I'm a fisherman, and working outside all those years did some damage."

"I'm glad that she could help you." I gestured to Simon. "This is Simon Lewis. He's a friend of mine."

Ron shook Simon's hand, too. "Nice to meet you." Ron reeled in the line and let it out again. The water sparkled on the bay like stars. "So what can I help you folks with?"

I watched the water lap at the shore. "I'm interested in learning more about Max Bixby, Daniel Russell, and your father. If you don't mind, can I ask, was your father a rum runner?"

"Course he was. Most fishermen out here ran liquor as a side job." Ron smiled. "They had some adventures. My dad loved those times."

I pointed to the estate. "I did some research that showed that Max Bixby and Daniel Russell were rum runners, too."

Ron reeled in his line and tossed it again. "Max provided the financial backing. He couldn't have outrun the coast guard if he had a jet. But he had a crew, and my father and Daniel worked in it. They did the hard work, took the risk of getting the booze from the three-mile limit to land and up the island to New York City speakeasies. They used the secret passages in the house and secret compartments in the trunks of Max's cars to hide the liquor so it could be transported."

So there was more than one secret passage? I'd have to check that out along with the secret compartments in the cars. "Did your father tell you about the murder of Daniel Russell in 1933?"

"Sure. Everyone knows about that."

"Do you think Daniel's murder had something to do with the rum running?"

"That's what the family wanted everyone to believe," Ron said. "My father said it had something to do with Daniel's wife, Rebecca. That's James Russell's mother. She worked for Max as a maid. Rumor was that Max was in love with her, but the feeling wasn't mutual. It was almost common knowledge that Max killed Daniel to get Rebecca for himself. But the Bixbys had a lot of power back then—all the way to the White House—and Max was never even investigated. Naturally, the case was never solved."

"I think that Daniel's murder may be connected to the murder of Roger Bixby, Max's son. Simon has been accused of the crime by the police."

"But I didn't do it," Simon said. "I really didn't."

Ron sized up Simon. "I don't know anything about you, but if Claire's niece here believes in you, you're probably okay." Ron reeled in his line, frowned at the empty hook, and tossed it back in the water. "If you're investigating this thing, you need to know that these people are ruthless both upstairs and downstairs. Max was meaner than a rattlesnake, didn't care who he hurt. And Daniel's son, James Russell, the caretaker, is every bit as cold-blooded as old Max was."

"James Russell is an old man now. You're saying he's dangerous?"

"He'll do anything to protect his place on that property. A few years ago, Max considered opening the estate to the public to earn money for upkeep on the mansion. James went up to the house with a shotgun and told him what he thought of that idea."

"I see what you mean," I said. James was now rapidly rising to the top of my suspect list.

Ron reeled in the line and stuck the fishing pole in the sand. He turned to look at us. "It's all about money, power, and pride on that side of the wall, so you two better be careful."

Simon had driven to the beach, so we parted there. I headed to the estate to find Jackson and tell him what we'd found. When I got to the mansion, I tried him on the walkie-talkie and told him where I was. A few minutes later we were sitting on the steps, talking. Qigong jumped on Jackson's lap.

"How is Tom doing?" I asked.

Jackson scratched Qigong behind the ears. "He's going to be okay, but he did have a concussion. Rick told him to take it easy. Today, they're concentrating on putting together a montage about Roger for the show, and show how his murder is similar to Daniel Russell's murder. He says it'll be good TV."

"I'd like to see that. Simon and I did some research this morning. We didn't find much in the books from the library, so he suggested we go to a museum. That gave me the idea to go to the Maritime Museum, and that led me to Ron Turner's son." I told him about our conversation.

"So you're going to talk to Lucas and James again?"

I nodded. "I also found something in the lavender diary." I opened the book to the passage that said, *MJ and R came over. Discussed TV shoot. Nothing new from R. Same B.S. This will be a problem. Talk to LB.*

"Sounds like James has a relationship of some kind with MJ and Rick. And who is LB?"

"That's what I'd like to know. Can you go with me?"

"Can't. Another production meeting."

"Ron also mentioned secret passages, so there must be more than the one we discovered. He also said the cars back then had secret compartments."

"Well, I don't know if any of the old cars are still around, but I'm guessing you want to go hunt for those other secret passages."

"You're getting very good at reading my mind." I grinned. "What's the schedule for tonight?"

"They're breaking at six because it's Saturday night and Pierre's birthday and they're taking him out to celebrate. Then, the plan is to shoot all day tomorrow and into the night. MJ wants to go back up to the third-floor bathroom after dark. So if you want to take a look, let's do it tonight."

"I'll meet you at six." I stood up and grabbed Qigong's leash.

Jackson kissed me. "Make it seven. That way everyone will be gone. Keep me posted about your visit to the Russells. Remember what happened last time."

I promised to check in with Jackson periodically as I set off for the Russells' house. After being shut in the shed and receiving the warning, I knew I had to be careful. So, I took Qigong with me and also decided to use my phone to record any conversations I might have.

When I got there, Sheila Russell was sitting in a rocking

chair on her front porch, having a cup of tea. She wore a faded housedress and flip-flops. She set her cup down on a little side table when she saw me. "Help you?"

"I'm Willow McQuade." I climbed the stairs to the porch. "I was here the other day."

"Right, to see Lucas."

Up close, I could see that her face was weathered and covered with fine lines, her hair more gray than blond. She looked as though she'd had a difficult life. "Is he around?"

"No, he's helping up at the big house." She pointed to her cup of tea. "Would you like a cup? It's freshly brewed chamomile. Very relaxing."

"My favorite, thanks. Do you use the plants you have around here? I saw some the other day."

"I'm not that adventurous. I use tea bags. But it will just take a moment."

"Sure, thank you."

She opened the door to the cottage and went inside. I took the chair next to hers, pulled out my phone, texted Jackson about what I was doing, then switched on the phone's recorder.

Sheila returned moments later and handed me a mug decorated with wildflowers.

"Thank you." A lavender-scented breeze wafted past my face. The view from the cottage was lovely. I could see the pond and off in the distance the sparkling aqua-blue bay beyond the retaining wall. "It's beautiful here. You must enjoy it."

She sat down and picked up her cup. "I try to, but James is not well. He has terrible migraines, two or three a week. And when they hit, he can't work, can't eat, can't sleep, can't do much of anything. It makes it, well . . . difficult."

"What does he take for his migraines?" I knew how devastating they could be.

"An aspirin or two. Mostly, he just waits until they pass."

This was unfortunate because there were many natural remedies for migraines (even eating two tart apples a day can help) and, if necessary, new prescription drugs as well.

"Lucas has them, too." She took a sip of tea. "Was there something you needed from him?"

"I met Ron Turner today. He told me that his father was a fisherman who worked for Max in his rum running business. Is that true?"

"Ron Turner," Sheila said softly. "I haven't seen that man for years. . . . Yes, it was Ron Sr., Max, and Daniel."

"So they did work together as rum runners?"

"Yes, they did. Although Max pretended he had no part in it. He had a reputation to maintain. Mr. Big Shot." Her voice dripped with disdain. So far, it seemed the only person who had anything good to say about Max was Mrs. Florrick.

"We also talked about the murder of James's father in 1933," I went on. "So, Max was a suspect?"

Sheila gave a bitter laugh. "Everyone from here to New York City knew he did it, and he was never even charged. I tell you, if I never hear about that again, it would be a blessing. James goes on and on about it. He's obsessed with the past."

I sipped the chamomile tea while I considered how to phrase the delicate question about Rebecca Russell. "Ron said that Daniel's wife, Rebecca, was a maid in the big house."

"Oh, yes, and didn't Mr. Bixby take advantage of that. He forced himself on her. James said that she was never the same after that."

"That's horrible. I didn't realize that she was raped."

"She was," Sheila said bluntly. "And to this day, James can't stop thinking about it. I do believe it's why he gets those bad headaches." She let out a big sigh. "Even worse, when he feels unwell, all the responsibility falls on poor Lucas. I wanted him to have his own life, to leave this place, but he can't because of James. It's been a hard life for him, for all of us living in the past."

"Perhaps if you moved away it would be easier for everyone."

"You obviously don't know my husband. James would never leave, and he doesn't like change. When Max wanted to open the grounds to the public a few years ago, he went crazy."

"Sheila!" James shouted from the inside the house. "What are you doing? Come inside, I want my lunch!"

Startled, she jumped up from her chair, and as she did, her teacup clattered to the ground and broke. "So much for teatime." She tried to smile as she knelt to pick up the pieces.

"Get in here, woman!"

"Why don't you let me pick those up?" I said quickly.

James shouted for her again.

"Don't worry about that. I'll clean it up later." She walked toward the screen door, pulled it open, and stepped inside.

I stood there for a moment, looking at their house and wishing I could rescue Sheila Russell from her husband. Was he physically abusive, too? Ron Turner had called him ruthless and cold-blooded. At the least, he seemed a man trapped in bitterness and anger. The question was, was it the kind of anger that could lead to the murder of Roger Bixby?

I started the golf cart, made a U-turn, and skidded to a stop because Amanda had pulled up in front of me.

"I've been looking all over for you," she said, sounding aggravated. She jumped out of the cart and came over to me. "I think you have something of mine, or rather of Sheila's, and I need it. Pierre and MJ want to see it."

"I don't know what you mean."

"I think you do. The diary? You took it from the production trailer. Can I have it, please?"

I had gone through the diary pretty carefully and probably didn't need it anymore. I wondered why MJ and Pierre wanted it. Were they, too, looking for clues to Daniel's murderer? In any case, I didn't want the shoot held up because of me. I took the journal from my purse and handed it to her. "Is this what you're looking for? I was just borrowing it."

"Sure you were," she said dismissively. "I know how nosy you are. You were even looking at my text messages yesterday."

"It's not what you think. I'm trying to help a friend."

"I know what you're doing. You're trying to clear Simon when he's the one who killed Roger! I don't know how you live with yourself." She climbed into the golf cart and took off.

chapter nineteen

Dr. Willow McQuade's Healthy Living Tips

If you've ever had a migraine, you'll never forget it. Over 30 million people in the United States have migraines, most of them women. The knifelike, throbbing nature of a migraine demands that you pay attention. You can feel the pain of a migraine in your forehead, temple, ear, jaw, or around the eye, usually one side at a time. You may also be overly sensitive to lights, sounds, and smells. Aromatherapy can be a gentle remedy to help address the pain. My friend Jade Shutes recommends this remedy:

> *Migraine-Stopper Gel*
> 5 drops peppermint essential oil
> 3 drops lavender essential oil
> 1 tablespoon aloe vera gel
>
> Mix all in a small bowl. Apply to the temples and the back of the neck. Avoid the eye area.
> Wash your hands after applying. If your headaches are interfering with daily activities, it's time to see your health practitioner.

Yours Naturally,

Dr. McQuade

Amanda drove off, leaving me to mull over what she'd said. She was angry because she believed that Simon had killed Roger, and I was trying to get him off. But how did she even know I was trying to clear him? Had Carly told her? I wondered if Amanda was the one who sent the threatening note, trying to scare me off the case. Was she the one who'd pushed me into the shed? None of that really made sense unless she'd been close to Roger.

I thought about the text messages I'd seen on her phone: *Nothing same since Roger died. I think C knows. . . . Also think C may have killed R or hired someone to do it!* Actually, they made perfect sense, I realized, if Amanda had been Roger's last mistress and now believed that Carly had found out about the affair and had planned Roger's murder—and had gotten Simon to carry it out.

I headed back to the cottage Saturday afternoon because I had clients to see. Carly was leaving Allie's room when I got there. I asked her how Tom was doing.

"Pretty good, considering. I told him he should come in for a massage. It would do him good. Allie has magic fingers."

Allie came out of her treatment room. "I heard that." She smiled. "I'm glad you think so. Take it easy the rest of the day, okay?"

Carly nodded. "It's Saturday already," she said softly. "Tomorrow will be a week since Roger died."

I followed Allie back into her room, where she began to strip the linens off her treatment table. "I hate to ask," I said, "but did she say anything else about Roger's murder?"

Allie started to make up the treatment table with fresh sheets. "I feel guilty repeating what a client has told me in confidence. But I know why you are asking."

"I wouldn't if I didn't have to, but Simon could go to jail for the rest of his life."

"Got it." Allie picked up a fresh pillowcase and put it on a pillow. "Carly was very upset about the attack on Tom, and, of course, she's worried about Simon. She's convinced that he didn't kill Roger."

"Of course. He is her boyfriend, after all."

"She also said that if she'd had the guts, she would have killed Roger herself a long time ago. He was a serial philanderer."

"Yeah, I've heard that he cheated on his first wife and Carly."

"Repeatedly, from what Carly said. It was one woman after another."

"So, why did she stay with him?"

"She loved him in spite of his wicked ways. She kept hoping that he would change. They even went to marriage counseling; that is, when Roger bothered to show up. On the night of her birthday in April, he left the party with someone else. She filed for divorce the next day."

"It must have been weird for them to work together on this project."

"It was, especially since they just separated a few months ago. But she said that being with Simon really helped. I think that took the edge off her pain."

Carly had as good a motive to murder Roger as anyone else—a woman scorned, and all that. And if she did kill him, it was unlikely that she acted alone. She was petite and couldn't have gotten Roger's body to the beach without help. It was the same problem that James would have encountered if he killed Roger. Was Amanda right? Had Carly murdered Roger with Simon's help—or hired someone else to do it?

I still couldn't believe Simon was involved, partly because he was too decent to ever do something that cruel. But also because Simon was kind of a wimp. The sight of blood made him feel faint; he didn't have the hard-core personality of a killer. Besides, why would Carly bother killing Roger now that she had filed for divorce and was happy with Simon? Didn't that sort of dilute the need for a crime of passion?

I spent the rest of Saturday afternoon seeing clients. I helped one of the cameramen with his tinnitus, an associate producer with hives, and the film editor who had carpal tunnel syndrome.

After I was done, I called Jackson to check in and told him about my run-in with Amanda. He told me to steer clear of her and that we were still on for a seven o'clock excursion into the Bixby mansion.

Since it was only five o'clock, I joined Nick's hatha yoga class. While I went through the asanas, I reviewed my conversation with Sheila, how James acted, and that Amanda had tracked me down for the diary. Normally, I keep a quiet mind in yoga class, but that was impossible today.

I arrived at the mansion at six forty-five that night, just as the last of the crew and staff were leaving. Jackson was in his truck on the phone, saying, "That's a big help. Thanks. I'll check in with you later." He put the phone down and leaned out the window. "Just checking on the doxies. The dog sitter is going to stay with them until I get home." He put his phone in his pocket and got out. "So how do you want to do this?"

"Why don't we start at the top of the house. If there's a secret passage on one side of the mansion, maybe there's another one on the other side, in the bedroom."

"Okay, but we've got to be careful. Remember what happened to Tom."

"Trust me, I haven't forgotten," I said. "Let's take Qigong

along. At least he can bark and let us know if someone's coming."

"Which would also give us away."

"I know, but I'll feel safer with him."

So with Qigong beside us, we entered the house and began climbing the stairs. On the top floor we headed into the bedroom. It had a depressing vibe. The furniture was covered in sheets, and the olive-green paint was peeling from the walls. The yellowing shades on the two windows were drawn. "This was Max's bedroom, right?"

"It used to be," Jackson replied. "According to what Mrs. Florrick told us, when he got older he took a room on the bottom floor. I think Roger used to stay here when he visited."

"But if it was originally Max's room, it would make sense that he'd have a secret way to get in and out."

"Maybe." Jackson opened the door of the closet. This one didn't have shelves but a rod with what had to be hundreds of hangers, holding coats, jackets, suits, shirts, and slacks, all jammed together so thickly that we couldn't even tell that a wall was behind them.

"I'm getting the feeling that Max never threw anything out," I said.

Jackson knelt down, turned on his flashlight, and crawled under the clothing. He disappeared for a couple of minutes. Then I heard him thump on the back wall of the closet.

"Sounds hollow. Let's take a look, but first we've got to get this cleaned out." He got to his feet and started removing hangers from the closet.

"Give 'em to me. I'll put them on the bed."

The clothes smelled musty and old. Qigong jumped up on the bed and burrowed into the pile of old wool coats. He seemed to be having fun so I didn't stop him. It wasn't as if Max would be wearing them again.

Jackson came out of the closet and dumped another load on the bed on top of Qigong.

"There you go, buddy. Have fun."

We cleared out enough of the clothing for us both to walk into the closet and examine its back wall. Sure enough, there was the faint outline of a door.

"Okay, now to find the latch to open this." I watched as Jackson felt around the door. A few moments later, with a click the door opened a few inches. He pulled it all the way open, clicked on his flashlight, and stepped inside. "It looks just like the other one. It probably leads to the side door on the ground floor."

"Let's see. C'mon, Qigong." Qigong jumped off the bed and ran after Jackson while I trailed behind.

Jackson pushed away the fraying cobweb at the top of the stairs and stepped down. This stairway was also built on a spiral and was even tighter and more cramped than the one in the bathroom. It felt claustrophobic, but I gripped the metal rail and stepped down. The air was musty and I started coughing from all the dust.

It felt as if we'd been descending for hours when we finally arrived at another door.

Jackson tried to turn the knob. "It's stuck." He kicked the door and tried it again. The door swung open. Thin evening light filtered through high windows ahead of us.

"Well, I'll be," Jackson exclaimed. "We're in the garage!"

We stepped inside the musty space. My flashlight picked out an old sit-down lawn mower; a Peg-Board holding hammers, screwdrivers, and pliers; old paint cans and brushes on workbenches—and two antique cars from the 1920s. One was a jet-black Crossley from England, and the other, a yellow convertible Model A Ford.

"I was wrong," Jackson said, his voice soft with amazement. "Those old cars were right here all along."

"Ron said that they moved the liquor to New York by putting it in secret compartments in the cars. Let's see what we can find."

Jackson walked over to the Crossley and started searching it. I went over to the Model A and did the same. Fortunately neither car was locked. We both started in the front and moved to the back. The Ford's front and back seats yielded nothing.

"Jackson," I said, puzzled, "this car has no trunk."

"I don't think they had built-in trunks then. This one has an attached trunk."

He was right. A black box—sort of like the kind of trunk you buy for a kid going to sleepaway camp—was attached to the back of the Crossly. Jackson jiggled a small padlock that was attached to it, and it opened. "Rust," he said. He opened the box, and I shone my flashlight into it as he ran his hand along the inside. I heard his breath catch as he touched the back wall of the trunk. Then he pushed a spot, and a small door popped open. He shone his flashlight inside and pulled out a dusty bottle with a handwritten label that said GIN, and a yellowed copy of an old local newspaper called the *North Fork News*.

The paper's headline reported Daniel Russell's death and the story that followed confirmed what I had learned so far, namely that the death was suspicious and that Max Bixby was a suspect. But someone had scribbled a message in the margin. We both leaned in closer to try to read it: *Edith Thorne*. What looked like a phone number had been scribbled over, so it was unreadable.

"Edith Thorne," I said. "That's the same name on the letter I found at Tom's house. She wanted him to contact her."

"It's an interesting find. But I'm not sure that it relates to

Roger's murder—or even Daniel's. Besides, I think we should go. We've been here long enough."

Jackson was right. It was an interesting find, but I had no idea if it was anything more than that. He carefully opened the garage door, and after making sure that no one was watching, we walked out.

I rounded the house and noticed activity inside the mansion. "Jackson, there are lights on in the study. Someone is in there." I tucked the newspaper in my back pocket. "I thought you said everyone had gone to celebrate Pierre's birthday."

"They did. It was a big deal. Everyone had to go. Got to keep the director happy."

"Not Mrs. Florrick."

Jackson shook his head. "It wouldn't be her. She only works in the house during the day. Nights, she's in her own cottage. Besides, those are small, moving lights. Whoever is in there is using flashlights. If Mrs. Florrick were in the house, I don't think she'd have to be sneaky about it."

We walked over to the window. "So, then who is it?" I thought about the article that I'd read in the *Suffolk Times*. "Maybe these are those burglars that have been going around town."

"Could be. If so, I need to stop them. Follow my lead and keep quiet." He took my hand and we crept toward the house. Jackson tried the front door. "It's open. I locked it when we went in before."

I felt my heart start to beat faster. What if it was the murderer in there?

Slowly, Jackson turned the knob and opened the door. I scooped Qigong up in my arms so the patter of his toenails wouldn't give us away. Then we crept into the hall, as silently as possible. When we were about ten feet from the study, we stopped and listened. It sounded like two people talking to each other.

Jackson strode into the study, reached for the light switch, and flipped it on.

There, ransacking the shelves and grabbing all the first editions and shoving them into boxes, were Arthur and Agatha Beasley.

"Stop what you're doing!" Jackson shouted.

Arthur and Agatha froze, clicked off their flashlights, and put the books down on the coffee table. Both of them wore white coveralls, bootees, and gloves.

"Who are you?" Arthur said.

"I'm Jackson Spade, head of security for the *MJ's Mind* shoot. Who are you?"

"I know who they are," I said. "Jackson, this is Arthur and Agatha Beasley. They're the owners of the Curious Kitten. I bought your anniversary present there. They also have plenty of expensive first editions. Did you steal them from the Bixbys? Is that how you got them?"

Arthur looked at Agatha and shook his head. "No, that's not true. Roger sold them to us."

Jackson walked over to the coffee table and pointed at the books. "And now that he's dead, you thought you'd help yourself."

"We're only doing this because Carly, his wife, wouldn't deal with us," Agatha said. "She's been very unreasonable."

"Oh, so you had no choice," Jackson said. "Give me a break."

"Why was Roger selling the books in the first place?" I asked.

"Roger was selling off family heirlooms to replace money lost from a risky hedge fund in the 2008 stock market crash,"

Arthur said. "This was on top of learning that Max had essentially left him a worthless house. He'd mortgaged the place within an inch of its life to pay for the elaborate séances he liked to hold. He used to fly in psychics from Europe and even Russia."

That confirmed what Simon had said about the house being worthless.

"So when he was murdered, you decided to just take what you wanted," Jackson said. "And you think that's okay?"

Arthur shrugged. "In this economy you have to do what you can to stay afloat. If we didn't take the books, they would continue to degenerate. We're giving them a good home and passing them along to people who really appreciate them."

Jackson took out his phone. "I'm calling the police."

"Do you have to?" Arthur looked distressed. "We promise not to do it anymore if you don't call."

Jackson started to punch numbers into his phone. "You won't do it again for sure if I do." He finished dialing and put the phone to his ear.

Agatha scurried over to him. "We know that Willow is investigating Roger's murder, and we have information that will help you if you'll let us go."

Jackson looked at me. I nodded. He stopped the call. "Okay, you've got our attention. Start talking, but if this information isn't helpful or is false in any way, I'm still calling the police." He motioned to the couch, and Arthur and Agatha sat down. I pulled out my phone and turned on the recorder.

Arthur leaned forward and put his elbows on his knees and laced his fingers together. "Max and my father, Fred, were friends when they were younger. Both of them were born and grew up in Great Neck. Max used to spend his summers out here at the family house, and sometimes my father was invited along for weekends and holidays. Even back then, my father said, Max Bixby had big dreams. When Max was a teenager, he always talked about working for his father's company. He wanted to make it a worldwide success. He had no siblings, and when his father died when he was twenty-seven, he inherited everything. He was ambitious and ruthless. He took over the company, fired employees who had been there for years, and brought in new ones. It caused a lot of resentment.

"When Prohibition came, Max seized the opportunity to become even richer. He worked with local fishermen and his caretaker, Daniel Russell, to move booze from the three-mile limit to New York."

So far this was similar to Ron Turner's story. "So your father knew Daniel Russell?" I asked.

"Yes," Arthur said. "He knew him. My father had opened his dental practice in Great Neck, but he still came out to Greenport on the weekends with my mother. This was before I was born. My parents liked to hunt for antiques. When my dad retired, he opened his own store, and I was fortunate enough to apprentice there."

"I hope this is leading to something that will help us," Jackson said, shifting from one foot to the other.

"I'm getting to that," Arthur said. "One weekend, about six months after Daniel Russell was murdered, my parents went out to visit Max on the weekend. It was a surprise; Max didn't know they were coming. As my father told it, the door was open when they arrived. So they walked into the house, and they heard voices, loud ones, a real screaming match. They never saw the woman, but someone was shouting at Max, telling him that he was a monster, that he'd destroyed her life. And he was telling her that she was a crazy woman who could never see the truth. That he only did what he did because he loved her."

"Rebecca Russell," I said.

Arthur nodded. "I'd say so. That's what my father thought."

"And?"

"And that was all. Max must have heard them come in because he charged into the entryway, accused them of eavesdropping, and ordered them off the property. They didn't speak after that."

Jackson ran his hand through his short, dark hair. "Well, that's interesting but not much help. Everyone back then was sure Max killed Daniel Russell. And no one could prove it."

"Except, I think there's one person who can," Arthur added quickly. "I told you my parents used to socialize with the Bixbys. There was someone else in that crowd, a woman writer. Years after the murder, I think it must have been the early 1960s, my father ran into her, and they got to talking about Max. He mentioned that time they'd been thrown out of the mansion, and how he always believed it was Rebecca Russell they'd overheard. And she said it was, and my father asked her how she could be so sure, and she said something cryptic about for every story you go to the source. But she wouldn't say any more."

"That sounds like she either got it from Max or Rebecca," Jackson said.

"What was this writer's name?" I asked.

Arthur drew his brows together. "I asked my father that same question. He didn't remember, exactly. But he said it had something to do with a rosebush."

"A rosebush?" Jackson echoed.

I pulled the old newspaper out of my back pocket. "Could it have been Edith Thorne?

Arthur snapped his fingers together and pointed at me. "That's it!"

"So how exactly does this help us with the case?" Jackson said.

Arthur shrugged. "I was thinking if you could find her, maybe she could help you figure out the real story behind Daniel's murder and that would help you solve Roger's murder."

"You don't know where she lives, then?" I asked.

Arthur shook his head. "No, but you're a smart cookie. You can track her down."

Jackson looked doubtful. "You think that's enough to get them off the hook?"

Arthur and Agatha gave me pleading looks. They were old and desperate and I couldn't help but feel sorry for them. Besides, I didn't want Koren asking questions about what we were doing in the mansion when everyone else was gone. "Sure. Let them go."

"Oh, thank you," Arthur said, and smiled at Agatha. They picked up their flashlights and stood.

"Just one thing," Jackson said. "Put the books back."

They did as they were told and left. After they did, Jackson said to me, "So how do you intend to track down this writer, Edith Thorne?"

I took out my phone. "I guess I'll start with the Internet." I accessed my browser and typed in her name. No result. "There's nothing here." I put the phone away. "If she's local, she'll be in the phone book. I'll check that when I get home. It's low-tech but it could work."

"If she's a writer, she could be anywhere. I'll contact a buddy of mine who's still on the force. If she's not local, he can track her down."

I stepped close to Jackson and gave him a kiss. "I'm glad you're on my side. We make a good team, don't you think?"

"Yes, we do, McQuade. We're like the dynamic duo."

chapter twenty

Dr. Willow McQuade's Healthy Living Tips

When your vocal cords become inflamed, it can make you lose your voice (laryngitis) or just have difficulty talking (hoarseness). Inflammation can be caused by everything from an infection to allergens and even heartburn. A steam inhalation can help you speak up. Just boil a pot of water and remove it from the stove. Add two drops of eucalyptus essential oil, and two drops of pine oil. Put a towel over your head and the pot and inhale. Also, as much as possible, rest your voice. Write things down if you need to communicate!

Yours Naturally,

Dr. McQuade

Jackson went home to take care of his dogs, and I headed back to Nature's Way. When I got home, I immediately went into the office, pulled the phone book out of the desk drawer, and went to the *T*'s. An E. Thorne was listed, but no address. It was too late to call tonight, but I would try her first thing in the morning.

I had a fitful night's sleep. I definitely slept better and felt more rested when Jackson stayed over. Several times during the night I heard creaking floorboards and hopped out of bed, went to the door, and looked out, but no one was there. When I got back in bed, I obsessively reviewed the facts of the case, especially the information that Arthur had provided. Edith Thorne was my new person of interest. I had to make contact.

Sunday morning, I woke up at seven thirty. The overcast day was one week since Roger was murdered. I did my yoga routine, took a shower, and headed downstairs. I found Merrily and Wallace in the kitchen, handling the breakfast crowd. Nearly all the tables were full. I headed straight for the coffee-maker. "How is everyone this morning?"

"We're doing fine," Wallace said.

"I've got a batch of organic raspberry muffins coming out if you want one," Merrily said as she put on an oven mitt and opened the oven. She pulled out a tray of muffins that looked perfectly yummy.

"I'd love one," I said. "Are you feeling any better?"

"Well, the tests came back positive for Lyme, and Dr. Cooper put me on doxycycline for two weeks. I started the dose yesterday, but it was still hard getting up this morning. All my muscles ache and I'm really tired."

"It may take a while for the symptoms to calm down."

"I know. Dr. Cooper said it could take a couple of months."

"Well, make sure you rest whenever you need to. The couch in my office is always available."

"Thanks. You may find me camping out in there."

"Not a problem." I grabbed a muffin and poured myself a cup of coffee. I put a nice dollop of organic butter on top of the muffin and watched it melt. "This looks delicious, Merrily. I may just have to come back for seconds."

She smiled. "Feel free." The door opened and two more customers came in. Wallace grabbed menus and led them to a table near the window. I took my coffee and muffin and headed into my office.

I sat down at the desk and put my breakfast aside for the moment. I wanted to call Edith Thorne. I reached for the open phone book, found her number again, picked up the office phone and dialed the number. But there was no answer.

I took my phone out of my pocket and checked my messages. Jackson had left a text at 8:01 Sunday morning saying that he was on his way back up to the estate and asking me to call him when I arrived. Amanda had e-mailed me the schedule for today without any comment on our conversation at the Russells'. Allie and Hector had appointments from three on, and so did I. This would give me time to take care of things here and check out one Edith Thorne.

I tried her again but there was no answer. I decided to pay a few bills and, that done, turned my attention to my blog on NaturesWay.com. I did some research and decided to tell readers about a new study in the *Journal of Pain Research* that showed that when women participated in a seventy-five-minute yoga class twice a week for eight weeks, it lessened pain and improved psychological functioning, mindfulness, and cortisol levels. I opened WordPress, posted the info, added a photo of women in a yoga class from iStock.com, and published it.

That done, I turned to the article about rashes that I was writing for *Nature's Remedy,* but I just couldn't concentrate.

MJ's Mind was leaving town tomorrow, and I still hadn't found Roger's killer. I picked up the phone and tried Edith again. No answer.

Wallace knocked on the door and came in. "We're almost out of a bunch of things in the kitchen. Should I work on a new order?"

"Sure." I put Edith's number in my iPhone and put the phone book away. I felt frustrated, and I guess it showed because Wallace asked me what was wrong. I gave him a brief overview of my investigation into Roger's murder, specifically what Jackson and I had found out from Arthur last night. "So now, I really need to talk to this writer, Edith Thorne. I've called her several times and she isn't answering."

"She doesn't always answer her phone," Wallace said. "Or she might be at Town Hall working on something. She likes to go in on Sunday when it's quiet to do her work."

"You know Edith Thorne?" I asked, surprised.

"Edith used to be my history teacher in high school in Northport. When she retired twenty years ago, she moved out here and became the village historian for Southold Town. She's friends with my mother. They have lunch every month either here or in Northport."

"Arthur said that she was also a writer."

"Yes, she wrote a book about rum running titled *East End Rum Running* about twenty years ago. But she didn't put her name to it. It's written by Anonymous. I don't know why."

"Arthur said she knew Max Bixby, and he implied that somehow she got the real story—either from him or Rebecca. Maybe it was for that book," I said. "I think she may be able to help me solve Roger's murder, which I need to do ASAP. Everyone is going back to L.A. tomorrow."

"Well, be prepared. She's very reclusive, to the point of

being a hermit. She's prickly and doesn't get along with most people. But I'm sure you'll find a way to charm her."

"I hope you're right."

I needed to talk to Edith, but a Sunday Labor Day rush at Nature's Way intervened. At nine thirty we got slammed, and all the tables in and outside were full. I was grateful for the business, but it was a scramble to get everyone fed at the same time. We decided that Merrily would stay in the kitchen and make up the dishes while Wallace and I served the customers. At eleven forty, I dropped off my last two plates of food at a table for two on the front porch. Fortunately, Southold was only about seven minutes away from Greenport, so I still hoped that I might catch Edith at Town Hall.

By this time, the sun had burned away the clouds and the sky was clear, with only mild humidity. It was the kind of day that reminded me of fall, which was only weeks away. To people who lived on the East End, fall was our best-kept secret (except for the pumpkin and corn-maze craze around Halloween). The roads weren't crowded, the towns settled back into nontourist mode, and the weather was glorious. It made me feel optimistic. Maybe I could solve Roger's murder and clear Simon before the production left town. Edith Thorne was the key.

So, I drove out of Greenport, past the high school and the gas station, the Lutheran church, up and over the new bridge, and followed the road past Mill Creek and farm stands into the town of Southold. After the light by the Capital One bank, I continued on past Feather Hill and parked in front of Town Hall. I'd just reached the door when a man dressed in a suit and tie came out of the building and said, "They're closed."

"I figured that, but do you know if there is a woman

named Edith Thorne in there working? She's the town historian."

"Mrs. Thorne works in the annex in the Capital One building. You may be able to catch her there, but I doubt it. It's Sunday."

I turned around and drove east back to the Capital One building, parked, and went into the lobby. But the door to the annex was locked. I did see someone working in the back, though, so I knocked. A few moments later a young guy in a polo shirt and jeans came to the door and opened it. "We're closed until Tuesday."

"I'm looking for Edith Thorne. Do you happen to know her address?"

"I do." He eyed me suspiciously. "But I can't just give it out. Have a good day." He closed the door.

I headed back to Greenport, frustrated because I hadn't been able to talk to Edith Thorne and because I'd forgotten the products I needed to treat my clients today. It was already 1:00 p.m. on Sunday afternoon, and I wanted to be back at the estate by two. I had just driven past Greenport High School when my cell phone rang. I glanced at it but didn't recognize the number. Thinking it might be important, I pulled over and answered it.

"Willow? Willow?" Simon sounded absolutely panicked.

"What's the matter?"

"They've arrested me. I'm in jail."

Oh, no, not that. "When, why?"

"I'll tell you when you get here. Can you come down? I need to talk to you. Please." He sounded on the verge of hysteria.

"I'll be right there." I felt my frustration double. Not only had I been unable to see Edith, but now Simon had been arrested. This was the very thing I was trying to prevent. Why now? I wondered. Had Koren discovered something that gave him grounds to arrest Simon? I gripped the steering wheel, tried to remain calm, and called Jackson. He didn't answer so I left a message and pulled back onto the main road.

A few minutes later, I arrived at the jail. I pulled open the heavy oak door, went to the counter, and asked to see Simon Lewis. At first, the imposing police officer with the shaved head said Simon couldn't have any visitors. But when I told him that Simon was my brother, he grunted and led me back to a small room with nauseating green walls, a table and two chairs, no windows, and the smell of BO.

The guard told me to sit down and went to get Simon. I took a few long, deep breaths. Because Simon was in a panic, I needed to remain as calm as possible. I had to find out what had happened and get up to the estate and find some answers.

Moments later, the guard led in Simon. He was dressed in his street clothes—a navy Izod polo shirt, khaki shorts, Docksiders—and handcuffs. He looked absolutely awful, unshaven and gaunt, with a haunted look in his eyes. "Willow, thanks for coming."

The guard said, "Sit," and pushed him into the chair oppo-site me. "No touching." He went to the door, closed it, and stood in front of it.

"What happened?"

Simon tried to run his hands through his hair but stopped when he remembered that he had handcuffs on. "The cops found this letter that shows that I was blackmailing Roger about his cheating on Carly."

"Simon, don't get offended, but I have to ask. Did you write it?"

"No, of course not. I make plenty of money of my own, thank you very much. Why would I stoop to blackmailing anyone?"

"Greed?"

"Oh, please!"

I remembered the bright green Post-it note from Roger that had been attached to the payment Tom had received: *This is blackmail, Tommy. But I trust you will keep your word and not tell Carly a thing. Destroy this note!—RB.*

"I believe you," I said. "I'm guessing the note was forged." It would have been relatively easy to forge a letter implicating Simon instead of Tom, except for the signature. "Is your lawyer having the letter authenticated?"

"Yes, but until then, I'm stuck here."

"But it makes no sense. If you were blackmailing Roger, why would you kill him? It's like killing the goose that laid the golden eggs. Not that you need the money."

"Exactly. But Koren came to my house last night. He told me I had motive, namely the controlling interest in Galaxy. Plus, means—I'm rich so I had access to whatever I needed to kill him; and opportunity—we were at the same party and we'd fought earlier in the day and now this weird letter. His brilliant theory is that Roger refused to pay me and I killed him.

"My lawyer is trying to get me out on bail. We had a hearing at the Suffolk County courthouse early this morning. The prosecutor didn't want me to have bail at all, says I'm a flight risk, but the judge didn't agree and set it at one million."

I gasped. "Do you have it?"

"I only need to come up with ten percent, or one hundred thousand, so, yes, I can afford it." He leaned toward me. "I need to know if you found anything that can help me out of this mess."

I gave him a quick recap of our trip to the estate last night and what Arthur had told us about Edith Thorne.

Simon shook his head. "Well, I'm not sure how getting info

on Daniel Russell's murder will solve Roger's, but it sounds like our only lead. You need to find her, Willow."

"I know that. I went to her office in the Capitol One bank in Southold, but it was closed and I don't have her address. But Wallace knows her. He may know where she lives."

"Ask him! Pronto!"

The guard walked over to us. "Calm down, Mr. Lewis. You have two more minutes." He jingled the keys to Simon's cell, went back to the door, and crossed his arms over his chest.

"I'll be at the estate all afternoon and I'm hoping I can solve this today," I said. "The show wraps tomorrow, so we don't have much time." I didn't relish going back up there. A murderer was on the loose, and the stakes were higher than ever before.

My anxiety must have shown on my face because Simon put his hand on top of mine. "You can do this, Willow. I know you can. You're super smart and you're a good friend, the best. I know you won't let me down."

We were certainly better friends than lovers. I actually liked him most of the time now, instead of constantly being frustrated by his inability to meet my needs.

"No touching!" The guard came over to us and helped Simon up from his chair. "Let's go, Mr. Lewis. It's time to go back to your cell."

Simon gave me a look of pure desperation as he headed out the door.

chapter twenty-one

Dr. Willow McQuade's Healthy Living Tips

Did you know that certain scents can also help you remember? That's because the nasal cavities are close to the brain. So, if you need to remember important information, inhale up to ten breaths of pure essential oils such as basil, lemon, lemongrass, lime, peppermint, or rosemary (ancient Greek scholars wore laurels of rosemary around their necks) to help imprint the information on your mind. When you need to remember the info, smell the same scent.

Yours Naturally,

Dr. McQuade

When I went back to Nature's Way, Merrily and Wallace were busy with the lunch crowd. The Saturday and Sunday of Labor Day weekend were always the most hectic. Today, Sunday, both the tables inside and outside were full. Wallace didn't have time to talk about Edith Thorne, so I packed up some more lavender essential oil, Rescue Remedy, and homeopathic remedies for stress, put them in the big, purple van, and headed back out to the estate. I decided to leave Qigong at home since I anticipated a hectic day. *MJ's Mind*'s production team had to get all the scenes it needed to shoot done between now and tomorrow.

On the way back to the estate I tried Mrs. Thorne again, and this time she actually answered. I pulled over into a parking lot so I could focus. "Mrs. Thorne?"

"Yes. Who is this?"

"My name is Willow McQuade. I run Nature's Way Market and Café in Greenport."

"What does that have to do with me?"

"Right now I'm working up at the Bixby estate, and there's been a murder. A murder that is very similar to the murder that took place in 1933 when Daniel Russell was killed."

She hung up.

I tried her again. When she answered, I said, "Mrs. Thorne? It's Willow." She hung up again. This was getting me nowhere. I called the store and Wallace answered. He sounded frazzled and rushed. "Nature's Way Market and Café. How can I help you?"

"Wallace, it's me, Willow. I just tried to call Edith Thorne. I don't think I charmed her. She hung up on me, twice."

"I told you that she's prickly." I could hear the clatter of plates in the background and the busy din of customers chatting.

"I see what you mean. Do you think you could call her and ask her to talk to me? It's important."

"I know it is. Just let me get through the lunch rush and I'll give her a call. I'll let you know what happens."

I thanked him and hung up. I hoped he could reason with her. I pulled the van back onto the road and headed to the estate. I arrived ten minutes later and pulled the van into the turnaround in front of the mansion. For some reason the house seemed more foreboding than ever. I didn't get a chance to open the door before Jackson came up to the window.

"Simon is in jail," I said.

"MJ's missing," he replied.

It was obviously not a day for good news. I sucked in a breath. "What happened?"

"She was here this morning. They were shooting some one-on-one close-ups to show her thinking and psychic process. She wasn't in a good mood and seemed stressed-out. Instead of leaving her alone, Tom started pushing her, telling her that they only had one more day to get everything. Pierre tried to step in, and the two of them started to argue. MJ said she was going back to her cottage to have lunch and rest, but when Amanda went to pick her up for this afternoon's shoot, she wasn't there and the Mercedes was gone."

"Maybe she just needed to get away for a bit. She is the star of the show. That's a lot of pressure and these aren't ideal circumstances."

Jackson shook his head. "Rick says she never does this. She's always on set when she's needed. And she didn't tell him where she was going."

I thought about it. Where would a psychic who wanted to get away from it all go?

"Maybe she went for a walk on the beach to clear her head. That's what I would do."

The two of us ran over to the seawall to check the beach. No MJ.

"Everything has come to a complete halt," Jackson said. "Rick is frantic."

"Should we call our favorite cop, Koren?"

Jackson shook his head. "He won't do anything. She's only been gone a couple of hours."

"True. Let's go check her cottage. Maybe she left a clue there as to where she was going."

"Good idea. I'll go get a golf cart."

A few minutes later, Jackson and I arrived at MJ and Rick's cottage. For some reason the door was ajar. Jackson went inside first, and I followed him. The place looked as if a small tornado had just come through. Dirty dishes were on the counter and in the sink, and clothes were strewn on the floor and draped across most of the furniture. The drawers on the cabinet in the living room were also open, and ripped-up paper littered the carpet like snow.

"Did someone break in here or are she and Rick just slobs?"

"Hard to tell," Jackson said, picking up a piece of paper. He showed it to me. "This looks like a page from her contract for *MJ's Mind.*"

I thought about it. "Maybe she was fed up and wanted to see what the contract said. You know, to see what would happen if she walked off?"

I heard a noise in the back of the house. Moments later, Mrs. Florrick came into the living room, dressed in a black-and-white maid uniform, her hair pulled into a tight bun. "What are you two doing here?" She gave us both a stern look.

"We're trying to find MJ," I said. "What are you doing here?"

"I am MJ's maid and neighbor." She pointed toward the

back of the house. "My cottage is behind this one. I'm here to tidy up." She picked up the clothes and carried them to a small utility room, where she started the washing machine.

"Do you have any idea where she might be?" Jackson asked.

She pushed the drawers back into the dresser and picked up the paper that was scattered on the floor. "No. How would I know that?"

"Maybe she mentioned something during your conversations," Jackson said.

"I don't have time for chitchat with just anyone." Mrs. Florrick took the pile of paper into the kitchen, stuffed it into the trash can, and put the dirty dishes in the dishwasher.

I went over to the counter. "Maybe you overheard something that would help us find her."

"I'm not a gossip." She turned toward me and gave me a withering look. "And I'm not nosy like you are. Granted you helped me with my varicose veins, but you are a snoop." She put detergent in the dishwasher and turned it on. "You'll never figure out who killed Roger."

"Do you know who killed him?" I asked.

"If you do, you should tell the police," Jackson said.

"I mind my own business, and you should, too. Both of you." She checked her watch and walked to the door. "I have to go. Please don't make a mess."

"We'll do our best not to," Jackson promised.

"She's quite a character." I watched her head back to her cottage. Moments later, she zipped by in a golf cart, holding a broom, looking like the Wicked Witch of the West in *The Wizard of Oz*.

"Yeah, but she's not helpful." Jackson went into the kitchen, grabbed the trash can, and began pulling out pieces of paper. "Let's go through this trash together." So, while he continued to pull paper out, I checked it for any clues to MJ's where-abouts. But I didn't find anything that related to the cancellation clause in her contract.

We were sitting on the couch trying to figure out what to do next when Rick and Tom walked in. Tom wore a Hawaiian shirt, jeans, and sunglasses. Rick wore a white shirt and white jeans and was smoking a cigar. "MJ's not here?" he asked.

"No, but Mrs. Florrick cleaned up the place," Jackson said.

"That's good," Rick said absentmindedly. He paced around the living room. "I have to tell you, I'm worried about MJ. She's never done this before."

"We did find this." Jackson handed him the scrap of paper.

Rick leaned against the counter, scanning it. "This is part of her contract with Galaxy. Roger set it up."

"She might have been checking it to see what would happen if she dropped out," I said.

"She wouldn't do that," Tom said. "Don't listen to her, Rick."

"You, shut up!" Rick said. "It's your fault that she is missing in the first place."

"I was just trying to help." Tom pushed his sunglasses up on top of his head. "You know, by giving her a firm hand."

"That's the director's job and my job, as executive producer," Rick said. "You're just the second assistant director, an AD."

"That's right. And Roger gave me that job. He knew I could handle it."

Obviously now that Roger was dead, Tom was revising recent history. When Roger was alive, he hadn't seemed to have much faith in his younger brother.

"I'm not going to get into that with you," Rick said. "Wait for me outside."

"They've turned you against me," Tom said, pointing to us. "You two need to mind your own business."

Rick pointed to the door. "Tom, outside, now!"

Tom slunk out and slammed the door.

"He's more trouble than he's worth, even though he did apologize to Pierre and me." Rick flopped on the couch and puffed his cigar. "Okay, so now what do we do?"

"Did MJ mention any places she wanted to visit out here?" I asked. "Somewhere she might go to be alone?"

"That's a good question." Rick blew a perfect smoke ring. "In L.A., she walks on the beach with our dogs—we have two black Labs—when she gets stressed-out. She says it clears her mind."

"There are plenty of beaches out here," I said. "She could take her pick."

"True," Jackson said. "But which one?"

Rick radioed Amanda and told her to start searching beaches. It was almost two thirty on Sunday afternoon, and my first client was Sarah at 3:00 p.m., so I left the hunt for MJ to them. I took the box of supplies from the golf cart and walked next door to the cottage, where I unpacked the products and put them on the shelves. I'd just put the homeopathic cures on the top shelf when my iPhone rang. It was Jackson.

"Hi, did you find her?"

"Not yet. Amanda just checked the town beach, and we're headed to Kenny's Road and Mattituck Inlet. But I've just heard that a hurricane is on its way here. It should hit land late tonight. It's not supposed to be huge, but it will still be messy, especially on the East End."

"A hurricane? That's just what we need while we're trying to wrap up this case by tomorrow."

"I know. So, anywhere else I could look for her?"

"Check out Greenport if you don't find her there. Maybe she's playing tourist."

"Okay, will do. I'll call you when I know something. Love you, McQuade."

"Love you, too." Calling me McQuade wasn't exactly romantic, but I loved it just the same. I ended the call just as there was a knock on the door. It was Sarah, and she was in tears. I let her in. "What's going on?"

"I need to talk."

I led her to the front porch, grabbed a few tissues, and handed them to her. "Sit down and tell me what's wrong." I picked up my purple legal pad and a black pen to take notes.

She looked at me. "Anything I tell you is in confidence, right?"

"Absolutely." I didn't mention that if she told me that she had murdered Roger, I'd have to report that to the police.

She pointed to the legal pad. "Please don't take notes."

I put the pen and pad on the coffee table. "I need to take notes so I can prescribe effectively, but if this is something personal, I won't. Don't worry."

"Thank you." She dabbed her eyes. "Back in L.A., I was seeing Tom until he broke it off."

"And?"

She blew her nose. "I really love him, but he wants Carly."

"Can you tell me what happened?"

"We'd been dating for about six months, ever since he came to L.A. to work with Roger. But he dumped me when Carly showed up on the set during preproduction. She'd been up in Vancouver, working on another series, and in Italy before that, and he hadn't seen her in a couple of years, and this time things were bad between Roger and Carly. Tom was thrilled. He figured he was finally going to get his chance with her. But then she started dating Simon. He hated Simon for that. And it got even more complicated when we came here and he began to worry about all the time Carly was spending with Roger. They were just working on the show, but Tom thought she was falling for him again."

"How do you know all this?"

"Cassidy told me. Tom tells her everything. They're pretty close, and she and I are best friends." Sarah put the used tissues in the trash basket at the end of the couch. "I guess Tom's had an alcohol problem for a while. But it's been so much worse since we've been here. He's completely out of control. When I drove him home the other night, he was like a different person—cold and hateful. He scares me now."

"He's scared me, too," I confessed.

"I'm worried that Tom may have killed Roger to get her all to himself. I mean, it all works out really well if he also manages to get Simon framed for it."

"But he was attacked and ended up in the hospital. Don't you think that pretty much rules him out as a suspect?"

"No. He's crazy enough to hurt himself to divert suspicion."

"Really?" It just seemed too far-fetched, though I was thinking that Tom *was* behind the blackmail forgery. "Are you sure? Did Tom admit to killing Roger?"

"No, nothing like that. I'm just starting to believe that he could have done it. Cassidy doesn't see it that way. She knows that Tom can be difficult but she loves him."

"Maybe you should talk to the police." At the least, that might help divert suspicion from Simon, who was, at this moment, sitting in jail.

She shook her head and tears started falling again. "I can't do that to Tom. I'm just upset about losing him and worried that he's done something really stupid." She plucked a tissue from the box on the coffee table in front of her. "I thought you could give me something that would help."

"First of all, I'd suggest keeping your distance from Tom. If what you say is true, he could be dangerous." I made a mental note to do the same. "I'd like you to try Saint John's Wort. It will relax you and can be very helpful when you are worn-out from crying. It's a good alternative to prescription medications. You can't take both together though."

I got up and went over to the bookcase and picked up Saint John's Wort, a vial of homeopathic Ignatia, and the flower essence Star-of-Bethlehem and handed them to her. "Ignatia can help when you identify with the person you lost and feel you can't go on without them. Take three pellets under the tongue three times daily as needed." I handed her the flower essence Star-of-Bethlehem. "Take two drops of this in a glass of water three times a day as you need it. It will soothe you."

"Boy, do I need that." Sarah looked at the little blue vials doubtfully. "You really think this stuff works?"

"These natural remedies will help comfort you. It's going to take time for you to feel completely better. But I'm sure once you leave here, it will get easier. You won't have to see Tom every day." I took out my iPhone and found the name of a therapist I knew who was based in L.A. I wrote down her name and number and handed it to her. "Dr. Carr is excellent. She can help you through this. You don't have to do it alone."

I escorted Sarah to the door and said good-bye. I greeted my next patient, one of the accountants, and showed her into my office. I was about to start the session when my cell phone rang. I saw that it was Jackson, so I excused myself and stepped into the kitchen.

"Did you find her?"

"Yes, we found her."

"Is she okay?"

"I think so. Get this. She's giving psychic readings to people," Jackson said.

"Where?"

"She's sitting on that bench outside the Coronet in Greenport."

"And why is she doing this?"

"She told us that she was super-stressed-out from shooting all week. She says she needs to get back in touch with real people, her audience."

"Is she going to come back?"

"Maybe. She wants to see you."

"Me? Why me?"

"I don't know. Can you come down?"

"I have a patient here but I can come down after that. Say forty-five minutes or so?"

"That'll work. She's got a line of people waiting to see her."

I completed my appointment with the accountant and gave her natural remedies for her adult acne. She was most concerned with unexpected breakouts, so I suggested she apply tea tree oil to the problem areas. I also suggested that she drink the juice of half a lemon in a glass of water one to three times daily to help the liver break down toxins. I walked her out and went to Allie's door and knocked.

Allie opened the door. "What's up?"

"MJ disappeared earlier today but Jackson and Rick found her. She's in Greenport, giving psychic readings."

"O-kay. Is she going to come back and finish shooting her TV show?"

"I hope so. She wants to see me for some reason, so I've got to go down there. When my five o'clock shows up, please ask her to wait for me. I'll be back as soon as I can."

"You got it. I'll hold down the fort until you get back." Allie smiled. "Go get her, girl."

chapter twenty-two

Dr. Willow McQuade's Healthy Living Tips

The immune system is your body's twenty-four-hour security system when it comes to zapping bacteria, viruses, fungi, yeasts, and parasites. It makes good sense to bolster your immunity any way you can, but especially if you are stressed, tired, and eating the wrong foods. While good nutrition, vitamins, and herbs are most important when it comes to boosting immunity, essential oils can help as well. Consider using immune-enhancing essential oils that have strong antimicrobial properties. These include cedarwood, cinnamon, clary sage, clove, garlic, grapefruit, juniper, lavender, lemon, lime, marjoram, orange, oregano, patchouli, peppermint, pine, rosemary, and tea tree. Add them to a diffuser or use them in the bath or in a massage oil. Breathe deep for better health!

Yours Naturally,

Dr. McQuade

Ten minutes later on Sunday afternoon, I rolled down Front Street in Greenport in the bright purple Nature's Way van. The town was packed with tourists holding shopping bags, eating ice cream cones, and enjoying the village. At the corner of Main Street, I spotted MJ dressed in flowing purple robes and a bright red turban, giving a psychic reading to a young woman in a tie-dyed T-shirt and a denim skirt. MJ had her eyes closed and was holding the young woman's hands. Jackson and Rick were standing nearby, watching her and looking extremely bored. I beeped the horn on the van, and Jackson spotted me and waved.

Taking a left, I went around the corner and tried to find a place to park. Usually, getting a parking space on Labor Day weekend was like winning the lottery, but today I got lucky. I drove into a parking lot just as a Jeep full of kids and dogs was pulling out.

I crossed the parking lot and headed south toward the waterfront on Main Street. The bay was already choppy, a sign of the impending hurricane, but the smell of sea air was delightful none the same. I took in a few deep breaths.

I passed the antiques store and Fiedler's art gallery. In the window was a lovely seascape watercolor I would have loved for my office.

I tapped Jackson on the shoulder. He turned around. "Hey, you made it. Can you believe this line?" He gestured to the dozen or so people waiting for a reading with MJ. "They're star struck."

"She is a star," Rick said. He puffed on a cigar. "And she's in her element now. This is what she likes best, putting on a show for her fans."

"Jackson said she wanted to talk to me?"

Rick shrugged. "I don't know what about. When I asked

her to go back to the estate, she said she wasn't going until she talked to you."

I couldn't imagine why she wanted to talk to me, but when she was between readings I walked over to her. "MJ, are you okay?"

"Willow! I'm so glad you came." She grabbed my hand and pulled me down so I was sitting next to her.

"Hey! No cutting," someone said.

MJ stood up and faced the crowd. "Please, dear ones, I just need a moment." She sat down again.

"MJ, how can I help?"

She smiled at the people who were still waiting. "Meeting my fans has energized me, but I have to admit that I haven't been feeling well. I think that's the reason that I couldn't reach Daniel or Roger. It was as if I'd lost my gift. So I had to get away and be with my people, recharge my batteries, and restore my confidence."

I lowered my voice. "Is it your hip that's bothering you?" I'd noticed her favoring her right leg.

"No, I've had that for years. It's this incessant ringing in my ears. I can't think of anything else and I can't sleep. I'm worn-out. It's making me crazy."

"When did this start? Were you injured?"

She frowned. "Not in my ear. But two months ago, I fell down the stairs at my home in Malibu and sprained my ankle. It was very painful."

I suspected that I knew what was wrong. "What were you taking for the pain—NSAIDs? Nonsteroidal anti-inflammatories like aspirin and ibuprofen?"

"How did you know? I was popping them like Skittles."

"Those kinds of meds can cause ringing in the ears. It's called tinnitus. If you stop or ease off those painkillers, it will go away. I'd also recommend taking ginkgo biloba three times a day, either in a tea, tincture, or capsule. It will improve nerve-signal transmission and increase your brain's use of oxygen. I'll get some for you."

"Oh, thank you! You are an angel."

I looked at the line of fans. "So, will you come back and wrap up the show?"

MJ looked at Rick and back at me. "Yes, I will. Just let me finish up here." She took my hand. "And, Willow, thank you."

I quickly stopped by the store to grab some gingko biloba for MJ. It would take time, but eventually she would feel much better. Hopefully, just knowing why her ears were ringing and that she was getting treatment would perk her up; that and her fans' adoration.

Late Sunday afternoon, I was back at the cottage, where I was surprised to find it full of people waiting for treatment. I said hello to everyone, grabbed the sign-in sheet, and went to Allie's room. She was stripping her massage table.

"What is going on out there?"

"Amanda called and told me quite a few people were headed over since MJ wasn't back yet. It's the last day to get treatments, so I guess they wanted to take advantage of that. I've cut my sessions in half so I can get everyone in. Hector did, too."

I checked my watch. It was 5:05. I scanned the sheet. Six people were here to see Allie, five for Hector, and four for me. I headed into the living room.

"Hi, everyone. We're going to try and get to you as quickly as possible." I called my first appointment in. An hour later, I'd seen three people. I didn't rush; I just got down to the nitty-gritty without much preamble. My last client was Pierre, the director, who was lounging in one of the easy chairs texting on his cell phone.

I called him and led him into the front porch. After he was seated, I asked what I could do for him.

"I can't wait to see my doctor in L.A. I've got nasty blisters on both of my heels. I made the wrong choice to wear a new pair of crocodile loafers today." He slipped off his expensive left shoe and showed it to me.

I stifled any comment about his choosing to wear animal skins on his feet and examined his heels. The blisters were red, raw, and oozing. They looked painful.

"Don't worry, I can help you with that." I went over to the bookshelf and picked up a small bottle of tea tree essential oil, organic aloe vera wipes, and Band-Aids.

"You've been a big help to the crew, and MJ, too," Pierre said. "People are a lot less stressed since you've been around. Rick was right to hire you."

"Can you sit at the end of the couch and put your legs up?" He did as I asked. I put on gloves and cleaned out both blisters with the wipes. "That's really nice of you to say."

"Allie gives a great massage." He looked off into space. "Roger would have dug that. He used to have a masseuse come into the L.A. office at least once a week."

"What was he like to work with?" I applied tea tree oil to the blisters.

"Great, well, most of the time. Roger was very smart and he knew the business. But he also could be moody and difficult, and then when he and Carly started to have problems, it was very tense."

"I can imagine. Did you two work together before this project?"

"Many times. MJ introduced Rick and me to Roger. She'd known him for years."

This was a surprise. So Rick had lied to me when he said he'd met Roger at Jerry's Deli in Studio City? But why? "How did MJ and Roger meet?"

"The two of them went to college together and afterwards were roommates in New York while they were out-of-work actors."

"MJ was an actor?"

Pierre nodded. "Sure, when she was in her twenties. Mostly off-off-Broadway stuff. Roger made a living making commercials. You know, he did that one for margarine. 'Better Than Butter.'" Pierre suddenly realized whom he was talking to. "Oh, that was before your time."

I mulled over Rick's lie as I applied bandages to each heel. "I thought that Rick met Roger first."

Pierre shook his head. "No, that was all MJ. She's one of those people who knows everyone—and introduces them to everyone else."

I took off my gloves and threw them into the trash. So MJ was a psychic, an actor, and a social butterfly? "Okay, you're all set. I'd switch shoes though. It will just aggravate the wounds if you don't."

"I've got a pair of sandals I can wear, thanks. I'll go barefoot for now and ask Amanda to pick me up." He pulled out his phone and texted her.

I walked him to the door. "When will you start shooting again?"

"We'll go tonight after dinner. We've got a bunch of pick-ups to do—you know, close-ups of MJ. Later we're going to reshoot the bathroom scene. It should be interesting—that is, if she connects this time with Daniel Russell and Roger. You should come by."

I thought about what he had said about MJ and Roger. "I'll do that."

Half an hour later Jackson and I were eating fresh crab cakes and organic sweet-potato fries with the crew and production staff under the big tent in front of the mansion. Allie and Hector were headed to New York to hear a lecture by Dr. Newsome, a nationally known holistic physician. They asked me to come, but I couldn't leave, not now. Fortunately, MJ was back, and lying down in her cottage, resting for this evening's performance. They'd begin shooting after the dinner break.

"So you're saying that MJ was the connection to Roger, not Rick?" Jackson popped a sweet-potato fry in his mouth.

"That's what Pierre said."

"But why would Rick lie?" Jackson ate a piece of crab cake. "This is good."

"I don't know. For some reason he didn't want us to know that MJ was the connection to Roger, but I can't figure out why."

"Maybe he needs to be top dog, you know, the guy that gets things done, so he wants everyone to think that he knew Roger first, that he made the whole deal happen. Some men are like that. You know, a big ego. Of course, *I'm* not that way." Jackson winked at me.

"Of course you're not, sweetie." I smiled. "You're one in a million." I ate a fry and thought things over. "I need to talk to MJ."

"Maybe you'll get a chance tonight."

"I have to. It's Sunday. They're leaving tomorrow." I looked out the door of the tent at the sky. It was definitely darkening. "I don't like the way the sky looks. What's the word on the hurricane?"

Jackson took out his cell phone and checked the weather channel. "It'll hit the East End around midnight." He glanced up at the tent's ceiling. "I hope they've got this thing tied down tight."

Carly, dressed in a black linen shift dress and orange flip-flops, spotted us and was coming our way. Jackson tilted his head toward her. "I forgot to tell you. I heard from my guy who checks financial backgrounds. Simon was telling the truth. She is a trust-fund baby. Her family is old money, the kind that would make the Bixbys, at their richest, look like paupers."

Carly came straight to our table. Her short blond hair was mussed, as if she hadn't bothered to comb it, and her eyes were red rimmed from crying. "I just saw Simon."

I put my hand on hers. "Are you okay? Is he okay?"

"He's talking about breaking out. He's acting crazy. That's why I need to talk to you. He said you haven't figured out who killed Roger, but are you close?"

"Hard to say." I sipped my lemonade. "But I'm working on it." I glanced at Jackson. "We both are."

"You've got to hurry," Carly said. "Once we wrap the shoot tomorrow, everyone will leave and we'll never get to the truth."

She was right. I needed answers. I reached into my purse and pulled out the photos from the disposable camera. "Speaking of the truth . . . did you take these photos?" I spread them out in front of her. She glanced at them and pointed at the one that showed her sweater and sunglasses. "Those are my things, but I didn't take these photos. Why do you ask?"

Before I could answer, her phone pinged. She pulled it out of her pocket and looked at a text message. "I have to go. We're starting to set up for tonight and Pierre needs me. You should be there. It might help you figure this out."

"I will be," I said.

"Good. It may be our last chance."

chapter twenty-three

Dr. Willow McQuade's Healthy Living Tips

If you are stressed-out, tired, anxious, or angry, it can result in a tension headache. If you have one, you'll feel pain or discomfort in your head, scalp, or neck along with muscle tightness. This natural cure will help to ease the pain:

> *Tension-Type-Headache-Buster Oil*
> 1 ounce apricot kernel or sunflower vegetable oil
> 5 drops of lavender oil
> 3 drops of peppermint oil

Yours Naturally,

Dr. McQuade

Two hours later on Sunday evening, Pierre and his crew were set up in the third-floor bathroom. MJ was dressed in a midnight-blue robe with tiny stars, and an elaborate silver headpiece. Pierre, Tom, and the cameraman were in the bathroom, while Rick, Carly, and Amanda stayed next to the door, and Sarah and Cassidy hovered in Max's old bedroom. Jackson and I stood on the landing at the top of the stairs. I could hear the wind picking up outside and the branches of the trees next to the house scratching the windows. The hurricane was getting closer.

"So what do you think about what Carly said?" Jackson asked me. "Do you think she was telling the truth about the photos?"

"I don't know. I guess it's possible that she left her things on the dock and someone else took the photos. But who and why?"

Amanda leaned over and whispered something in Rick's ear. He whispered something back and turned and looked at us.

"What is it?" Jackson said. "Is there a problem?"

Rick took a cigar out of his pocket and lit it. "Amanda says that Willow took the diary that Sheila Russell gave her. I told her you were just trying to help."

"That's right," I said. "If you have a problem with that, Amanda, you should talk to me, not Rick."

"Forget it. I'm just the lowly assistant." She turned her back on me.

"That's not true, Amanda." Rick squeezed her arm. "Sorry, Willow. She's just trying to do her job."

So am I, I thought, but I said, "I have a question for you, if you don't mind."

"Go ahead." Rick blew out a perfect smoke ring. "Anything to help."

"I had a talk with Pierre this afternoon and he told me that you met Roger through MJ, not at Jerry's Deli in Studio City."

Rick looked puzzled. "I don't know why he would say that. It's just not true. I actually met Roger before I met MJ."

Whom to believe—Rick or Pierre? Which of them had something to hide?

"Okay, folks, we're going to start," Pierre said. "Rick, you need to shut down that cigar."

"We'll need to talk about this later," Rick said, stepping into the bathroom to douse his cigar in the sink.

I whispered in Jackson's ear, "I can't figure out who is telling the truth."

"You need to talk to MJ," he whispered back.

Rick stepped back out in the hall. Amanda whispered something to him. He smiled. What was going on between those two? He stepped back into the bathroom. "I want to be in here with MJ."

"Honey, that's not necessary," MJ said.

"It is, if he wants to run the special effects," Jackson whispered to me.

"That's fine, Rick. Just stay out of the way," Pierre said. "Now, I'm going to ask questions as we go along, MJ. I think it might help."

"That's all right with me," she said. "But if I'm onto something, let me follow it."

"Right," Pierre said. "Let's go."

"We're rolling," the cameraman said. "Speed!"

"Action!" Pierre yelled, and pointed at MJ.

MJ walked over to the bathtub and stood still. "This is a dark place. Evil things have happened here. Two murders. Both for passion, both for love." She closed her eyes and took a few deep breaths. "The murderers killed because they were desperate. They felt that this was the only way to get what they wanted."

"What did they want?" Pierre asked.

"Love and possession." MJ stepped back from the tub and took a deep breath. "Both of the men who were killed were lured up here. Both of them were tricked."

"By whom?"

MJ took another deep breath. "I don't know that."

"Are the victims here now?"

"I'll check." MJ walked slowly to the middle of the room. "Daniel Russell, are you here? Daniel?" At first there was no response. Then the windowpanes began to rattle, gently at first and then more loudly. I was willing to blame the wind for that, but seconds later, water began to pour into the bathtub. If this was a trick, it was pretty good. MJ walked over to the tub. "Daniel? What is it you want to say to me?"

The windowpanes stopped rattling and the water seemed to turn itself off.

"Go ahead, Daniel." She circled the room. "I hear you." She stopped and listened. "He's saying that he was betrayed. He says that the Bixby family is evil."

"But Roger Bixby was the second victim," Pierre said.

MJ held up her hand. "Later. I'll call Roger later. Now it's Daniel whose spirit is present."

A low hum began to resonate from the room. MJ seemed startled and walked over to the closet. "I'm opening the door." She turned the handle and pulled the door open. As she did, an inky-black shape swept into the room and swirled around the ceiling. MJ looked aghast. "What are you doing? Daniel? Stop this!" The inky-black shape descended from the ceiling and headed right for MJ, but at the last moment it zoomed past her back into the closet and the door slammed shut. The lights went out and the bathroom and hallway were plunged into thick, black darkness. The door to the room opposite the bathroom slammed shut.

"Willow, stay close to me," Jackson said. "We don't know what's going on here."

"Okay," I said, trying to reach for his hand. But before I could, someone stepped between us, grabbed me by the shoulders, and pushed me hard. I screamed as I tumbled down the stairs.

My shoulders and hips and ankles were hitting against the stairs, and I was crying out. Then suddenly my head slammed against the railing, and my body rolled to a stop.

The next thing I knew I was on my hands and knees, sobbing and trying to get my breath. I could tell that the floor was flat beneath me—I had to be on the next landing—but it was spinning. Everything was spinning. I saw stars and crumpled into a heap.

The lights came back on, and I heard footsteps clattering down the stairs. Then Jackson was beside me. "Willow! Are you okay?"

I tried to get up but my legs felt wobbly and my head was still spinning. "I think I have a concussion. My brain feels like it's swimming in my skull."

Jackson helped me to my feet. "We're going to the ER, right now."

I leaned on Jackson. "Someone just tried to kill me."

"No kidding." He put his arm around me. "Now, step down, carefully."

I looked back up the stairs and saw MJ, Rick, Pierre, Tom, Amanda, Sarah, Cassidy, and Carly watching. Everyone looked concerned, even Tom, everyone except Amanda, who wore a look of smug satisfaction on her face.

Because it was Sunday night on Labor Day weekend, Jackson and I waited for two hours before anyone in Eastern Long

Island Hospital in Greenport could see me. The ER waiting room was full. I was bruised and dizzy and aching, but I wasn't as sick as the woman who had just had a heart attack or the guy who was injured in a car accident. So we sat, me slumped against Jackson's shoulder. It hurt to think, but I knew I had to try to make sense of what had happened.

"Amanda has to be the one who did it. Did you see her face?"

"Not necessarily," Jackson said. "She might have just been pleased that you got hurt."

"That's sick."

"Some people are." Jackson held my hand. "It also could have been someone who hid in the closet, like James or Lucas, and then, when the lights went out, came out and pushed you down the stairs. Regardless, you are obviously getting too close to the murderer." Jackson gave me a long look. "The other things—the phone call, the branch, the letter, even shutting you in the shed—I think all those things were designed to scare you off. But this was different. The killer is getting serious now, and he or she is perfectly willing to take you out."

"You're right." I tried to keep my voice steady, though I wasn't doing a convincing job of it. "But I'm not going to give up."

Jackson sighed. "You only have about a dozen suspects, and you're not sure of any of them."

"I know. But I am sure that this all has something to do with the past. The murders are just too similar. I need to talk to Edith Thorne." I pulled out my phone and checked my messages. Wallace hadn't texted me, so I texted him again: NEED TO SEE EDITH THORNE ASAP PLEASE!

"No word from Wallace," I said. "I want to do some research on MJ and Roger, too." I clicked on Safari, a Web browser, and typed in MJ's and Roger's names.

But before I could get the results, a nurse called me into the examination area and told me to turn off my phone. I handed it to Jackson and we went into an examination room. I was seen by a young physician's assistant, tall, with a scruffy beard and wild hair. I told him what happened and he examined me and ordered a CAT scan of my head and an X-ray of my wrist. We waited for the results. Forty-five minutes later, he came back.

"Nothing is broken, but you do have a severe concussion. You should have someone stay with you tonight and follow up with your own doctor."

"I'll stay with her," Jackson said. "She won't be alone."

"Good. You can take Tylenol if you have any aches and pains. Try to take it easy the next day or so. Give yourself a chance to heal."

I said okay, knowing perfectly well that any healing was going to have to wait until I found Roger's murderer and got Simon out of jail.

We headed out of the ER and walked across the parking lot against the ever-increasing wind that was coming off the water. The hospital was right on the bay, and the salt water seemed to mix with the rain; I could feel its sting on my skin. Finally, we reached Jackson's truck, and he helped me inside. I pushed my hair out of my face, fastened my seat belt, and turned my phone back on. It rang immediately.

"Willow?"

"Hi, Wallace. Did you talk to Mrs. Thorne?"

"I did. You can go see her now." He gave me her address.

I glanced at my watch. It was almost midnight. "At this hour?"

"She just texted me and said it was okay. She's a bit of a night owl."

"We're on our way. Thanks, Wallace."

Jackson started the truck. "What's that all about?"

"Edith Thorne will see us now."

We headed out of Greenport after midnight. A steady rain from the hurricane had started, so Jackson flipped the wipers on high. Wind from the storm pushed his truck around on the road as if it weighed nothing. Thick branches and power lines were already down, and Jackson had to be careful to drive around them. It was an obstacle course. I tried to use the time to do a Web search even though I was dizzy and nauseated, but the server was down, too.

By the time we got to Southold, the storm was already much worse. Jackson had to slow down and use his bright lights when there wasn't any oncoming traffic to see through the rain. We finally arrived at Edith Thorne's house. It was almost one o'clock in the morning. Her house, an aging Craftsman, was located down a winding private road in Southold off Bayview Avenue, about a block from the water.

Her house had seen better days. The shingles were mildewed and falling off, and so were the tiles on the roof. Vines covered the fence that surrounded the yard, and the path to the door was cracked and uneven. The paint on the blue front door was peeling. One light was on downstairs. Jackson held his jacket over our heads and we ran to the door through the torrential rain. I knocked and we waited for what seemed like hours. We soon found out that this was the time that it took Edith to come to the door on her cane.

She opened the door and eyed us suspiciously. A tiny, bird-like woman, she had short, gray hair and small, round glasses. She wore light blue sweatpants and a sweatshirt that said ASJA. AMERICAN SOCIETY OF JOURNALISTS AND AUTHORS. WE WRITE THE

BOOKS YOU READ and had a line drawing of a typewriter with a piece of paper in it.

"Mrs. Thorne, Wallace sent us. I'm Willow McQuade, and this is Jackson Spade. May we talk to you?"

"I've been expecting you," she said, as if unhappy about it.

"I'm sorry it's so late, but the roads were a mess. Wallace said you wouldn't mind."

"I'm up until all hours. I just can't sleep like I used to, especially with this storm. Come in."

"Thank you."

We entered a dark and damp-smelling hallway cluttered with dusty antiques.

Mrs. Thorne pointed to a room on the left. "We can talk in here." She followed us into the small room, which was lined with bookshelves. It had a couch and two easy chairs and a small television set perched on yet more books. The blinds were closed. A fire burned in the fireplace. Edith took her perch on the easy chair closest to the fire and motioned us to sit down. We sat on the couch opposite her. She pulled off her glasses and rubbed her eyes, which looked puffy.

"Are your eyes bothering you?" I asked.

"They're always burning and itchy. I'm a writer. I do a lot of reading and research."

"Perhaps I can help. I'm a naturopathic doctor." I was hoping this might smooth the way to her being more cooperative, although that wasn't my first concern.

"A what?"

"I'm a doctor who specializes in natural remedies."

"Never heard of that before. But what do you suggest?"

"A parsley-leaf tincture is helpful for eyestrain. You can also use violet leaves in a compress or an eyewash for sore eyes. It has antiseptic properties. I have them all at my health food store."

She scrutinized me. "What's this, some kind of pitch? You want me to buy something from you?"

I glanced at Jackson, who seemed amused. "No, no, just trying to help. No charge to you."

"No charge? All right then." She put her glasses back on. "It's a good thing you know Wallace Bryan. He was one of my best students. Otherwise I wouldn't have let you two in."

"I know that. I really appreciate the fact that you're seeing us."

"Doesn't he say anything?" She motioned to Jackson.

"I'm just here to help, Mrs. Thorne." Jackson smiled.

"Help who?" Mrs. Thorne arched an eyebrow.

"A friend of ours, Simon Lewis, has been accused of murdering Roger Bixby. The odd thing about Roger's death is that it was almost identical to the way Daniel Russell was killed years before. We were hoping if we could learn more about the past, about Daniel Russell's murder, it might shed light on what happened to Roger Bixby last Sunday night."

She sat in her chair and thought about this for a bit. We could hear the wind whining and the rain pounding the ground. I noticed a trickle of water in the corner by the window and, below it, a blue bucket. Jackson and I waited.

Edith got up, grabbed her cane, and went over to the wall of books to the right of the fireplace. After some searching, she plucked a dusty volume off the shelf and brought it back with her to her seat. "I've known the Bixby family for many years. Our families purchased summer homes here at the same time. Later, when I was older, my husband, Harold, and I used to meet Evelyn, Max's second wife, along with Roger and Tom down at the Laughing Water beach. Of course, Max was always working. Roger and Tom were darling boys. We never had children of our own so we became very fond of them. Of course, when they got older, they had no use for us. Still, it's a shame that Roger is gone." She gazed out the window and seemed to become lost in her thoughts.

"You were saying?" I prodded her. We didn't have much time to help Simon.

She turned back to us. "But before that, one night in January of 1953, Max came to see me. He wanted to talk."

"About what?"

She gestured to the fireplace. "We sat here by the fire for a long time before he got to what was bothering him. That's when I learned the truth about what happened on the estate in 1933."

"You mean the year that Daniel Russell was murdered?"

"Yes, but first Max forced himself on Rebecca, Daniel's wife, in January of 1933." She paused and looked thoughtful. "You would call it rape now. Back then women had no rights and Max was powerful. He wanted Rebecca for himself. He told her to leave Daniel, but she refused. So . . ."

Jackson leaned forward. "So?"

"So, he killed him three months later, in April. He drowned him in the bathtub upstairs and took him down the secret passage to the beach. It was easy for him to get away with it. He had power back then. The family was respected. They tried to pass it off as an accidental drowning, but a sharp cop named Fletcher figured it out. The problem was, he could never get enough evidence to put Max behind bars. But Max lived with that guilt the rest of his life. He ended up a bitter, lonely old man. Roger was in L.A. and never visited; neither did Tom, even though he was only in Cutchogue. Very sad. Although you could say it was what Max deserved. It was his penance, you could say, living in that dreadful mansion with only Mrs. Florrick to keep him company."

"What happened to Rebecca?" I asked.

Mrs. Thorne shook her head. "Rebecca was never the same after Daniel's murder. Her death in 1953, twenty years after she had been raped, was the reason that Max came to see me that night. He told me that before Rebecca died from cancer, she confessed to him that he was James's father, and that James was the rightful heir. If he wouldn't acknowledge James as his son, she begged him to look after James after she was gone. Since I was an old family friend, he wanted my advice.

"I told him that he should be in jail, but if he wouldn't confess, the least he could do was look after his own son. So, he made James the caretaker even though he was only twenty and gave him a cottage on the estate. It eased his conscience."

I was trying to process all this. "So James should have been Max's heir. Does he know?" If he did, that would give him the perfect motive for murder. And he'd also be the prime suspect.

"I don't think so. But he was convinced that Max killed Daniel. Most people thought the same back then, but he was never arrested."

"I know. He told me that."

"What about Roger and Tom?" Jackson asked. "Aren't they the rightful heirs?"

"No, you see, Max's will left everything to his 'oldest son.' James was born in 1933, but Roger wasn't born until after Max divorced his first wife, Madeline, and married Evelyn in 1966. She was much younger than Max, and she had Roger in 1968, then Tom in 1972. So James was his oldest son, except that Max never legally acknowledged him." Mrs. Thorne pulled a thin piece of paper out of the book and handed it to me. "This is a letter of confession that Max wrote. He told me to open it upon his death. Until you came, I didn't know what to do with it. But now I do."

chapter twenty-four

If you have nightmares, you don't sleep easily. Sometimes nightmares can even make you afraid to go to bed at night. Often, the sensation you get when you have a nightmare follows you when you wake up, leaving you feeling strange. To sleep easier, herbal teas and sachets made of basil, chamomile, dill seed, and rosemary can help dispel disturbing dreams. You can also hang sprigs of these herbs over the bed. Sweet dreams!

Yours Naturally,

Dr. McQuade

January 16, 1953

To Whom It May Concern:

I am writing in my own hand what transpired in 1933. I hired a young couple as caretakers in 1932, Daniel and Rebecca Russell. From the moment I met Rebecca, I was enchanted. She was the most beautiful woman I had ever seen. I wanted her. She claimed she wasn't interested in me. But I am not the kind of man who takes no for an answer.

One night in January of 1933, when Rebecca was working in the manor house, I made love to her on the living room divan. Afterward, I told her that she needed to leave her husband and marry me. She refused. I told her that if she didn't leave him, I would make him disappear. But I don't think that she believed I would do it.

Three months later, in April, I murdered her husband, Daniel, by drowning him in the upstairs bathroom. I carried him down the secret passage and left him on the beach. When he was discovered, Rebecca knew I had done it. But she was afraid of me and lied to the police.

We lived with that secret for 20 years. Before her death in 1953, she confessed that James was my son and heir and asked me to make financial arrangements to take care of him. I have done so but never told him the truth. I am sorry about the mistakes I have made and beg God to forgive me.

As God is my witness,

Max Bixby

I had the letter from Max in my hand and the directive from Mrs. Thorne in mind as we left her house after 2:00 a.m. Monday. She told us to go and talk to Mrs. Florrick, Max's house-keeper. "Florrick can confirm everything I have said. Max told me that when he gave me the letter."

While Jackson drove, I decided again to search the Internet for information about MJ and Roger, too. The more info, the better. I got several hits, but before I could check them out, I lost my connection. Rain pounded against the truck, and high winds buffeted it to and fro. We'd just reached a turn by a horse pasture when we came to a pothole that looked like a small lake.

Jackson slowed. "We could stall out. I've got to take it easy here." He put his foot on the gas and we moved through the giant pothole foot by foot. When we'd reached the other side, Jackson tested the brakes. "We're good." We rounded the corner and kept going. The estate was only about a mile away when we came to our next obstacle—a huge tree branch in the middle of the road. Jackson checked the road behind him for traffic, grabbed the flashlight, and jumped out to examine the fallen limb. Moments later, he was back in the truck, soaked to the bone. The rain was fierce now. He reached behind him, in the open space behind the two seats, and pulled out a rope. "I'm going to tie this around that limb. When I signal to you, back up and head to the side of the road. That way," he said, gesturing to the north side of the road.

"Okay." I waited till he got out, then climbed over the gear-shift to the driver's seat. Jackson tied the rope around the end of the limb. When he was done, he waved to me to back up. I put the truck into reverse and slowly inched toward the side of the road. Rain sluiced down the back window. The visibility was zero, and I didn't want to back into a ditch. Slowly, the truck tugged the heavy branch across the asphalt. Jackson followed it, guiding it onto the side of the road. I watched as he untied the rope from the branch. He ran back over, tossed the rope into the open truck bed, and came around to the driver's side. I opened the door for him, then clambered back into the passenger seat.

After Jackson wiped his face with a towel from the glove compartment he took the wheel. I pulled out my phone. He drove slowly because we were close to the turnoff to get to the estate. No cars were coming so he took the left, forded another deep pothole, and headed south, toward the water. High winds buffeted the cab, and even though he had the wipers on high, it was all but impossible to see through the heavy sheets of rain.

While we inched along, I did another search. This time the Internet connection held, and I found what I needed. I told Jackson.

"So that's it, then," Jackson said. He took a right at the stop sign and headed down the rutted road, which was all mud except for what seemed to be one ditch after another, each a miniature lake. It was slow going, but we stayed on track. We got to the guard booth, drove through, and parked in front of the house. It was almost 3:00 a.m. We planned to get the golf cart and head to Florrick's cottage, but when I got out of the truck, I spotted the beam of a flashlight by the stairs that led to the beach.

Jackson came around the truck and I grabbed his arm and pointed to the seawall.

"Someone's over there!" I shouted over the storm.

"Let's move!" Jackson yelled. "Something must be going on. They wouldn't be out here otherwise!" He flicked on his flashlight and kept it low to the ground. We ran toward the retaining wall and peered down at the beach. There were two flashlight beams. "It looks like two people are down there."

Voices carried on the wind, but I couldn't make out what

they were saying. I was already soaked to the skin and freezing cold, but I forced myself to ignore all that. "Let's go down. We've got to get closer."

Jackson looked in the direction of the steps to the beach. "We'll take the steps. Stay low and hold on to the railing. When we hit the beach, go for cover."

We made our way down the stairs. At the bottom, we hustled behind the tall beach grass, trying to catch what was being said. Suddenly, the moon came out from behind the clouds and I could see who it was: Rick and Sheila, James Russell's wife.

I'd expected to see Rick since the photos I'd found online, all from celebrity-gossip sites, showed MJ and Roger as a happy couple, out on the town in New York and in Los Angeles before she married Rick. The text in several of the articles intimated that their working on *MJ's Mind* had rekindled their love affair. I figured that if Rick had killed Roger, it was out of jealousy. But my research had also shown that Rick had declared bankruptcy the year before, so that might be a factor, too. Maybe Rick thought that by his killing Roger, Rick and MJ would assume control of Galaxy. But he didn't know about Simon's shares and that Simon would control the company if Roger was dead. I didn't know what Sheila was doing here.

Sheila shone her flashlight on Rick. "What do you mean, you don't have any money for me? I helped you get rid of Roger! You owe me!" She balled her hands into fists and lunged at him. Rick tried to step away but fell down into the wet sand instead. His flashlight rolled away from him, and he struggled to get up and retrieve it.

"I'm contacting Koren," Jackson said. He pulled out his phone and texted him.

"The two of them were working against me!" Rick said as he picked up the flashlight and shone it into Sheila's eyes. She tried to shield her face. "They wanted to cut me out of Galaxy—it wasn't just that she was having an affair! And don't forget, I've already helped you. If it wasn't for me, Roger would have sold the estate and revoked your lifetime tenancy!"

"That would have killed James! I couldn't let that happen. You promised me you would stop it. You told me you would talk to Carly, but you didn't! 'Darlin', I'm sorry, but she told me today that she's still planning on selling the place!'" Sheila mimicked Rick's Texas twang perfectly, then reverted to her own voice. "You didn't live up to your end of the bargain." She pulled out a small pistol and pointed it at Rick's chest. "This is what happens when you don't keep your promises."

Though she was aiming the pistol at Rick, her hands were shaking, almost uncontrollably.

"Sheila, listen to me!" Rick's face was pasty white. The rain had soaked his white pants and shirt, plastering them against his skin. He pushed his hair out of his face. "We can still work this out! We have to stick to the plan!"

She cocked the pistol. "Forget your plan. You had your chance." She took aim, but as she fired the gun, a bolt of lightning cracked the sky, startling her. She stepped back and the shot went wide. Rick dove for her and knocked her to the ground. She groaned, and the gun skittered away on the sand toward the water.

Jackson went for the gun, but Rick saw him and went for it, too. He tackled Jackson and the two of them went down. They struggled, each trying to pin the other, and began to roll into the water. Jackson got there first and stood up. Rick grabbed him by the knees and Jackson plunged in the water. Rick got on top of him and tried to hold him under.

I knew I had to save Jackson. Adrenaline pumping, I darted out from behind the tall grass, jumped on Rick's back, and put my arms around his neck and squeezed.

"Get off me!" he yelled, and tried to throw me off.

Jackson's head popped up out of the water. He gasped for air, took two steps, and punched Rick in the nose. Rick fell in the water with me on top of him. I let go, and Jackson and I ran for the beach.

"Where's the gun?" Jackson yelled. Both of us scanned the beach but it wasn't there. "Where is it?"

"I have it," Sheila said, aiming it at us.

"Throw it to me!" Rick called as he trudged out of the water. "If you want to get out of this without going to jail, throw it to me! I know what I'm doing, Sheila."

Despite their earlier confrontation, she threw the gun to him. He grabbed it and trained it on us. Unlike Sheila's, Rick's hand wasn't trembling. He held the gun easily, like someone who knew how to shoot.

Jackson lifted his hands in the air. "Don't do anything, crazy, Rick. The cops are on their way."

Rick smirked. "Sure they are." He pointed the gun at me. "You have been a grade-A pain in my you-know-what. Now, here you are again."

"So you're the one who's been threatening her and trying to get her out of the way?" Jackson said.

Rick nodded. "Someone had to try and stop you. I didn't have a choice about you being on the set. That was MJ's decision, and you don't argue with MJ if you want the show to come in on schedule. So once MJ decided she wanted you both here, I had to do what I could to get you to back off."

"So the call, the letter, cutting that branch, pushing me down the stairs, that was all you?" I felt anger bubbling up inside me.

"Yep." Rick actually started chuckling. "And Sheila, here, took your precious doggy and locked you inside the shed."

Sheila pointed to Rick. "It was his idea. He said to look for ways to make you back off. I'm really sorry. I wouldn't have done any of this. I was just, well, desperate. I had to do it, for James."

"What about Tom?" I asked Rick. "Are you the one who beat him up?"

Rick touched his still-bandaged nose. "I told you, I owed Tom. Besides, he's no angel. He didn't want you here either, and he couldn't wait to pin his brother's murder on Simon. But, yeah, I'm the one who decked him. Then, I dragged him into the secret passage and locked both doors."

I knew I needed to keep Rick talking until Detective Koren arrived. "What about those strange happenings in the house—the whispers, the lights dimming, books flying from the shelves, the cracked mirror, and the chandelier crashing to the floor. Did you do all that, too?"

"You and Amanda," Jackson added. "With the help of that control panel in the bathroom cabinet?"

"So, you know about that," Rick said. "Very good. Well, we used it to create the whispers and the lights, yes. But as for the rest, well, I guess you'd have to blame the rest on the ghosts. You'd have to ask MJ, but, of course, you won't get the chance." He cocked the gun.

"Wait!" I shouted. I was so cold I could hear my teeth chattering, but I had to keep him talking. *Where was Koren?* "If you're going to kill us, at least tell us why you killed Roger."

"Now why would I do that?" Rick gave me a sly look. He seemed like an entirely different person, but this was who he really was all along. How could MJ not have known?

Panic was ricocheting through my body, but I came up with one more delaying tactic. "Wait! Let me tell you my theory. You tell me if I'm right."

Rick looked at me in disbelief, then said, "Okay, I could use a laugh. Go ahead tell me what you think I did."

"I think you took photos of the estate and the beach to help you plan the murder. I found the disposable camera."

"That was nothing. Just some vacation photos. What else you got?"

"I think last Sunday night, you lured Roger up to the bathroom to talk about the logistics of shooting there, or maybe you convinced him to show you the goodies in the medicine cabinet."

"Boring. What else you got?"

I looked toward the stairs. *No Koren yet. He was probably stuck in some stupid pothole.* "I think you knocked him out and put him in the tub and drowned him. Once he was dead, you stashed him in the secret tunnel and waited until the party was winding down. Then you carried him across the lawn to the beach. When you got to the cottage, you put the idea in MJ's head that something was wrong on the beach. So she went out to look."

"You're so stupid. That's not what happened at all. Roger asked *me* to go upstairs. He wanted to show me the medicine cabinet. When we got up there, he told me that he was in love with MJ and he wanted her all for himself. He tried to kill me! I had to defend myself."

"You buy that?" I said to Jackson.

"I like your version better."

"I do, too," I said. "But what I'd like to know is why you made Roger's murder seem just like Daniel Russell's. You killed Roger the same way Max killed Daniel and for the same reason. For love."

Rick looked bewildered. "Max killed Daniel? Roger never told us that."

"But Amanda must have," Jackson said, trying to inch toward Rick. "You and MJ had her researching everything that ever happened in this house."

"Stay right there, Spade." Rick kept the gun on him but turned to me. "Okay, I copied the 1933 murder to make Roger's murder seem supernatural. I thought it would work for the show. Goose the ratings, you know? The secret passage was also a great way to get the body out of the house. I wanted to throw the cops off the scent, and it worked. I even wound up with the perfect patsy. Your ex-boyfriend is going to go to prison for Roger's murder, probably for the rest of his life. I tell you, of all the plans I ever made, this one is the finest."

"*We* hatched the plan together when you came out here to scout the location," Sheila corrected him. "If you remember, Rick, everything except Simon's involvement was *my* idea."

"Shut up," Rick said, floating the gun over to point at her.

"Weren't you afraid MJ would find out?" I said.

Rick laughed, and I was again in the gun's sights. "That would only be a problem if MJ were a real psychic. Did you really believe all that stuff she did in the manor? Most of that was thanks to Amanda. She's good with that technical stuff. She showed me how to do it, too. The scene up there tonight was mental! That black smoke and the other stuff worked just the way I planned it. The audience will eat it up. We'll definitely get an order for next season."

"So you did it to hold on to MJ, keep your stake in Galaxy, and to make your show successful. Wow, you were going for the trifecta."

"Right." Rick aimed the gun at Jackson. "I need you to stand right next to her. I want you both in my sights." Moving slowly, Jackson stepped sideways so he was standing right next to me. It would have been a comfort, except I knew what was coming next, and I felt my whole body go tense with terror. "Enough talking," Rick said in an amiable voice. "Time to go."

He cocked the gun, and in that instant lightning split the

sky. Rick, like Sheila, was startled and stepped back. Jackson didn't hesitate. Moving faster than I thought was humanly possible, he charged Rick and dropped him to the wet, hard sand. Once again, the gun skittered away, sliding across the sand toward the water. But this time I grabbed it.

I whirled around to see that Jackson had grabbed Rick with one arm and Sheila with the other. I pointed the gun at them. "Stay right where you are. It's over."

epilogue

The police arrived minutes later and took Rick and Sheila into custody around 4:00 a.m. I gave Detective Koren the letter from Max and told him what Mrs. Thorne had said about Mrs. Florrick, too. Then Jackson and I filled him in on Rick's confession. Koren gave me his usual speech about staying out of police business, but both he and I knew it was just talk. I'd solved another mystery, and he didn't like it.

Jackson and I headed back to my house, took a steamy hot shower together, and climbed into bed around 5:00 a.m. with the dogs and cats. Home, at last.

We woke up five and a half hours later, at ten thirty Monday morning. I rolled over, grabbed my iPhone, and checked my e-mail. There was just one message, from Carly, sent at 5:00 a.m. *Simon has been freed from jail! Thank you! We'll meet you at the estate for the wrap party at noon! Love you both, XO Carly and Simon.*

"Don't tell me. It's Simon, right?" Jackson mumbled from the other side of the bed.

I snuggled over to him and held the iPhone in front of his face. He read the message and rolled over to kiss me. "You are truly amazing."

I kissed him back. "You are. What other boyfriend would help his girlfriend help her ex-boyfriend?"

Jackson thought about this for a moment. "You're right. I

am amazing. I'd have to be to put up with Simon." He smiled and kissed me again.

"I'm just glad it's over. Now I can concentrate on my business again and, of course, you."

"Sounds good to me." He inched over to kiss me once more, but Rockford stuck his little snout in between our faces. "Who do we have here?" He gave the dog a kiss on his nose. Seeing this, Columbo and Qigong jumped on top of Jackson and slathered him with wet doggy kisses. Jackson started laughing and I did, too. It was good to have things back to normal. Or the new normal. I felt truly blessed.

A little before noon on Monday we parked in the driveway in front of the Bixby mansion for what we both hoped was the last time. Jackson turned off the ignition and looked at me. "Are you ready for this?"

I took a deep breath. "Yes. I want to make sure MJ is okay with all that's happened. I need to talk to her." I also needed to pick up my stuff from the healing cottage. We walked down toward the tent, but before we even got there, Carly and Simon came running to meet us.

"Willow! You're here!" Carly hugged me tight. "You are a genius! We can't thank you enough!"

"Jackson was just as much a part of this as I was."

"We know, we know. Thanks so much, man." Simon gave Jackson a hug, then turned to me next. "And you, you saved my life." Simon hugged me tight. "Thank you, Willow! I owe you big-time!"

"You are very welcome." I noticed an Irish Claddagh ring on Carly's left hand. "Is this something new?"

Simon took her hand. "I asked her to marry me, but she

wants to take it slow. I got this for her instead from a little boutique in town, the Gem. But Carly's the gem. She stuck with me through this whole horrible ordeal." He kissed her.

Carly admired her ring. "I love it. It's a pre-engagement ring."

I silently wished them luck, hoping it would last.

"You guys hungry?" Simon asked. "It's an all-organic buffet, thanks to Carly."

"Between the yoga classes and the treatments, you've renewed my belief in natural remedies," Carly explained. "We're having only organic food on our sets from now on."

"I'm sure Tom will appreciate that," I said, giving Jackson a look.

"Don't worry about him." Carly led us into the tent. "He's in rehab and isn't expected to be out for a few months. Turns out he has a problem with alcohol *and* cocaine. That's why he was always broke and always asking Roger for money."

"I'm glad to hear he's getting help," Jackson said. "He'll be a better person when he's clean."

"One can hope," Carly said. "Shall we eat?"

The four of us got in line for the organic buffet—a beautiful display of fresh greens for salads, veggies and fruits, vegan lasagna, and Asian-inspired dishes made with tofu. We filled our plates, grabbed two passion-fruit iced teas, and found a table near the door so we could see the water.

I spotted Lucas at the buffet line and waved him over. He brought his plate over and came to sit next to me. "How are you doing, Lucas?"

"Not great. My mother is in jail, and I just got back from visiting my dad in the hospital. It's a damn mess."

"What happened to your dad?"

"Well, at about four a.m. last night, the police came by to

tell us that my mother had been arrested and was going to be charged as an accessory to murder. My dad just collapsed. The ER doc said it was a stroke. He's very weak and is having trouble talking and moving his right hand."

"I'm so sorry." I couldn't help thinking how Max's original crime—raping Rebecca—just kept claiming victims, destroying lives.

Lucas shrugged. "Well, it's not all a disaster." He gave Carly a shy smile. "Carly invited me to the appointment she had at a lawyer's office. I stopped there on the way back from the hospital. Tom was there, too, with a friend. He called him his sponsor."

"It was a meeting about the estate," Carly said. "I had to schedule it after Roger died. We read the will. Roger hadn't updated it recently so, as his wife, I was still the main beneficiary." An unreadable look passed between her and Lucas.

"And?" Jackson prompted.

Carly sighed. "Well, I never liked the estate. It has always creeped me out. The truth is, I don't want it or need it or care much what happens to it. But Lucas does, and so does Tom. And really, Max was wrong to leave everything to Roger. He should have split it among his sons, Roger, Tom—and James. So I asked the lawyer and Lucas and Tom if there wasn't some way we could make things right."

"At first Tom didn't like that idea," Lucas said. "But his sponsor suggested that he try to work with me, to do the right thing, to make amends, so we figured something out. When that letter you gave the detective is authenticated—and Mrs. Florrick says it will be—my dad will be a rightful heir to the property. But he's not well enough to manage the estate, so Tom and I will do it together. We'll be co-directors of the Bixby Trust." Lucas picked up his fork and motioned outside. "We're giving the house to the state. The lawyer is pretty sure they'll turn it into an historical site, what with all the rum-running history plus the lavender farm. It's got all sorts of potential as a tourist site. So some of the money will get used to pay for whatever care my dad needs and my mom's legal costs. And Tom wants to build a nice big studio with plenty of light so he can sculpt when he gets out of rehab."

"What about you?" I asked. "Are you going to stay in your family's house?"

"For now. But if we can work out the finances, I'm going to knock down my parents' place and build a new house—something bright and cheerful—for my dad and me."

MJ didn't come to the party. Carly told us that she'd checked herself into a hotel on the South Fork for a few days.

Life for the rest of us returned to normal. Labor Day was crazy busy in the store and café. Merrily was starting to feel a little better so that helped a lot.

Two days later, on Wednesday morning, MJ came in the door. I walked over to her and gave her a hug. "It's good to see you. How are you?"

"Better now. I needed to get away. It was too crazy here. I'm still having trouble processing what happened."

"It's a lot to take in. Do you have time for a cup of herbal tea? Anything you like."

"Chamomile would be great, thanks."

As I got up to go in the kitchen, Jackson walked in the front door with Columbo and Rockford. He came over to me and gave me a kiss and said hello to MJ.

"The dogs look so healthy," MJ said as she petted them. "I can see they have a good home."

Jackson pulled some papers out of his back pocket. "Pretty soon, I'll be able to give more dogs a home. I just applied for a permit to create a sanctuary at my house. It should be set in a month or so. Columbo and Rockford will soon have plenty of friends."

"That's fantastic!" I said. "I'm so proud of you."

"How wonderful." MJ scratched the dogs behind the ears.

"I've got to go home and make some calls about this, but I just wanted to stop by and share the good news." Jackson turned to MJ. "I'll leave you gals to your chat."

"I'll call you later," I said as I walked him to the door. "Maybe we can have an organic BBQ at your house."

"Grilled tofu? I think not. I'll come up with something else that's healthy and appealing."

"Sounds good." I kissed him good-bye.

After he left, I said, "I'm going to get us that tea." I went into the kitchen and put on the teakettle. A few minutes later, I returned to the table with two cups of piping hot tea and some organic chocolate chip cookies.

"You've been through an awful lot. Losing Roger and now Rick. How do you feel about what Rick has done? Are you angry?"

"Yes, I'm angry. Rick was wrong to do what he did. It wasn't necessary. I loved Rick but I loved Roger, too. Roger and I knew we were soul mates the minute we met each other at NYU. But he loved other women too much. So I married Rick. I know that Roger did some bad things, and I know his family weren't good people. So, perhaps justice was served. But I will miss him. I'll miss them both." She took a sip of tea, then gave me a wry smile. "You know what the worst of it is?"

"What?"

"That Rick killed Roger and I didn't know. I mean, I was on that estate, sharing my bed with a murderer, and I didn't have a clue. Some psychic, huh? It's made me question every assumption I've ever had about myself. Now I don't know what I'm gonna do."

"Maybe it's like the way doctors are told they should never treat their own family. When you're too close to someone, you don't have any objectivity, and you can't always see the truth about them. It's not necessarily a reflection on your abilities."

She reached out and patted the back of my hand. "Well, that's a very generous take on it. Thank you."

"I was wondering about something. I had a chance to look into James Russell's diary, and it said that 'MJ and R' had come to visit. I thought it was Rick, but it was Roger, wasn't it?"

She nodded. "I went with Roger to see James. He wanted to talk to him about selling the estate. The house was worthless, but if Roger sorted out his father's mortgages, the land could be worth a fortune. James, however, wasn't having any of it. He threatened to sue and told us he would talk to his lawyer, Les Barber."

So that was LB.

"So you and Roger were having an affair?"

She nodded. "We'd become involved again, but I thought we were discreet. I don't know how Rick found out."

"It was probably Amanda. She seemed as protective of Rick as she'd been of Roger."

"Maybe." MJ took another sip of tea. "Or maybe Rick had a sixth sense about me. That man spent a lifetime reading and catering to my every mood."

I got up from the table, went over to the counter, and picked up a box of the Fresh Face cream. "My aunt Claire created this. I want you to have it. I think you'll find it soothing." I told her briefly what had happened in June. "I think I could have really used your help."

She opened the jar and put some of it on her face. "I would have been glad to help you. I can feel the healing and love in this cream." She put the top back on, put it back into the box, and closed the lid. "Willow, I came here to tell you something. I want you to know that your aunt Claire is well and she is proud of you. I thought you should know."

I was stunned. "How do you know that?"

"I knew that you didn't want to do the work with me, so I had a talk with her myself one night. She's so glad you've taken her advice and are living more in balance."

I could hardly breathe. "Those were the exact words Aunt Claire had used in a letter she wrote to me. Nick gave it to me after she died."

"I know."

"So you are a real psychic, after all?"

MJ considered my question for a moment, then said, "I know that Rick and Pierre and the crew are skeptical about my abilities. That's why he had Amanda use all that hocus-pocus, like the lighting effects and the noises. It's a TV show, so you need a certain amount of drama. But the bottom line is, I am a true psychic. Sometimes people's spirits are like trapped energy and just need a helping hand to move on."

"I believe that, too." I gave MJ a penetrating look. "So, Aunt Claire, she's okay?"

MJ took my hand. "She's fine. And she loves you."

Printed in the United States
By Bookmasters